Eric Wilder

Garden of Forbidden Secrets

Gondwana Press

Edmond, Oklahoma

Other books by Eric Wilder

Ghost of a Chance
Murder Etouffee
Name of the Game
A Gathering of Diamonds
Over the Rainbow
Big Easy
Just East of Eden
Lily's Little Cajun Cookbook
Of Love and Magic
Bones of Skeleton Creek
City of Spirits
Primal Creatures
Black Magic Woman
River Road
Blink of an Eye
Sisters of the Mist

Gondwana Press LLC
1802 Canyon Park Cir. Ste C
Edmond, OK 73013

For information on books by Eric Wilder
www.ericwilder.com

Front over by Andres Grau

ISBN: 978-946576-07-1

Acknowledgments

I would like to thank Donald Yaw and Linda Hartle Bergeron for beta reading, helping me edit the book and providing valuable input involving timeline and character development.

For Marilyn

Garden
of Forbidden
Secrets

A novel by
Eric Wilder

Chapter 1

The only way to deal with a bad situation is to embrace the problem and kiss it on the mouth. Taj Davis was beginning to doubt his lifelong philosophy as he followed a bellman down the hallway of a New Orleans hotel.

Though only thirty-four years old, Taj was ancient by NBA standards. His surgically repaired left knee still ached whenever he jumped. Arthritis had begun affecting his fingers, though none of his coaches or teammates had yet noticed the knots deforming the digits of his shooting hand. As he followed the hall of the French Quarter hotel, he felt every year of his age.

Taj had hoped to play in Cleveland during his final years in the league. An early morning call from an assistant coach had informed him his dream was not to be. He'd had about three hours to pack his apartment before taking a taxi to the airport and flying to New Orleans, the NBA city that had acquired him in an unexpected mid-season trade.

The bellman stopped in front of a door, the odor of must and age greeting them as he followed the little man into the room. The bellman, dressed in a red velvet coat, sat the suitcase on the bed and smiled as he palmed the twenty Taj handed him.

"You're Taj Davis."

"Right on. What's your name?"

"Tommie. You way bigger than you look on TV. How tall are you?"

"Six-nine. You like basketball, Tommie?"

The little man massaged the stubble of beard on his chin. "Nothing much I like better. My favorite team is the Pels. One of these days, they gonna be champs."

"Hope it's sooner rather than later," Taj said. "I've dreamed of a championship ring. I'm running out of time to find a winning team to help get me there."

"I hear that," Tommie said. "Hope you're good enough to replace Zee Ped. He been filling up the baskets lately."

"I have no idea why the Pels traded their best player for me," Taj said.

"Nobody around here knew a thing about the trade until a few hours ago," Tommie said.

"Neither did I. An assistant called this morning and told me to meet him in the locker room. He had my locker already unpacked, a plane ticket and itinerary for me when I got there. I didn't even have a chance to say goodbye to anyone. I had to leave most of my stuff unpacked in my apartment."

"You serious? You mean today was the first you heard about the trade?"

The curtains on the large room's windows were open. Taj nodded as he glanced out at the flashing neon of the French Quarter and running lights of boats out on the river.

"No clue," he said. "I know it's late. Any chance of scoring something to eat around here?"

"You kidding? This the Big Easy. Most places in the French Quarter don't even get started good until at least midnight."

"I mean here in the hotel. This move has me dogged totally out. All I want to do is eat, take a hot bath and then crash."

"I hear that. Tell me what you want. I'll have someone bring it to you."

"Rib eye, rare, and a bottle of your driest cabernet."

"If you like Cajun and Creole, the chef makes the best gumbo in town," Tommie said.

"Just steak. I'm not much on seafood."

"Better learn to like it," Tommie said. "You could be here awhile, and this is the gumbo capital of the world."

"Hope you're right about me spending some time here. This is my third team in the past five years. I was hoping to play my final season in Cleveland. Tell you the truth, I've never eaten gumbo," Taj said.

"I'll bring you a cup, along with the steak. Give it a try. Nothing else like it on earth."

"If you say so," Taj said.

"Ever stayed at Hotel Montalba before?"

"First time. When the Cavs are in town, they stay in one of the newer hotels on Canal. How old is this place?"

"Going on two-hundred years. The oldest hotel in the French Quarter."

"Love it," Taj said. "The elegance, architecture, and service are impressive. What's not to like?"

"Maybe the evil spirits lurking around every corner," Tommy said.

"Do you believe in ghosts?"

"Me and everyone else in town. You will too after you been here awhile. Hell, you might not make it through the night before you see one."

"You know something I don't know?"

Tommy massaged his chin again. "I already said too much. I better go put your order in."

"Not so fast," Taj said. "You have something to tell me?"

"This old hotel ain't just haunted it has more ghosts than St. Louis Cemetery No. 1 over on Basin Street."

"And . . . ?"

"This room, 1413."

"Go on."

"It's really room 1313. This is the thirteenth, not the fourteenth floor. The hotel stopped using this room before I started working here."

"How long has that been?" Taj asked.

"Almost thirty years."

"Bet you have lots of stories to tell," Taj said.

"On just about anything you want to know about New Orleans."

"If the hotel doesn't use this room anymore, then why am I staying here?"

"We're extra busy with people coming into town to see the Christmas lights. Management put you here because they couldn't turn down a call from the Pels. This was the only room that wasn't booked."

Taj stared at the panorama through a corner window. "Even if it's haunted, it has to be the most beautiful suite in town," he said. "I can't imagine a better view of New Orleans. Why on earth would the hotel let a few spirits of the night stop them from using it?"

"Maybe because someone was murdered here," Tommy said.

"Whoa! Somebody was killed in this room? Are you making this up?"

Tommy's smile had disappeared. "Guess I should have shut my mouth when I had the chance."

"You started it, now finish the story."

"You're not gonna get me fired, are you?" Tommy said.

"Course not," Taj said.

"A cleaning lady found a body in the bathtub. The murdered woman's head was missing."

"Crime of passion?"

"No idea," Tommy said. "The murder was never solved."

"How is that possible?" Taj asked when Tommy grew silent. "Wasn't she a guest?"

"Like I said, it happened before I started work here." Tommy handed Taj the antique key to the room. "I better put in your dinner order."

The little bellman hurried away down the dimly lit hallway. It was the weekend, the Pels on a road trip out west. Taj had until Monday to report to the training facilities. He'd visited New Orleans often during his tenure in the NBA, though he'd never ventured far from the Smoothie King Center, or his hotel room. Tomorrow, he intended to change all that.

After another glance out the window, he shut the curtains. Mid-December, the weather had turned cold. Though not as frigid as temperatures in Cleveland, the humid climate in New Orleans was uncomfortable. Taj turned up the thermostat, opened his suitcase, found a sweater, and pulled it over his head.

Checking his email on the cell phone entertained Taj until a white-smocked waiter knocked on the door. The serving cart he pushed sported a white tablecloth, fine china, and silverware. After opening the bottle of wine and filling a glass with a ceremonial flair, the waiter accepted Taj's twenty, departing after saying almost nothing.

"Nice," Taj said, sipping the cabernet.

As Taj twisted the tap on the antique porcelain tub and tested the water with his palm, he'd forgotten Tommy's story of murder. When it grew hot, he returned to eat his steak. He turned up his nose at the steaming cup of gumbo, pushing it aside without tasting it.

As steam wafted up from the tub, Taj sat the wine bottle and his glass on the barbershop tile floor, and then stripped off his clothes. Not bothering to check the temperature, he slid over the side, sinking into the water to the top of his head.

Taj had a powerful frame for such a big man. Used to battling in the paint, he had a chest covered with bruises, contusions, and even a few cuts. The hot water soon began to soothe his sore body, and he finished drinking the wine straight from the bottle. After draining the last drop, he closed his eyes and fell asleep.

Sometime later, Taj's hand relaxed, and he released his grip on the bottle. His eyes popped open when it shattered on the tile. He didn't know how long he'd been asleep, though the water had become tepid. Worse, the lights had gone out, the only light coming from a crack in the curtains. When he got out of the tub, he stepped on broken glass.

Finding a towel, he wrapped it around his bleeding foot and hobbled to the window. Unable to find a light switch, he pulled open the curtains, red flashing neon from the French Quarter flooding through the window.

The room had grown icy cold. Sticky globules dripped from a windowpane and Taj recoiled when he touched the gooey substance. The inhuman sound of something coming up behind him caused him to wheel around.

Not a person easily startled, Taj backed against the wall. Heavy feet shuffling across the floor, along with the rattle of chains, made him do a double take. As he drew a gasping breath into his lungs, what he saw almost caused him to choke.

Neither man nor beast, it was a cloud of white light with flashes of reds, yellows, and blues. Something alive, though anything but human, the thing reeked of death as it floated toward him. The droning noise emitting from the specter sounded like the muted whine of a revving chainsaw.

With his fists clenched in a fighter's stance, Taj took a swing at the advancing demon. When his hand passed through the apparition, he realized he needed to run instead of fight. Sidestepping the entity, he stumbled to the door. As he glanced over his shoulder at the demon, he couldn't get it to open.

Taj slammed his fists against the door, trying to break it and get away from the supernatural being behind him. When it opened of its own accord, he fell on his face into the hallway. With the bloody towel still wrapped around his cut foot, he sprinted into the arms of an inebriated couple returning from a French Quarter bar.

Taj towered over the man and woman. Despite the alcohol they'd both consumed, nothing had prepared them for a meeting with a naked giant with a bloody foot. They were both screeching as they hurried away. A dozen doors opened, staring out at the naked man with wild eyes and coated with blood. Hearing the commotion, Tommy came running.

When Tommy saw Taj standing naked in the hallway, he grabbed a bathrobe from a service cart and tossed it to him. Before Taj could secure the tie around his waist, Tommy had pulled him into an elevator and punched the down button.

"What the hell, man? You gone crazy?"

"Son of a bitch!" Taj said. "You weren't kidding. That room is haunted. I'll be damned if I'm going back there."

"Good God! What did you do to your foot?"

"Stepped on broken glass," Taj said.

"You're bleeding all over the carpet. Until I can get you downstairs, we need something to slow the flow."

Tommy stopped on a lower floor and found a handful of towels in a linen closet.

"Damn glad it was you that showed up and not the police," Taj said. "My first day with the Pels might have been my last."

"Got that right," Tommy said. "You look like you been in a knife fight and got the worst of it."

In the fluorescent lights of the elevator, Taj could see the little man was correct. Blood already covered the bathrobe, and he felt light-headed.

"You'll be okay," Tommy said. "We got a doctor on staff downstairs. He'll fix you up. What you got in your hand?"

Taj didn't realize he was holding anything until he looked and saw it.

Recoiling, he let the object drop to the floor. "What the hell is that thing?" he asked.

Tommy stared with his mouth open as he nudged the gruesome item with the toe of his polished shoe.

"Good God almighty!" he said. "Looks like a voodoo doll that somebody dunked in a bucket of blood. Where'd you get it?"

"No earthly idea," Taj said. "I know nothing about voodoo."

"Then what about your tattoo?" Tommy asked.

The bathrobe had splayed open across Taj's broad chest, revealing a strange tattoo.

"I've had this thing since I was old enough to remember seeing it. Where it came from, I can't tell you. You think you know what it is?"

"Hell yes, I know. It's a voodoo symbol," Tommy said. "Around here they call them veves."

"Voodoo symbol? You're shitting me," Taj said.

"No, I'm not," Tommy said.

Then what the hell is it doing on my chest?" Taj asked.

Tommy wrapped the bloody doll in a towel and picked it up. "The witch doctor who marked you with it is the only person that knows."

Chapter 2

Though Taj Davis wasn't oblivious to pain, he'd learned to live with it during his thirteen years in the NBA. He hadn't flinched when the hotel doctor deadened his foot before stitching up the wound. Used to boots and casts, the thick sock over his bandaged foot and special sandal he wore seemed mild to him.

Tommy had retrieved Taj's bags from room 1313. After changing into a Cavs warm-up, the tall basketball player had fallen asleep in a comfortable chair, in the lobby of the old hotel. Tommy was still at work when Taj awoke the next morning.

"Management's real sorry about what happened last night," Tommy said. "We moved your bags to a room on the second floor."

Tommy smiled and shook his head when Taj asked, "Are there ghosts on the second floor?"

"Ghosts are everywhere in the Big Easy. Don't matter none. Your new room is the safest one in the hotel," he said.

"Why are you still at work?" Taj asked.

"Everyone in town loves the Pels. The hotel's paying me overtime to stick around and get you settled in your new room. Ready to check it out?"

Taj grimaced when he got out of the chair and put weight on his foot.

"Dammit!" he said. "One day with the Pels and I'm already on the injured list."

"Doc White said the cut isn't deep. You'll be fine in a day or two."

"No severed tendons or nerves?"

"Nope. Just a little soreness. Doc fitted you with a specially padded sandal."

Taj tested it with his weight. "You're right. It's a little sore, though not bad."

"You sure? The hotel has a wheelchair you can use."

Tommy's offer brought a grin to Taj's face.

"No wheelchair, or crutches for me," he said. I'll be fine."

After following Tommy to the elevator, Taj wasn't so sure. Instead of an antique key, the little bellman opened the door with an electronic card. When they entered, there was no smell of must or age. Except for the view that didn't hold a candle to the one he'd had the previous night, everything was perfect.

Taj's suitcase was waiting on the bed, his hanging clothes on a rack. He almost panicked when he realized he didn't have his wallet. Tommy grinned when he handed it to him.

"Lucky for you, I'm not a thief," the little man said. "Must be a couple thousand dollars in there."

Before tossing the wallet on the bed, Taj gave him a twenty from it. "I'm not much on credit cards," he said.

"With the money you fellas earn in the NBA, it must be nice."

"I've had a couple of big paydays. Now, I'm on a veteran's minimum salary."

"Still a million bucks, or more, I'll bet," Tommy said. "I'll never make that much my whole life."

"Just dumb luck on my part," Taj said. "Not everybody is six-nine."

"Ain't many big men can ball like you do," Tommy said.

"Kind words are music to my ears. You just earned yourself an extra twenty," Taj said.

Taj grabbed his wallet and handed Tommy another bill from it.

"Hey, thanks," Tommy said. "If everything's okay, I'm on my way to the house for a little sack time. At least if my old lady don't want to go dancing."

Taj grinned at Tommy's retort. He stopped the little bellman before he could get out the door.

"One question before you go," he said.

"Ask me," Tommy said.

"I don't have to report to the team until Monday. Where can I get some info about the tattoo on my chest, and the bloody voodoo doll I was carrying last night?"

"Some things are best left alone," Tommy said. "What happened last night is probably one of them."

"Ain't happening," Taj said. "I need answers. Forgetting about last night isn't an option."

"Your balls and not mine," Tommy said. "Lots of voodoo shops, mostly tourist traps, in the Quarter. There's one a few blocks from here on Dumaine. Might be someone there that can help you."

You think the voodoo doll came from that shop?"

"You're asking the wrong person," Tommy said. "I don't have a clue."

"Sure about that?" Taj asked.

"There are lots of people that practice voodoo in Nawlins. I ain't one of them."

"What about the blood? Where did it come from?" Taj asked.

"From that cut on your foot," Tommy said. "Where else could it have come from?"

"How did the damn doll get into my room, and why didn't I know I was carrying it when you found me?"

"This is New Orleans," Tommy said. "Live here as long as I have, and you come to expect the unexpected."

"Not the answer I'm looking for," Taj said.

Tommy glanced at his watch. "Maybe someone at the voodoo shop can give you some answers. Me, I'm fresh out and tired as hell."

"What's the name of the voodoo shop?"

"Dr. Voodoo's Spells and Hexes," Tommy said, hurrying out the door without waiting for Taj's next question.

❦

Taj took a cab to Dumaine. After signing an autograph for the star-struck cabbie, he stood outside Dr. Voodoo's Spells and Hexes, staring at the voodoo dolls, African masks, and drums in the picture window. A cold breeze was whistling down the street. As two lightly dressed tourists brushed past him on the sidewalk, he pulled the black leather trench coat tighter around his neck.

A bell on the door, pealing the theme song of some horror movie Taj barely remembered, sounded when he entered. As the door shut behind him, welcome warmth and the odor of pungent incense accosted his nostrils. The sound of voodoo drums emanated from speakers hidden behind the rows of African masks and grotesquely carved effigies. The little shop was empty of tourists and Taj jumped when someone behind him spoke. A portly man with a cookie duster mustache was grinning at him when he wheeled around.

"Didn't mean to scare you, big guy. Hep you?"

13

Taj showed him the bloody voodoo doll. "I'm wondering if this doll came from your shop."

"Whoa, don't hand it to me. Where'd you get that thing?" the man asked.

"My hotel room. I was hoping someone could tell me something about it."

"Aren't you Taj Davis?" the man asked.

"I am. You?"

"Tammany Louis Lafourche III," he said. "I'd shake your hand, but I don't want to touch that thing you're holding."

"You have voodoo dolls all over the store. What's wrong with this one?" Taj asked.

"It's covered in blood. Most of my dolls come from China. I can see right off the bat the one in your hand is the real Magilla."

When Taj leaned forward, Lafourche took a step backward.

"Even if I'm big and black, I promise I won't hurt you," Taj said.

"I'm not worried about you," Lafourche said. "It's that thing in your hand. It's bad news."

"How so?"

"From the looks of that bandage on your foot, I'm guessing the blood on the voodoo doll is yours. Am I wrong?"

"It's mine. So what?"

"You got that wound by design, is my guess."

"An accident," Taj said. "Stepped on broken glass."

"Someone has hexed you, is what I think," Lafourche said.

Taj glanced at the shopkeeper, searching for a grin, or some other sign he was having his leg pulled. Lafourche wasn't smiling.

"You don't believe in that sort of thing, do you?"

"I was born and raised right here in New Orleans. Not only do I believe it, I know it's true."

It was Taj's turn to smile. "Who would have a reason to hex me?" he asked. "I've only been in town since last night."

"I heard," Lafourche said. "Everyone's talking about you joining the Pels."

"Is that bad or good?"

Lafourche hesitated before answering. "Mixed feelings, mostly bad. Zee Ped's an All-Star. Everyone knows you're good but . . ."

"But what? You think I'm too old?" Taj said, finishing Lafourche's sentence.

"Almost ten years older than Zee Ped. He's the best player on the Pels. At least he was."

"Sorry," Taj said. "I had no choice in the matter. I'm as confused as you are about what I'm doing here."

"May have something to do with that thing in your hand," Lafourche said.

"What the hell do you mean by that?"

"Someone may have wanted you here."

"For what reason?"

"Maybe unfinished business. You'd know the answer to that better than me," Lafourche said.

"I don't know anything. I came here for answers, not more questions."

"I'm as in the dark as you are," Lafourche said.

"You know about voodoo dolls. It's how you make a living. What makes you think this one is real?"

The drumming soundtrack segued into an African chant as Lafourche leaned back against a display case filled with polished wooden masks and pottery effigies.

"I've owned this shop for eighteen years. While most everything here is little more than tourist souvenirs, I've learned a thing or two about voodoo," Lafourche said.

"So you're telling me this is a real voodoo doll?"

"It didn't come from this shop."

"What about another shop in town?" Taj asked.

"That doll didn't come from a shop. A real voodoo houngan or mambo made it. A ceremony was performed, you can bet good money on it."

"How do you know?" Taj said.

"Your doll's made of bleached cloth wrapped around two sticks of different sizes. Those sticks represent the cross. Bet they're even made from the same kind of tree they used to crucify Christ on."

"What's Christianity got to do with voodoo?" Taj asked.

"Vodoun is a religion brought over by slaves from West Africa. When they reached the West Indies, it began changing. Vodoun, Catholicism, and pagan Carib beliefs got all mixed up at the sugar plantations and morphed into what we now call voodoo. At least until it reached New Orleans, and then it changed even more."

"You're white. I always thought voodoo was only practiced by blacks."

"You'd be wrong about that," Lafourche said. "A Jew was once the most powerful voodoo practitioner."

"Do you practice voodoo?" Taj asked.

"I bought this shop from an old voodoo woman. A real voodoo woman. Voodoo dolls are my main business, and I learned everything I know about them from her."

"Just the dolls or all about voodoo?"

"Few people know what voodoo is really about. Practitioners can be powerful, and dangerous. I've purposely kept my nose out of their business."

"I don't have that luxury," Taj said. "What's the deal with this voodoo doll?"

"When it's cold outside, my business is slow," Lafourche said, glancing around the shop.

Catching the drift, Taj reached for his wallet and handed him a twenty.

"Does that warm things up for you?" he asked.

"I'm still a little chilly."

Taj handed him two more twenties. "Warm enough?" he asked.

Lafourche stashed the bills in the pocket of the cracked leather vest he wore over his threadbare Western shirt.

"Like I said, the two sticks represent the cross. Bleached cloth is wrapped around the sticks to form the doll."

"That it?" Taj asked when Lafourche paused.

"The cloth is the property of the victim of the doll. The person who made the doll either stole it from the intended victim or paid someone to steal it. Once the houngan or mambo gets it, they bleach it in a voodoo ceremony. Then they use it to make the doll."

"Get real!" Taj said.

"The more personal the connection, the more powerful the spell. The rotations around the sticks, the direction it's wrapped, and where it's tied off, all have meaning to the person that made the doll. The more precise the construction, the more powerful the spell."

"Surely, you don't believe all that malarkey," Taj said.

The African chant coming through the speakers transitioned back into drumming. Lafourche glanced around the little shop as if expecting to see someone listening to the conversation.

"Let me just say I wouldn't want to be the person this doll was made for. If it's you, then you got a problem. Hell, the whole damn town's been hexed, because the team lost its best player to get you."

When Lafourche turned to walk away, Taj grabbed his shoulder.

"Wait just a minute," he said. "I paid you sixty bucks. Is that all you got?"

"Like you said, I'm white. What the hell do I know?"

"More than me," Taj said. "I paid you, and I have more questions." Taj pulled three more twenties from his wallet and thrust them at Lafourche. "Will these help jog your memory?"

Lafourche shook his head. "Keep your money. I've told you all I know."

"At least, point me in the right direction."

"There's a cemetery tour starting in twenty minutes. Maybe the tour guide can help you fill in the blanks. Want me to sign you up?"

Chapter 3

Realizing Tammany Louis Lafourche III was unable or unwilling to answer any more questions, Taj let the shop owner sign him up for a tour of the St. Louis Cemetery No. 1. Lafourche disappeared in the back and didn't return, even when the same young couple he'd passed on the sidewalk entered the shop to the chiming of bells.

"Are we in the right place for the cemetery tour?" the young woman asked.

"It's what I'm waiting for," Taj said.

The couple looked no older than mid-twenties, the woman's Midwestern accent hinting they weren't locals. Her denim shorts, and the lightweight maize and blue coat, zipped open enough so he could see her University of Michigan tee shirt, suggested she'd expected warmer weather in New Orleans. The stunning young woman had long, red hair, creamy-white skin, expressive blue eyes, and stood about five-feet-seven.

The slender young man was wearing an identical coat and had his head in a guidebook. When he glanced up and saw Taj, he pushed his John Lennon glasses onto his forehead. They weren't into sports, because neither of them recognized him.

"I'm Amy," the young woman said. "This is Brian. We're students at Michigan and decided to visit New Orleans over the Christmas break."

"I'm Taj," he said, shaking the young woman's hand.

"Are you from out of town?" Brian asked.

Before stashing the voodoo doll in his trench coat, Taj had stuffed it into a baggie Tommie had given him.

"Something like that," he said.

Amy with the wavy red hair was smiling. Brian had a look of terror on his baby face. Taj was used to the reaction. People aren't always prepared to meet a physically imposing six-foot nine-inch black man dressed in a knee-length black leather trench coat.

"I'm a history buff," Taj said. "I heard these cemetery tours aren't to be missed."

Brian's concerned expression vanished. "Us too," he said. "I'm majoring in American history and hope to teach someday. It's my passion."

"What about you, Amy?" Taj asked.

"Don't know yet what I want to do for the rest of my life," she said.

The chime on the door sounded before Amy could ask him what he did. An older man, wearing a yellow vest over his jacket, rubbed his hands together to warm them. The plastic nametag hanging from his neck pegged him as the tour guide.

"Sorry I'm late," he said. "Wind has picked up out there, and I had to run back home and get a heavier coat. I'm Garlen, your tour guide."

Taj noticed the dirty look Amy flashed Brian at Garlen's mention of a heavier coat. Her reaction lasting only a moment, she was smiling when she shook Garlen's hand.

"I'm Amy," she said. "Brian is the one who looks like an aspiring college professor. Taj is the gentleman in the black coat."

"Pleased to meet you," Garlen said. "Hope that windbreaker keeps you warm enough, young lady."

"Brian said the weather in New Orleans would be mild this time of year."

"It is," Brian said. "At least when compared to Ann Arbor."

Amy gave Brian another dirty look.

"The humidity in New Orleans makes every little chill seem much colder than it really is," Garlen said. "At least we'll be out of the wind when we reach St. Louis Cemetery No. 1."

Garlen, like Amy and Brian, apparently had no idea who Taj was. As he followed them down the Basin Street sidewalk, it was all right with him. Though Taj knew most of the graves in New Orleans were above ground, he wasn't prepared for the eerie feeling of déjà vu warming his neck upon seeing the brick and stone monoliths. Garlen was correct. The wall around the cemetery blocked the wind when they entered the gate.

"This is the oldest cemetery in New Orleans," Garlen said. "The spiritual home of many famous citizens. Mark Twain called our cemeteries "Cities of the dead.""

"This place is amazing," Brian said. "The tombs are so large and ornate and the paths between them so narrow, they seem to close in around you. What do you think, Amy?"

"My skin is crawling," she said.

"You can't be serious. This place is awesome. What's the matter?"

"Spirits of the dead; I can feel their cold breath on my neck," she said.

"You're shivering," Brian said.

"Brian, I don't like it here. I want to go."

"You're irrational," he said. "It's broad daylight. There are no ghosts."

"You stay. I'll walk back to the car and wait for you there," she said.

Casting a distressed look at Garlen, Brian shrugged his shoulders and followed her out the gate.

"So sorry," he said.

As cold rain began to fall, Garlen turned to Taj. "Under the circumstances, I'm calling off the tour. They'll give you a rain check at the shop."

"Wait," Taj said. "I have questions I need someone to answer for me."

"Next time," Garlen said. "It doesn't just rain in New Orleans, it pours."

Rain began dimpling the dark leather of Taj's coat, as he watched the tour guide disappear through the front gate. An unexpected voice startled him back to reality.

"Get in here before the sky opens up."

An older black man was holding open the door of an outbuilding Taj hadn't noticed when they entered the cemetery. As the rain began falling harder, he followed the man into the little building.

There were no windows, the air stale, the little room lighted only by a blazing potbelly stove and a few candles. There were a couple of ramshackle chairs and an old cot draped with pillow and bedclothes. The floor was dirt. Through the crack in the door, Taj could hear the drumming of rain growing heavier by the minute.

"Who are you?" Taj asked.

The man chuckled. "The keeper of cemeteries and lost souls."

"You're the caretaker?"

"Something like that."

"I'm Taj. What's your name?"

"People call me lots of things. You can call me Sam. You told that man you got questions."

"And I was hoping for some answers," Taj said. "Guess I'll have to find them someplace else."

Sam chuckled. "You weren't going to get the answers you need from him. Hell, the girl with the prissy boyfriend knows more about spirits than he do."

"How do you know that?" Taj asked.

"Old Sam here knows lots of things."

"But she's white."

"Not much difference between white and black in Nawlins."

"That girl's from Michigan and not New Orleans."

Sam fluffed the pillow on the cot. "Some people don't have the foggiest idea where they're really from," he said.

Taj let the comment pass. During his tenure in the NBA, he'd developed an eye for his opponents' height, weight, and age. Sam was about five-eight and probably somewhere north of fifty years old. Despite the gloomy day, he had a pair of dark sunglasses perched atop his head. The stub of his lit cigar came out of his mouth only when he talked. Moving the pillow aside, he plopped down on the cot, propping his feet up on a packing crate. Taj grinned when he noticed the holes in his dirty white socks.

"Gonna be raining awhile," Sam said. "Take a load off and grab a chair. Like I say, that white man don't know a damn thing about voodoo, anyway."

"Think I'll stand," Taj said, glancing at the rickety chair he doubted would support his weight.

"Want something to drink?" Sam asked.

"Sure. My body is wet, but my mouth is kind of dry."

Sam retrieved a gallon jug of red wine from behind his cot. After unscrewing the metal cap, he slung the bottle over his shoulder and slugged the cheap wine straight from the container.

"Nothing much better than a pull of MD 20-20,"

Taj took the bottle, laughing before he took a swig. As wine dribbled down Taj's chin, it was Sam's turn to laugh.

"Haven't had any Mad Dog since I was a freshman in college," Taj said.

"Good for what ails you," Sam said. "Have another taste."

Taj waved off the offer as he handed the jug of wine back to Sam.

"One pull was all I needed."

"Suit yourself," Sam said.

The rain had begun falling in sheets, humid air flooding through the partly open door.

"How'd you know my question was about voodoo?" Taj asked.

"Hell, boy, your silk shirt is open to the waist. Even in the dark, and half covered by that big old gold chain around your neck, I can see the veve tattooed on your chest."

Sam chuckled again when Taj said, "You know what it means?"

"Only the houngan or mambo that put it there knows the answer to that. And maybe the loa they're attempting to influence."

"That's what I heard," Taj said. "How do you know so much about voodoo?"

"Who says I do?" Sam said.

"Do you?"

"Ain't no one from Nawlins that don't know something about voodoo."

Taj reached into his coat for the voodoo doll. "What can you tell me about this?" he asked.

Sam, unmindful of the blood, took the doll. "Somebody got it in for you."

"Because?"

"Cause this is your doll."

"How do you know that?"

Sam removed a hair from the doll and handed it to Taj. "Looks like it came from your beard."

"That's crazy talk. It probably stuck to the doll when I was handling it," Taj said.

"What about this?"

Rain continued falling outside the little room as Sam dropped something into Taj's palm.

"A fingernail. What makes you think it's mine?" Taj asked.

"Is it?"

A sliver of purplish skin hung from the fingernail. Taj glanced at the ring finger on his left hand at the blackened nail he'd damaged in a recent basketball game.

"If it is mine, how would anyone have gotten it?"

"Voodoo practitioners have long arms. Might surprise you who could have got it for them. For a price."

Taj recalled the woman he'd met in a bar after the game that night. An overly friendly young woman with a southern accent.

"I'm having trouble believing all of this," he said.

"You believed it enough to come looking for answers," Sam said.

"You think someone's trying to kill me?"

"Getting hexed with a voodoo doll don't always mean a person's trying to kill you."

"Then what does it mean?"

"Somebody is trying to control your actions."

"A voodoo witch doctor?"

"Practitioners make their living casting spells. More than likely, someone hired them to do it."

"And why on earth would they do that?"

Sam shook his head. "You wronged anyone lately? Screwed someone else's wife, or took something that didn't belong to you? Hell, man! It could be almost anything."

"I'm not a perfect person, though I can't think of anyone I've wronged lately," Taj said.

"Then search your soul. You did something to somebody, and they're pissed off about it. That, I can promise you," Sam said. "Or . . ."

"Or what?"

"Somebody might be trying to send you a message," Sam said.

The heavy door banged against the wall as a gust of wind blew it open. Sucking the air out of the room, it extinguished all the candles as it slammed shut again. Sam padded across the dirt floor, relighting the candles with what looked like a flame coming directly from his fingers. Taj waited until he'd returned to his perch on the cot.

"I need help," Taj said. "I'll pay you well if you can help me."

"I don't need your money, and I've already told you a bunch. What you need is the right person to help you," Sam said. "A smart houngan or mambo."

"Can you refer me to one?"

"There's a powerful mambo I've dealt with," Sam said. "I'm betting she can help you."

"Please tell me who she is."

"Her name is Mama Mulate."

Chapter 4

Clouds had turned an angry shade of gray, rain having ceased as Taj left Sam's shack. Two seagulls floated in lazy circles above him as he pulled the leather coat around his neck and hurried up the sidewalk.

Except for a wino looking for shelter from the weather, the streets were deserted. Taj handed the derelict a twenty as he walked past. He saw someone he recognized when he reached Dr. Voodoo's Spells and Hexes. It was Amy, shivering as she stood on one leg against the wall.

"What the hell!" he said. "You could get killed out here all alone. Where's your boyfriend?"

"The little prick left me here."

"You gotta be kidding? Why in the world would he do that?"

"It wasn't his idea to spend Christmas in New Orleans. It was mine."

"So?"

"Brian comes from a wealthy Long Island family that always celebrates Christmas together. His mother called and told him to get his ass home."

"Why didn't you just go with him?"

"Because he hasn't bothered telling his mother about me yet. He offered to drop me at the airport."

She smiled for the first time when Taj said, "That was mighty white of him."

"He gave me a hundred bucks. Probably not even enough for a bus ticket to Ann Arbor."

"I have money," Taj said. "I'll cover you for a plane ticket home."

"I'm not going home. I was drawn here for a reason. I'm staying until I find out what that reason is."

Taj removed his leather coat, draping it around the young woman's shoulders.

"Don't want you to catch a cold," he said. "Why are you still at the voodoo shop?"

"Waiting on you. The first time I saw you I knew we had a cosmic connection. Can I stay the night with you? I have no other place to go."

Taj took a step backward. He was an attractive big man who had wielded an almost hypnotic attraction on women since he was in his teens. Even so, Amy's words caught him by surprise.

"You're moving way too fast," he said. "I'm not looking to shack up with anyone tonight."

She grabbed his wrist and pulled him closer. "Neither am I," she said. "I have something you need to see."

A rush of adrenaline warmed Taj's neck when Amy raised her University of Michigan tee shirt. She was braless, though it was something other than her breasts that caught his attention. The veve situated between them, though smaller, was identical to the one on his own chest. After lowering her tee shirt, she stared at him.

"That's the same mark I have on my chest," he said. "Were you born with it?"

"Yes, and my name isn't Amy. It's Adelajda. My relatives and friends call me Adela."

"Then why did you introduce yourself as Amy?"

"Because Brian thought Adelajda sounded too

ethnic."

"What a jerk," Taj said.

"It's not the reason I encouraged him to drive off without me. When I saw the symbol on your chest, I knew I had to talk to you about it. Did you come to New Orleans for the same reason as me?"

"Not exactly," he said. "You hungry?"

"Starved," she said. "And I was freezing until you lent me your coat. Thank you."

"What are you hungry for?"

"Anything. I haven't eaten since we got here. Brian was a stickler for staying on schedule. If you missed a meal, you just went hungry until the next one rolled around."

"Jerk," Taj said. "My hotel isn't far away. Their food is pretty damn good. We can warm up, talk, and get something to eat and drink."

A damp chill permeated the air around them, the sound of tourists growing louder as they approached Bourbon Street. Flashing neon failed to mask the pink pastels of the winter sky as the sun disappeared behind old French Quarter buildings.

Except for a few half-drunk college students, the chilly weather had kept most of the tourists in their hotel rooms. A strip show barker standing in an open doorway called to them, trying to attract some business.

"Naked ladies. Gotta come see. First drink, half price."

"Next time," Taj said, clutching Adela's arm as they hurried past.

Music poured from the doors, vibrating the fine mist that was wafting up from the street. Adela pulled Taj to a halt, turned around and stared at the blocks of neon-lighted antiquity.

"Bourbon Street's like an adult fantasyland," she said.

"I hear that," Taj said. "Let's hurry. It's starting

to rain again."

Rain began dampening their shoulders, lights of the hotel casting a welcome glow through the gloom as they followed a side street to Royal. A stretch limo was dropping off people in front of the hotel. Festively dressed in holiday colors, they looked as if they were on their way to a Christmas party. Tommy was back on duty and spotted them as soon as they entered the bustling lobby.

"Tommy, my man," Taj said. "This is Adela. She's my sister."

"Sure she is," Tommy said. "Pleased to meet you, Miss Adela."

"We need your help," Taj said. "When you get a minute, can you come upstairs?"

"Sure," Tommy said. "Got an errand I need to run first."

"No hurry," Taj said.

Everyone in the lobby turned to watch the tall black man and the young woman with long, red hair, disappear into the elevator. Five minutes after arriving at the room, Tommy, carrying two menus and a bottle of red wine, joined them.

"Figured you might need these," he said.

"Same as last night for me," Taj said. "Steak, baked, and another bottle of your finest red wine. I've had a tough day."

"You got it, Mr. Taj. What about you, ma'am?" Tommy said. "We got some of the best gumbo in town."

"I've never eaten gumbo," she said.

"Then you're in for a treat," he said. "It's like ambrosia of the gods."

"That sounds lovely, Tommy. I can't wait to taste it."

"You like Cajun food?" Tommy said.

"I've never eaten any."

"You like seafood?"

"Love seafood," she said.

Beaming, Tommy said, "Then you'll love Cajun food. I'll have the chef prepare a sampler plate for you. What to drink?"

"Red wine for now, though Chardonnay sounds good with the seafood."

"You bet it is. You'll have a bottle of our best," Tommy said. "What else?"

Taj began peeling hundred dollar bills from his roll of cash.

"Adela is from out of town. She didn't come dressed for December in New Orleans and needs jeans, blouses, boots, socks, underwear, and a suitable coat. You get the picture?"

"Keep your money," Tommy said. "The concierge has someone on staff who shops for our rich clients. I'll send her up to get Miss Adela's sizes and have the hotel put it on your tab. Let the Pels pay for it."

"We'll also need another bed for Adela. Can you handle it for me?" Taj asked.

"Course I can. Guess you forget who took care of you last night."

Taj handed Tommy two twenties. "I won't forget about that. I predict there'll be front-row tickets waiting for you next time you want to see a Pel's game."

Tommy's eyes grew large. "You mean it?"

"You bet I do," Taj said.

"My man," Tommy said, giving Taj a high-five before exiting the room.

❧

The extra bed was in place, the shopping lady having come and gone, as Adela finished the last morsel of her bread pudding. Taj topped up their wine glasses before speaking.

"Feel better?"

"Wonderful," she said.

"We have things to discuss. Seems like an unbelievable coincidence both of us have identical voodoo marks on our chests and that we arrived in New Orleans at more or less the same time. I have no memory of how I got whatever this thing is. What about you?"

Adela shook her head. "No idea. My parents are good Christians. I feel certain they didn't put it there."

"I was adopted as a baby," Taj said. "I grew up in New Jersey."

"Michigan for me," she said. "I got a full academic scholarship after high school. I'm studying to be a botanist though I have no clue if it's what I want to do for the rest of my life. How about you?"

"I also got a full ride out of high school, though mine was by way of an athletic scholarship. I'm thirty-four. You have to be in your twenties."

"Twenty-five," she said. "I bummed around a few years before starting college."

"You're white, and I'm black. We're obviously not related."

"Then why do we have identical symbols on our chests?" she asked.

"Wish I knew," he said. "What's your last name?"

"Kowalski," Adela said. "Very Polish."

"You don't look Polish," Taj said.

"How's a Pole supposed to look?"

"With your red hair, freckles, and light colored skin, you look more Irish to me," Taj said.

"Adelajda is Polish, just like my last name. Is Davis your real name?"

"Real to me, though I'm sure it's not my birth name," Taj said.

Adela gazed out an open window at the lights filtering up from the French Quarter.

"The colors from up here are mesmerizing," she said. "I knew I had a connection to this city the moment I walked into that old cemetery. My head was all abuzz. It was as if I could hear the moans of the spirits. It was deafening."

"I feel the same way about New Orleans."

"Why were you on the cemetery tour?" Adela asked.

"Because of this," he said.

He reached inside his trench coat Adela had thrown across the bed and showed her the voodoo doll.

"What the hell is it?" she asked.

"Voodoo doll," he said.

"Is the blood on that grotesque thing yours?"

"Afraid so," he said. "The hotel was crowded when I arrived yesterday. They put me in a room on the thirteenth floor that hasn't been used for decades. I drank a bottle of wine and fell asleep in the bathtub. A demon from hell woke me."

"You're making this up."

"It chased me out the door."

"Were you frightened?"

"I'm not afraid of much. The demon I saw scared the hell out of me. Enough so, I didn't bother getting dressed. I stepped on glass when I got out of the tub and was naked and bleeding when Tommy found me. I had this in my hand. I went to the voodoo shop to try and find out what it means."

"Did you?" she asked.

"Both the shop owner and a man I met at the cemetery said someone had made it especially for me."

"How on earth would they have known that?" she asked.

"The doll had a hair from my beard and a fingernail I'd lost in a basketball game."

"Are you sure?"

"The nail from the doll fit my finger like a missing puzzle piece. I have no doubt it was mine."

"You're saying someone made a voodoo doll

that's supposed to be you? Why would they do that?"

"The cemetery caretaker seemed to know a bunch about voodoo. He said it could mean almost anything. One thing he was sure of. Somebody has put a hex on me."

"A cemetery caretaker told you that? Sounds crazy to me."

"Pretty much what I thought, at least until you showed me the veve on your chest," he said.

"What should we do?" Adela asked.

"The cemetery man gave me the name of a voodoo woman named Mama Mulate."

"This is too weird," Adela said. "I've had an urge to visit New Orleans, and I have no idea where the notion came from."

"Maybe you're part of the hex," Taj said.

"But that's just crazy," she said.

"It is crazy," Taj said.

"What happens if we do nothing?" Adela asked.

"Either find out the hex means nothing, or else suffer the results of it," Taj said. "My career is already affected. I have a cut foot, and now I've met someone with an identical mark on their chest as the one I have. I don't want to worry when I go to sleep at night I'll wake up with a demon in my face. We need to get to the bottom of this hex. The only way I know how to proceed is to contact the woman Sam told me about."

Distant thunder rattled the old building, the steady drumming of rain beginning to beat a tympani on the windows. Adela's vivid eyes flashed when the electricity failed for just a moment.

"How do we find her?" Adela asked.

"Maybe Tommy can help us."

Chapter 5

December had arrived in the French Quarter. I realized as much when I walked downstairs from my apartment above Bertram Picou's on Rue Chartres and saw him hanging Christmas lights over the bar.

"About time you got your ass out of bed, Wyatt Thomas," he said. "You so rich now you don't need to work?"

Bertram was of French Acadian descent. One-hundred percent coonass and he played it to the hilt for his visitors from out of town. After mopping his forehead and thinning hair with his trapper's hat, he pulled up a stool beside me.

"I work for myself, and it's Saturday," I said. "I can sleep late if I feel like it."

"Yeah, yeah," Bertram said. "Sleep all damn day for all I care. Just as long as you pay your rent."

I'd recently won lots of money betting on the ponies at the local racetrack. First thing I'd done was prepay the rent for twelve months in advance.

"Business slow?" I said, not taking his bait.

"Damn rain's about to bankrupt me," he said.

A steady drizzle of rain was falling outside. Through the windows, I could see a Lucky Dog wrapper floating down the flooded street. The sidewalks were empty, rain keeping the tourists in their hotel rooms.

"You'll survive," I said. "You haven't bought anything new for this place since I've known you. What do you do with all the money you make in this little goldmine?"

Bertram brushed a dark wisp of hair that had fallen down over his forehead, and then tweaked his mustache.

"You seen my bills lately?" he said. "I'm lucky if I break even every month."

"Quit whining, Bertram. I don't believe a word you're saying."

Bertram ducked under the bar, poured himself a shot of Cuervo and an icy glass of lemonade for me.

"Seen Eddie lately?"

"He's keeping a low profile, trying to decide whether to marry Josie Castellano."

"Frankie and Adele were here last night. Sounded to me like Eddie don't have much choice."

Adele was a friend. Assistant Federal D.A. Eddie Toledo and I were eating in Adele's Italian restaurant in Metairie the night local mob boss Frankie Castellano had walked in the door. Love had ensued, the couple still enamored with each other after two years of marriage. Josie was Frankie's strong-minded daughter who had fallen in love with perennial bachelor, Eddie.

"Maybe that's why we haven't seen him in a while. I can't see Eddie ever settling down with any woman, no matter how attractive, rich, or intelligent she might be."

"You could be right," he said as he slugged the shot and then poured himself another. "It bother you how much Josie looks like Desire?"

"At first it did."

"You over her yet?" he asked.

"I'll never be totally over Desire. At least I've

resolved her loss in my mind."

"She's one drop-dead gorgeous woman. Too bad things didn't work out," Bertram said. "What has happened to her?"

It took me a moment before I could answer. "Missionary work in Africa. I doubt she'll ever return to New Orleans."

I'd met Desire Vallee while working on a problem for her father, Gordon. The case had ended badly, both Gordon and Desire's twin sister dying tragically. Their deaths were also the end of my short-lived affair with the most exciting woman I'd ever known.

"Sorry to bring it up," Bertram said. "Have a new woman on your radar?"

"I'm done with relationships. Everyone I've had lately has ended badly."

"Gotta admit," Bertram said. "You're pretty tough on women. What about Mama Mulate? You two ever hooked up?"

"Though we've come close a time or two, our business relationship is more important to us than a love affair."

"I hear that," Bertram said. "How's it working out for you?"

"We haven't done anything businesswise in a while," I said.

"I can't remember how you got to be partners," Bertram said.

"Mama performed a voodoo séance for a rich client of mine. He was so impressed, he told all his wealthy friends about us. For a while, we had more paranormal related business than we could handle. Clients wanting us to contact dead relatives, or find lost graves."

"You've done lots of cases that didn't involve Mama Mulate," Bertram said.

"It's just a loose partnership," I said. "Mama's still an English professor at Tulane, and I've continued working cases even when she isn't involved."

Before I could expound further about my relationship with Mama Mulate, someone Bertram and I both knew entered the bar. It was Eddie Toledo looking professional in an expensive pin-striped suit.

"Well, look what the cat drug in," Bertram said. "We were just talking about you. What the hell are you doing here on a Monday morning?"

"I just got fired, and I need a drink."

Eddie's words came as a shock. He'd worked for the government since graduating as valedictorian from the University of Virginia law school. I'd fully expected him to retire with the Feds. From the look on his face, so did he. Bertram quickly poured Eddie a double scotch and pushed the glass across the bar.

"What the hell happened?"

"The powers downtown apparently thought I'd gotten a little too close to Frankie Castellano," he said.

Eddie had dark hair and eyes, his hair a bit too long to fit the image of a federal prosecutor. Women had a hard time resisting him, and he couldn't resist women. Though he'd fallen hard for the beautiful daughter of a mob boss, my money was betting he'd wind up as a life-long bachelor.

"You've always kept that relationship with Frankie at arm's length," I said. "What changed?"

"The rumor I was marrying the Don of the Bayou's daughter."

"We heard it was more than a rumor," Bertram said.

"I have to admit, I was resigned to taking the plunge," Eddie said.

"You changed your mind?" I asked.

"Josie changed it for me. She said she would never marry a cheater. I told her I had changed. My best defense failed to convince her."

"Bummer," I said. "Frankie and Adele had their hearts set on an April wedding. How are they taking it?"

"They both feel sooner or later Josie will change her mind. Me, I'm not so sure about it."

Eddie slugged his drink, and Bertram poured him another.

"What now?" I asked.

"I have no job, no car, and my resume just took a professional hit. I do have an opportunity on the table," he said.

"Oh?" I said.

"Frankie must have known what was going down because he called me with an offer this morning."

"One you can't refuse?" Bertram said.

"I have alternatives. I could put out my shingle and go into private practice."

"Because of your position with the Feds, you've probably met every influential person in town," I said. "You could make a killing in private practice."

"Don't know if I'm cut out to represent white collar scumbags."

"Why not?" Bertram said. "You'd soon be driving a Porsche, living in the Garden District, and golfing at the country club on the weekends. Hell, they might even make you president of the Boston Club."

"Funny, Bertram," Eddie said.

"What sort of offer did Frankie have for you? His consigliere?"

"Adele and Frankie still want me to marry Josie. They both know she'd have no part of me if I became Frankie's mob attorney."

"What then?" I asked.

"A developer built a weekend getaway destination east of here in the late twenties. It's on an island with access by water to the Mississippi

River, Lake Pontchartrain, Lake Bourne, and it abuts the Gulf of Mexico. It had a marina, a restaurant, and a dozen or so vacation homes. The development gradually declined because of its lack of infrastructure."

"What's the name of this place?" I asked.

"Oyster Island."

"And?" Bertram said.

"Frankie offered to give me the restaurant and bar, and all the property that goes with it."

"In exchange for what?" I asked.

"He wants to redevelop the property and for me to be the mayor."

"What good is a restaurant and bar if you ain't got no customers?" Bertram asked.

"The place is like a little resort community. Frankie says if we update the infrastructure and then advertise the hell out of it, customers and new weekend homeowners will flock there."

"What about hurricanes, flooding and global warming?" I asked.

"Frankie paid a consulting firm to do an engineering and geological study of the island. Seems it's located in just the right spot to receive a yearly influx of new sediment coming from down river. The island is sheltered by barrier islands and rises six feet above sea level. The study satisfied all of Frankie's questions about risking millions of dollars on development."

"So he's giving you the restaurant and bar?" Bertram said.

"I have to pay him back out of profits, but the loan is non-recourse. If the plan doesn't work, I walk. No harm, no foul."

"Except you'll be out the months or years you put into it," I said.

Bertram poured Eddie another scotch and a shot of Cuervo for himself.

"That's why I'm here," Eddie said. "I was

hoping Bertram would visit the island with me and give me his assessment of whether or not the plan has a snowball's chance in hell of succeeding."

"Asking for 'ol Bertram's help means you ain't half as dumb as I thought you was. When you want to go?"

Ignoring Bertram's remark, Eddie said, "I've got nothing on my dance card. How about now?"

Bertram glanced around the bar, and then at me. "Can you hold the fort down while I'm gone?"

"Why not?" I said. "The place isn't exactly overflowing with customers."

When Bertram whistled, his dog Lady, a beautiful cognac-colored collie, sauntered out of the kitchen, wagging her tail when she saw Eddie and me.

"Come on, girl. We're gonna take a little road trip with Eddie. Be back when you see me," Bertram said as they disappeared through the kitchen.

⳥ⳤ

A month had passed since I'd collected a retainer from a paying customer. Like Eddie, I had nothing on my dance card and was behind the bar polishing a glass when Mama Mulate walked through the door. I hadn't seen her in a while, and I ducked under the bar to give her a big hug.

"Where's Bertram?" she asked.

"Long story," I said.

"Give me a synopsis."

"On a wild goose chase with Eddie Toledo. I'm stuck tending bar until they return. What's up?"

"Tickets to the Pels game tonight," she said, flashing them for me to see. "Can you go with me?"

"You kidding? I love the Pels, and I haven't been to a game this year. Who gave you the tickets?"

"They arrived in the mail, along with ten new hundred dollar bills. There was a cryptic message."

"That said?"

"Mama, I need your help. Please accept these tickets and the money as a retainer. After the game, meet me on the top floor at the Riverfront. It's signed T.D."

"Wow! The Riverfront's one of the most expensive restaurants in town," I said.

"Check out these seats," she said. "Courtside. They had to cost a few thousand dollars each."

"Double wow," I said.

"Who do you think we're dealing with?" she asked.

"Someone with lots of money. Maybe a professional athlete. The Riverfront is a favorite hangout for pros from almost every sport."

"I've never been there," Mama said. "What's it like?"

"Never been there, either, though I hear it has a magnificent view of the river. The cuisine, I hear, is Creole and Italian."

"Then are you in?"

"You bet I am. I wouldn't pass up a free pro basketball ticket even if it were in the nosebleed section. I've never had a seat so close to the floor."

"What if Bertram isn't back?" Mama asked.

"I'll find someone to watch the place," I said.

"Then I'll pick you up out front, around six," she said.

She waved as she hurried out the door, a blast of chilly air flooding into Bertram's empty bar behind her.

Chapter 6

ertram Picou's Ford truck, the first new vehicle he'd ever owned, was bright red. Though he wouldn't admit it, he loved the big vehicle. Having the entire backseat to herself, so did Lady.

"Your truck is awesome," Eddie Toledo said. "I thought you'd never get rid of Old Betsy. What made you do it?"

"I wouldn't trade old Betsy for nothing," he said. "She's in my garage, under a canvas cover. It was Lady that wanted this one."

"How's that?"

"Cousin Ezra sells Fords. He come up for a visit in his new truck. Lady loved it so much, I thought she was gonna go home with him. He made me a family deal I couldn't pass on."

"You did good," Eddie said. "This truck is a beauty."

"You right about that," Bertram said.

Lady barked in the backseat as if seconding Bertram's assessment of the new truck. A drizzling rain had followed them out of New Orleans, the wipers of the Ford beating a slow tympani as they tooled down the rural road. They'd exited the main highway shortly after leaving the city. So far, Bertram hadn't consulted a map.

"You sure you know where you're going?" Eddie asked.

"I got kinfolk all over the state," Bertram said. "I know these roads like the back of my hand. My daddy and me visited Oyster Island when I was a kid."

A cypress swamp bordered one side of the byway, rain dimpling the coffee-colored water. A flock of brown egrets was landing, joining a handful of cows grazing in the open pasture on the side of the road.

"Which way is the river?" Eddie asked.

"That ridge you see is a natural levee. The river's on the other side of it. Indians had a trail on the ridgeline. This road follows the old Indian trail."

"There were Indians around here?"

"You bet they was," Bertram said. "Long before the French and Spanish ever got here."

"Where are they now?"

"Hell!" Bertram said. "I'm part Indian myself. They just kinda mingled in with the population, I guess."

"I guess," Eddie said. "How much farther to Oyster Island?"

"The old bridge is over the next rise," he said. "We're almost there."

Bertram's memory had faded over the years. It was another five miles further before they topped a small hill and saw the island that gave the old settlement its name. The low-lying bridge was just large enough for one vehicle at a time. The crystal water beneath them was shallow, large fish clearly visible.

A sandy beach stretched from the rolling countryside down to the blue water of the Gulf of Mexico. It wasn't the pristine beach, the gulls flying lazily overhead, or the solitude of the scene that caught Eddie's attention. It was the wooden edifice sitting on stilts and the boat docks of the marina surrounding it.

"Surely, that can't be the restaurant," Eddie said.

"Sure it is," Bertram said. "I seen picture postcards of it before in gift shops."

"It's huge. It'll cost a fortune just to air condition it."

"That ain't half your problem," Bertram said. "Like I said back in New Orleans, there are no paying customers within an hour of here."

Eddie drew a deep breath before replying. "That is a concern. What'll I do?"

"We're here, now. Might as well take a look around."

Frankie's engineering assessment of the island appeared correct. Atop the rise, above the bay, sat a lighthouse painted with a fresh coat of yellow and white. A picket fence circled the lighthouse, and the rear of an old Ford Bronco protruded from a covered shelter. Because of the Bronco and the well-manicured shrubbery around the fence, it seemed likely someone lived in the lighthouse. They turned their attention to the restaurant.

The large building, a partially covered veranda surrounding it, was circular and several stories tall. The wind had damaged the cupola topping the building, and the entire structure was in desperate need of a fresh coat of paint. Outside stairways led to the deck on the top floor.

"Good God Almighty!" Bertram said. "That thing is every bit of fifty thousand square feet. It'll cost a fortune to renovate. Even if you got customers waiting in line, I can tell you right now you're never gonna make that dog hunt."

"I have eyes," Eddie said.

Seeing Bertram and Eddie standing beside the walkway leading to the restaurant, the lightkeeper came through the white gate, down the broken shell pathway, to the bay. A large pit bull followed behind him. Eddie was the first to notice.

"Must be the caretaker. He's expecting us. Frankie said he'd give us a tour of the facilities."

"Uh oh!" Bertram said. "That looks like one mean dog he got with him."

"Let's hope not," Eddie said.

Though the brindle beast looked dangerous, it sprawled on the pathway as the man bent down and gave Lady's head a pat. With her tail wagging, Lady approached the big pit bull, rubbing noses with him. Seeing the concern on Bertram and Eddie's faces, the man smiled and waved his hand.

"Brutus wouldn't hurt a soul," he said.

"Sure about that?" Bertram asked.

"You got my Louisiana guaranty on it. I'm Jack Wiesinski," he said, shaking Eddie's hand.

"I'm Eddie, and this is Bertram. The gorgeous collie is Lady. Looks as if she likes your big pit."

"And he likes her too, though he's too lazy to get his big butt up off the ground and greet her like a proper gentleman."

Jack Wiesinski was short, probably no taller than five-six or seven. He was wiry, closely shaven, with brown hair buzzed almost to his scalp. From the odd shape of his mouth, it was hard to tell if he was smiling or frowning.

"Sure glad Brutus is friendly," Bertram said. "That big dog could do some major damage if he wanted to. I don't recognize your accent, Jack. You from around here?"

"Massachusetts. Grew up on Cape Ann. I like gumbo, but I'm still partial to Cape Ann chowder."

"Got no problem with that," Bertram said. "I'm partial to gumbo, but I've never turned down a good bowl of chowder."

"Mr. Castellano told me you'd be coming to take a look at the restaurant."

Jack scratched Lady behind the ears. She

must have liked him because she couldn't stop wagging her tail.

"Frankie said you live on the premises," Eddie said. "Up on the hill?"

"That's my other baby," Jack said. "Mr. Castellano pays me to watch his property, the state pays me to operate the lighthouse. After putting in thirty years with the Navy, I'm on government pension from them. I'm one lucky S.O.B."

"Sweet," Bertram said. "If you had someplace around here to spend all that money."

Jack flashed him a crooked smile. "Me, I don't need much."

"How about a shot of Cuervo?" Bertram said, pulling a silver flask from his light jacket.

"Man after my own heart," Jack said, taking a drink from the flask. "Ready to see the old queen?"

"That's what we're here for," Eddie said. "Lead the way."

Bertram and Eddie could see just how short and wiry Jack Wiesinski was, as they followed him to the covered walkway leading to the old restaurant. Dressed in khaki pants and shirt, he indeed looked like a naval retiree that couldn't quite get the service out of his blood. Only his black flipflops belied the image.

The restaurant sat a hundred feet from shore, the walkway the only way to reach it. The ring of keys Jack kept on his belt rattled as he opened the three locks securing the gate of the covered walkway.

"Watch your step," he said. "Some of the old boards need replacing."

"We'll follow you," Eddie said.

Buoyed by rusting oil barrels, the walkway swayed beneath them as they followed Jack to the front deck encircling the restaurant. Even though the paint was faded and everything dusty as hell, the grandeur of the old restaurant far exceeded anything either Eddie or Bertram had expected.

"This place must have been like a palace back in the day," Eddie said.

"That it was," Jack said. "People came from all over to get their pictures made here. It was quite the showplace."

Separate dining areas surrounded the main ballroom highlighted by the most beautifully carved wood bar either Bertram or Eddie had ever seen. The room was huge, the ceilings high and ornate. Even in its present state of dust and disarray, the building was regal. Jack pointed to the large bar.

"Carved by Italian artisans from giant cypress trees cut in a swamp near here. Mr. Castellano calls it a significant work of art."

"Impressive," Eddie said.

Brutus and Lady were nuzzling each other, their tails wagging. Lady barked, apparently agreeing with Eddie's assessment of the beautiful piece of sculpture. Bertram rubbed his hand across the wood.

"Needs a little furniture polish," he said.

"The whole place needs work," Jack said. "It's been more or less abandoned for seventy years."

"What do you think, Bertram?" Eddie asked.

"Even if you got this place back into apple pie order, there ain't enough customers in this whole parish to keep you in bidness."

"Frankie must realize as much," Eddie said. "He said he has a plan."

"There's lots more to see," Jack said. "An interesting level up these stairs. This deck has a history unique to the Prohibition Era."

A circular tier comprised of tiny rooms looked down on the bar and ballroom area. Tattered curtains covered the openings to the rooms. Jack pulled open a curtain, showing Bertram and Eddie the inside of one of the empty cubicles.

"During Prohibition, this place was a casino and speakeasy. Mobsters would bring their mistresses here for drinks and dinner. No one knew who was up here except the waiters and waitresses who served them."

"Must have been quite a scene," Eddie said.

Jack didn't respond, leading them into a staircase that wound to an even higher level of the old structure. He exited to the observation deck that looked out over the bay. Eddie and Bertram stared at the water with wide eyes and open mouths.

"Is that the Gulf of Mexico?"

"Yes." Jack handed Eddie a pair of binoculars. "You can see ships and offshore rigs if you use these."

Through the powerful lenses of the binoculars, the Gulf came alive. Gulls soared high above the water, floating in and out of the dark clouds. It seemed like a living diorama.

"Quite a view," Eddie said, handing the binoculars to Bertram.

Jack nodded. "Barrier islands protect this cove. Centuries ago, it was a haven for pirates. Local legend says there's a fortune in gold buried someplace on this island."

"I don't doubt it," Eddie said. "It's so secluded and pristine, it's hard for me to believe this place is even inhabited."

"It ain't," Bertram said. "Except for Jack and his dog. That's your problem."

Bertram and Eddie both seemed surprised when Jack said, "There's more to see. It's starting to sprinkle again. Let's go inside before the bottom falls out."

They climbed higher, by way of a circular staircase, and entered a room at the tallest part of the building. Windows circled the area affording a three-hundred-sixty-degree view. Polished teak and mahogany paneling evoked the look and feel of the bridge of a ship.

"The person that designed this deck must have liked to play sea captain," Eddie said.

"He was a retired sea captain. He used this private hideaway to escape from the crowds of people downstairs," Jack said.

"From up here, you can see for miles in every direction," Bertram said.

"Except for the lighthouse, there's no better view on Oyster Island. Want to see the living quarters?"

The deck below the bridge housed a large apartment, complete with galley, master bedroom, living area, pot-bellied stove, and bathrooms. Dust covers protected the original furniture still in place.

"Everything a man could need," Jack said.

"Cozy," Eddie said. "Anything else?"

"This old building has dozens of nooks, crannies, and secret passageways in the walls. You could spend a month here and not see everything there is to see."

"Secret passageways?" Eddie said.

"And the building is haunted. I've never seen a ghost, though others have."

"Sounds creepy," Eddie said. "The marina is so large. Where are all the boats?"

"There are only two," Jack said. "A sloop and a trawler. Both are seaworthy and have traveled more than once from here to islands in the Caribbean."

"Pleasure trips?" Bertram asked.

"Business," Jack said. "They were both rum runners. Even during Prohibition, patrons to Oyster Island could sample the best scotch, rum, or Canadian whiskey, courtesy of those two vessels."

"Who owns the boats now?" Eddie asked.

"You will. The boats go with the restaurant," Jack said.

"Are they still operable?"

"You bet they are. One of my duties is caring for the two boats. You could sail from here to the Bahamas tomorrow in either one of them if you wanted to."

"If I could sail, or knew how to operate a boat," Eddie said.

"I can teach you," Jack said.

"Don't know about that," Eddie said. "I'm still not sure if this is the job for me. I don't even have a car."

"A Land Rover comes with the restaurant. It's ten years old and still purrs like a kitten. It's something else I take care of for Mr. Castellano."

"Maybe you better talk to Frankie about this whole thing," Bertram said. "If you ask me, it looks like you'd be painting yourself in a corner."

"That's why I brought you along," Eddie said. "You know I value your opinion."

For the moment, the rain had ceased, though the skies had continued to grow ever darker. Jack glanced up the hill toward the lighthouse.

"You boys hungry? I got a kettle of oyster chowder simmering on the stove."

Chapter 7

The rain had returned, a cold breeze blowing up from the Gulf as Bertram, Eddie, Jack, and the two dogs hurried up the rocky pathway to the lighthouse on the sandy hill. Thunder shook the old wooden and mortar structure, as Jack held the door open for them. Welcoming warmth and the enticing aroma of oyster chowder greeted them as they entered the living area of the lighthouse.

The only furniture in the open living area was a single chair, and an old couch draped with an orange Afghan. There was also a pot-bellied stove and a desk, complete with computer and ham radio. Everything in the minimalist setting seemed to have a place and pegged Jack as a person who demanded order in his life. Warming their hands, Eddie and Bertram huddled close to the stove.

"Cozy place you have here," Eddie said. "Must get kind of lonely."

Outside the old lighthouse, the rain had begun falling in bucketloads. Sheer curtains that seemed a bit too dainty for a career Navy man covered the three windows, lightning flashing through them.

"I spent the best part of thirty years at sea," Jack said. "I like solitude."

"That chowder smells mighty good," Bertram

said. "Been cooking long?"

"Thirty years."

"Then I guess you never been married," Bertram said.

"Tried it once," Jack said. "Didn't last long. Women tend to want their man home at night, not off at sea somewhere. What about you, Bert? Ever been married?"

"Come close a time or two."

"You, Eddie?"

"Not yet," he said.

"Mr. Castellano says you're sweet on his daughter."

"The feeling isn't mutual," Eddie said.

"Maybe when you get Oyster Island up and running, she'll change her mind."

"Is that what Mr. Castellano told you?"

"No, but I'm pretty good at reading between the lines. You boys find a place to sit. I'll get us something to drink."

"I think Lady likes it here," Bertram said.

Brutus had crawled up on a woven rug in front of the pot-bellied stove, Lady joining him. A bell-shaped opening separated the galley from the living area of the lighthouse. Bertram and Eddie sank into a comfortable, old couch as Jack returned from the galley with two mugs and a pitcher filled with an alcoholic beverage.

"Hope you boys like rum," Jack said, filling their mugs from the pitcher.

Bertram took a sip. "This is the best rum I ever tasted. What brand is it?"

"Don't remember," Jack said. "Just some cheap swill I picked up at the liquor store. I like to serve rum with my chowder. Old Navy habit, I guess."

"Can I have a look at the bottle?" Bertram asked.

"Threw it away, already," Jack said. "I always

serve my grog from a pitcher."

"Old Navy habit?" Eddie asked.

"Exactly. Don't like getting too far away from my routine."

When the cuckoo clock on the wall sounded, Jack opened the front door and glanced out. A man was there, a colorful Indian blanket covering his head.

"Well, don't stand out there in the rain," Jack said. "Come in before you get soaked."

A large man with gray hair that draped to his broad shoulders ducked as he came through the door. His curved nose and facial features pegged him as a Native American. The imposing person stood at least six-foot-six, and he remained impassive as Jack introduced him.

"Gentlemen, this is Grogan La Tortue though I just call him Chief."

Chief draped his blanket over the back of a chair and then bent down to pat Brutus and Lady. Lady's tail was wagging as she licked the stranger's hand. Chief placed the legal folder he was carrying on a counter in the galley before returning to meet Eddie and Bertram.

"You about a big one. I'm Bertram, and he's Eddie. Better get yourself a mug of Jack's rum. It's the best I ever tasted.

Chief's expression changed into what was likely a smile as Jack handed him some rum.

"Pleased to meet you. Don't mind if I do." He smacked his lips after taking a drink. "Tasty. Jack, here is too cheap to buy good booze, so I'm usually forced to drink the swill he serves. You two must be special because this is his good stuff."

"And you'll probably drink every last drop of it," Jack said. "Indians aren't supposed to be able to hold their liquor. Chief, here, could drink the three of us under the table."

"What tribe are you from?" Bertram asked,

ignoring Jack's racial slur.

"He's an Attakapas," Jack said.

"Never heard of that tribe," Bertram said.

"Because they aren't around anymore. Chief, here, is the last of the Attakapas," Jack said. "Good thing because they were cannibals."

Seeing the looks Bertram and Eddie were casting, Chief said, "Jack has nothing to worry about. He's so small, he wouldn't even make a good snack."

Jack continued stirring the oyster chowder. "He doesn't mind eating my cooking and drinking my booze," he said.

"You two must be good friends," Eddie said.

"I got no choice," Jack said. "He's the only person living within twenty miles of here."

Chief didn't miss a beat. "Jack may serve cheap hooch, but he has one great dog."

"Don't mind him," Jack said. "Chowder's ready. Let's eat."

"Don't have to ask me twice," Bertram said.

Jack began ladling up chowder into bowls and putting them on a heavy wooden table that occupied much of the lighthouse's galley area. Eddie, Chief, and Bertram pulled up chairs, waiting for Jack to join them, which he did after topping up their mugs from the pitcher.

"Can't enjoy a Navy meal without a mug of grog," Jack said.

Bertram tasted the rum and smacked his lips. "Like I said, this is the best rum I ever tasted. What kind did you say it is?"

"Like I said, I don't remember. Didn't know I was going to have a rum connoisseur for dinner."

"I'm a bartender," Bertram said. "When it comes to alcohol, there ain't much I don't know."

Eddie, a consummate former prosecutor, didn't miss the looks of concern exchanged between Jack and Chief upon hearing Bertram's reply.

"When I was still in the Navy, I picked up a couple of bottles of special reserve from a distillery in the Dominican Republic. Thought I'd try one out on you boys."

"You had me going there for a while," Bertram said. "As many years as I've owned a bar, you can believe me when I tell you I know the difference between cheap swill and good hooch."

"I brought Bertram down to look at the place with me because of his expertise at running restaurants and bars," Eddie said. "From the looks of things, I'm not going to need him."

"Oh, and why is that?" Jack said.

"The restaurant is too big and too run down. Even if it weren't, there aren't enough customers around to fill even the smallest dining area."

"Amen to that," Bertram said.

Chief grabbed the bottle of rum from the galley counter and topped up Bertram's mug.

"Looks as if you need more grog, Bert," he said.

"Don't want to drink all your fine rum," Bertram said. "We have to drive back to New Orleans. Me, Eddie, and Lady wouldn't want to wind up in a bar ditch."

Jack opened the door a crack and peeked out. The storm had intensified, a gust of wind blowing water through the opening and dampening Jack's flipflops.

"It's raining so hard, you'll have a problem seeing past the hood of your truck. This old lighthouse has four bedrooms. Enjoy the rum and chowder, and stay here for the night."

"Wish we could," Eddie said. "I'm meeting with Mr. Castellano tomorrow to either finalize plans for taking over the restaurant, or else telling him I'm not interested."

"Then you better have some more of Jack's grog," Chief said, topping Eddie's mug.

"Another bowl of chowder?" Jack asked.

"Don't mind if I do," Bertram said. "Can't say as I've ever tasted better."

"I hope you reconsider taking over the restaurant and marina. Mr. Castellano has a plan for renovating everything," Jack said. "Lots of boats pass within a short distance of here. He wants to modernize the marina and draw in the boating customers."

"Won't that interfere with your solitude?" Eddie asked.

"I'll still have all I need up here on the hill."

"Did Jack show you the bungalows?" Chief asked.

"We didn't get that far," Eddie said.

"They're special," Chief said. "Mr. Castellano plans to build more, both for rentals and weekend retreats. A successful development could easily add several thousand people to the local population."

"You sound as if you work for Mr. Castellano," Eddie said. "Do you?"

"Just an interested bystander," Chief said.

After dinner, they returned to the living area. Jack glanced out the door again. Heavy rain continued to fall. The former sailor got on the ham radio and called for a weather report.

"There'll be a break in the weather in about half an hour," he said. "May as well relax until then."

"Why are you so anxious for me to take over the restaurant and marina?" Eddie asked. "What's in it for you?"

"Not a damn thing," Jack said.

Eddie and Bertram relaxed on the couch, watching Jack and Chief play pinochle on an old coffee table. Bertram was tapping his toe on the wood floor and glancing at the cuckoo clock on the wall.

"Has the storm passed yet?" he asked. "If it has, then we need to get going."

"The rain has slacked to just a trickle," Jack said after peering out the door. "If you hurry, you'll be almost home before it starts up again. And Bertram, I have a gift for you."

Jack handed him a brown paper sack with something inside it. From its shape, Bertram could tell it was a liquor bottle.

"You're giving me some of your rum?"

"I got more in back," Jack said. "Enjoy."

The rain had slackened, the road to New Orleans dark. Lady was asleep in the back, and Eddie had also dozed off. The lights of New Orleans were glimmering on the horizon when he awoke and blinked the sleep out of his eyes.

"Are we there yet?" Eddie asked.

"Almost," Bertram said. "You had a good nap and missed most of the drive."

"With everything going on in my life the past two days, I was beat. Sorry I didn't help you stay awake. Can you drop me off at my place?"

"You bet I can. What'd you make of them two scalawags back there?"

"Strange ducks," Eddie said. "Seems like they have an agenda I can't quite put my finger on.

Bertram reached in his jacket and pulled out an empty rum bottle. "Good observation, Mr. Ex-federal attorney. Take a look at this. Jack had thrown it in the trash."

Eddie held it up to the dashboard lights. "An empty bottle of Dominican rum. So what?"

"Check out the date it was bottled."

Eddie fumbled for the overhead light. "This can't be right. It says 1929. That's impossible."

"Maybe not," Bertram said. "I told you it was the best rum I ever tasted."

"But that would make it almost ninety years

old. What's a bottle of any liquor that old worth?"

"A whole bunch of money," Bertram said.

"Why do you think he didn't tell us?"

"Maybe because he stole it," Bertram said. "The bottle of rum he gave me had no label on it, though it's the same shape as the one in your hand."

"Jack doesn't strike me as a thief," Eddie said.

"Don't mean he ain't. Even with his government pension and working for Frankie Castellano, I doubt he makes money enough to serve thousand-dollar bottles of rum with his homemade oyster chowder."

Eddie pondered the thought a moment. "If he stole it, then why did he take a chance serving it to people he just met?"

"Probably because he figured we wouldn't know the difference. Or, maybe he wanted something from us and was trying to butter us up."

"Like what?" Eddie asked.

"Don't know. What I do know is that while I was in the kitchen, I had a look in the folder Chief brought with him."

"Something important?"

"A packet of information put out by NOAA."

"Such as?"

"Water depth, tide schedule, storm activity; pretty much anything you might ask for if you were interested in Oyster Island and the water around it."

"What's that all about?" Eddie asked.

"Something to do with the rum, I'm betting," Bertram said.

Chapter 8

Mama Mulate was the most eccentric person I knew. She drove a fully restored, baby blue 1959 Bugeye Sprite. If she'd known how much it was worth, she'd probably go into shock. The drizzle of rain had continued throughout the day. Mama had raised the canvas top on the tiny car when she arrived to pick me up. Though only six-feet tall, I had to resort to contortionism when I crawled into the front seat.

"When are you going to trade in this pygmy and get an SUV?" I asked.

"Never," she said. "I love Baby too much."

"Baby doesn't have an air conditioner," I said. "She's also too uncomfortable to drive in July and August."

"Stop nagging, or I'll let you walk to the Smoothie King Center," she said.

"I'll shut up."

"Good," she said, completing the short drive to the arena in silence.

Too cheap to pay for parking, Mama found a dark spot behind a trash dumpster about a block away from the arena.

"Glad I brought an umbrella," I said.

"Bet I can give this ticket away at the door to someone that's not so critical."

I knew by Mama's dirty look that I'd almost gone too far. "And deny me the chance to watch the Pels with the most beautiful woman in New Orleans?"

Though Mama said, "Shut the hell up," she was smiling as she did so.

The atmosphere inside the arena was electric, the team slowly beginning to come together as a coherent unit, after a slow start to the season. Mama was as tall as I was. She had long, flowing hair, an athletic body and the bone structure of a Sports Illustrated model. Resplendent in her multi-colored African-print dress, every eye was on her as a friendly usher led us to our seats.

"This is wonderful," I said. "I've never sat this close to the floor."

"Me either," Mama said. "I can almost reach out and touch those big, handsome men's tushes."

"Don't get us kicked out. We'll never get seats like this again."

"I know. I'm in heaven."

"Too bad the team traded Zee Ped," I said. "This is the best squad I've seen in years. With him in the lineup, we could have gone deep in the playoffs. Without him. . ."

"Taj Davis is one good-looking man, though I think he's on his last leg as a productive player," Mama said.

"Is he playing tonight?" I asked.

"Word on the street is, he cut his foot. He's not even sitting on the bench."

"Doesn't sound like a basketball injury. How did he cut it?"

"No idea," she said. "Why don't you be a sweetie and fetch Mama a beer and a pretzel?"

"Pretzel? You'll spoil your appetite before we get to one of the most expensive restaurants in New Orleans."

"I'll take my chances," she said.

By halftime, I'd returned through the throng of ardent fans, crowding the arena to the concession stand, twice and was starting to feel like Mama Mulate's errand boy. The last quarter was close. She forgot about beer and pretzels and concentrated on cheering the team. New Orleans won in a double-overtime thriller, with a buzzer beater that sent the sold-out crowd into a frenzy. I glanced at the Rolex on the wrist of the man sitting next to me.

"It's late. Let's get the hell out of here before we get caught in the crush," I said.

Twenty minutes later, Mama was fumbling for her keys in the darkness. We drove the short distance to the tall building overlooking the Big Muddy that housed the Riverfront Restaurant. Mama fussed with her hair and dress as we took the elevator to the top floor. The restaurant captain, wearing a white tuxedo coat and black pants, greeted us at the door.

"We're meeting someone," Mama said.

"And whom might that person be?" the man asked.

"We weren't told," she said. "I'm Mama Mulate, and this is Wyatt Thomas."

Gas lamps lighted the large, open room bordered on all sides by floor-to-ceiling windows. The view of the river was nothing less than spectacular. White tablecloths draped the tables, each lighted by a single candle. Mama pinched my elbow.

"Oh my God!" she said. "There are at least half-a-dozen celebrities in here. I think I'm in heaven."

A man appeared, directing us to follow him before Mama could opine further about the restaurant's clientele. Glass walls separated a private room from the main dining area. After opening the door for us, our usher departed.

Mama caught her breath when she saw who was sitting at a regally-adorned table. A very tall man dressed in dark slacks and sportscoat, and a white silk shirt open to the waist, stood and smiled as he waited for us to join him.

"You must be Mama Mulate," he said. "I'm Taj Davis."

"I know who you are. I've been watching you play basketball since you came into the league."

"Then you're a basketball fan?"

"The biggest," she said. "This is my business associate Wyatt Thomas. I brought him along because he's the best investigator in New Orleans. He's also a huge sports fan."

"This is Adela Kowalski. Please join us," Taj said.

Adela was a red-haired knockout, dressed in a little-bit-of-nothing, lime-green dress held in place by spaghetti-straps. I whistled to myself when I saw her. Mama sat beside Taj. I took the chair next to Adela as a waiter appeared to take our drink orders. Mama was soon nursing a very dry martini.

"Thanks for the front row seats to the game," she said.

"Glad you enjoyed them," Taj said. "I guess you're wondering why you're here."

"Very curious," Mama said.

"Take a look at this and tell me what you think," he said.

Taj opened his silk shirt and showed Mama the veve on his chest. Without hesitation, she moved closer, touching the symbol.

"Where did you get this?"

"No idea. It's been there for as long as I can remember. Adela has an identical veve on her chest."

Without asking, Adela lowered her low-cut top to reveal the veve between her bare breasts. After glancing around to see if anyone was looking,

Mama drew closer to compare the two veves.

"They're identical," she said. "How long have you known about each other's veves?"

"Adela and I met for the first time yesterday," Taj said.

"Interesting," Mama said. "You called the mark a veve. What else do you know about voodoo?"

"Almost nothing," Taj said. "Adela and I met while on a tour of St. Louis Cemetery No. 1. The groundskeeper told me what it is. He's also the person that gave me your name."

"I didn't know the St. Louis Cemetery No. 1 had a ground's keeper."

"His name is Sam. Sam said everyone in New Orleans knows something about voodoo."

"While it's true that everyone in New Orleans has heard about voodoo, few people know much about it," Mama said.

"That's what I'm finding out."

Taj laughed when Mama asked, "Are you and Adela related?"

"You can see we're not. A week ago, I didn't even know Adela existed. Something prompted us to arrive in New Orleans at the same time, causing us to meet and realize our connection."

"I see," Mama said. "Why did you visit the cemetery?"

"Because of this," Taj said, producing a voodoo doll. "Sam said it's my effigy and that someone used it to put a voodoo spell on me."

"Where did you get this?" Mama asked.

"My first night in town, I stayed in a room on the thirteenth floor of the Hotel Montalba. I fell asleep in the bathtub, cutting my foot on a broken wine bottle when I got out of the tub. A demon chased me out of the room. When the bellman found me, I had this in my hand."

"Oh, my!" Mama said.

"I know," Taj said. "It scared the hell out of

me."

"So what is it you need Wyatt and me to do for you?"

"Help us get to the bottom of this mystery. If I'm cursed, I need to find a way to break it. I don't ever want to wake up again and face a demon." Taj slid an envelope across the table. "As a retainer, there's a cashier's check for twenty-thousand dollars in the envelope. There'll be more if you need it."

Mama pushed the envelope back toward him. "That's too much money."

Taj gave it back to her. "You said you're a sports fan. If so, then you know I have more millions than I can ever spend. Take the money. All I ask is for you to devote all your energy to helping us solve our mystery."

"No problem for me," Mama said. I'm on semester break."

"My slate is clean," I said.

"Then let's enjoy drinks, dinner and this gorgeous view of the river," Taj said. "We can discuss how you plan to proceed as the evening progresses."

The cuisine at the Riverfront was as good as advertised, and then some. Despite what Taj had said about discussing the case during dinner, the subject never arose. What did arise was the mutual attraction between Mama and Taj. It became more apparent by the minute. I noticed, and so did Adela.

Adela, her long red hair draping to her shoulders, was quite the stunner. Admiring the view, Mama and Taj had walked to the window, Mama pointing to Algiers on the opposite side of the river. Adela glanced at my lemonade.

"You're not drinking?" she asked.

"I'm a recovering alcoholic. Every now and then I fall off the wagon."

"My dad was an alcoholic," she said.

"Was?"

"When he died of a heart attack, he wasn't even fifty."

"I'm so sorry."

"Dad gave me all the love I needed. He just couldn't control his drinking."

"I can relate."

"Taj seems infatuated with Ms. Mulate."

"She's doing nothing to rebuff his infatuation," I said. "She likes tall, good-looking athletes and it doesn't hurt anything that he's wealthy."

"Are you married?" she asked.

"No, are you?"

My question brought a smile to her pretty face. "I don't think I'm marriage material."

"Don't apologize," I said. "I know the feeling."

"Taj and I didn't know Ms. Mulate was bringing someone with her. What is it you do?"

"Solve mysteries," I said. "The tougher, the better."

"What's your background?"

Though I was taken aback by Adela's directness, I tried not to let on.

"I was a lawyer in another life. Political maneuvering is rampant in the Big Easy. I was disbarred and decided not to fight it. My strong suit is research, and I know lots of influential people. I've managed to support myself by doing investigations."

"You're good-looking enough to be a movie star. Has anyone ever told you that?"

"Only people trying to set me up. What's your angle?" I asked.

"It's Taj who is paying you. I'm just trying to make sure he gets his money's worth. What's your plan?"

"See if we can develop a common thread for what's happening here."

"Do you believe in magic?"

"Real magic and not just illusion?"

Adela sipped her wine without answering my question. Heavy rain had begun hammering the windows. A foghorn sounded from a towboat on the river. Mama and Taj were in their own little world, neither of them paying attention to either us or the weather.

"My parents always said I have a sixth sense. Maybe they were right. I think you also do. What's your feeling about me?" Adela asked.

"You look more Irish than Polish. Adela is an Irish name, not Polish."

"So, what are you saying?"

"I don't know. Maybe you were Irish in another lifetime," I said.

"You believe in past lives?" she asked. "What's that have to do with New Orleans?"

"New Orleans has had a large Irish population for more than a century. One of our neighborhoods is called the Irish Channel."

"So you think I was Irish and living in New Orleans during a past life?"

"Maybe," I said. "Though it doesn't pay to jump to conclusions, it's something to check out."

"When do you start?" she asked.

"The moment Taj gave Mama the retainer," I said.

Sipping her wine, she crossed her legs and glanced at the window as lightning lit the dining area.

"I thought we were just getting to know each other better. I didn't realize you were deposing me."

"Sorry if it appears that way," I said. "I sometimes have a hard time forgetting I'm not a lawyer anymore. Forgive me?"

For the first time since I'd met her, Adela's features softened. When she took my hand, I realized what a physical attraction I had for her. It was a definite no-no between an employer and an employee. Not seeming to care, her lips drew within six inches of my own.

"You like me, don't you?"

I tried not to wince at her pointed, though correct remark.

"Very unprofessional of me," I said. "Maybe I should bow out of this case and let Mama handle it alone."

"Don't do that," she said. "We can work together on this."

"Not if you don't stop staring at me with your hypnotic eyes," I said.

Adela loosened her grip. "I think I could become attached to you."

Chapter 9

Before I could respond to Adela's titillating remark, Mama and Taj returned to the table. Neither took a seat and Taj motioned for the check.

"Taj knows nothing about New Orleans' nightlife," Mama said. "I'm going to give him an introduction. He's a music fan, and I'm taking him to my favorite venue for jazz. Can you take Adela to her room at the Hotel Montalba?"

"Sure," I said.

Mama tossed me the keys to her car. "And will you take care of Baby for me? Taj is too big to fit into the front seat. We're taking a cab."

"You trust me with your car?" I asked.

"You put one little scratch on Baby, and you'll be comparing voodoo spells with Taj. Don't wait up," she added as they headed for the door.

"Guess we've been deserted," I said. "Ready to return to your room?"

"Not really. At least you and I discussed the case."

"Trust me, Mama's all over this. She'll have a plan before morning."

"Looks as if she has other things on her mind."

"So does Taj," I said. "Did you catch the smile on his face?"

"We probably won't see them before noon tomorrow."

"I promise, Mama will know all about your problem long before noon."

"If you say so," Adela said.

The rain continued as we huddled beneath my umbrella during the short walk to Mama's car. Adela gave my arm an extra squeeze when we reached it.

"This is it," I said. "It's not locked."

"I've never seen a car like this," she said. "What kind is it?"

"Austin Healey made it. It's a Bugeye Sprite, a British sports car."

"What year was it made?"

"Long before you were born."

"I love it," she said. "Can I drive?"

I handed her the keys. "Why not? I'm sure you're a better driver than I am."

Once behind the wheel, Adela was like a kid in a candy shop, revving the little engine and spinning the tires in the puddles of water that had formed on the cobblestone streets. The car's tiny wipers barely kept the windshield clean as she tooled down the dark thoroughfare. It wasn't far to Jackson Square, Adela reacting when she saw it.

"What's that big building?" she asked.

"St. Louis Cathedral, the most photographed structure in town. The park behind the iron fence is Jackson Square. That's Andy atop the horse."

"I want to touch it. Can we stop?"

"You'll get your pretty outfit wet," I said.

"It'll dry and so will I. I sense many important things have happened here."

"You're right about that," I said. "There are parking spots across the street. They're probably all open, because of the rain."

Light from the streetlamps reflected off the rippled puddles as we ran toward the entrance to

Jackson Square. Adela was the first to reach the gate and frowned when she pulled on it.

"It's locked," she said. "Why is it locked?"

"To keep street people from sleeping there at night. Now, they just sleep outside on the sidewalk. We're getting drenched, and I forgot the umbrella."

"To hell with the umbrella," she said. "I haven't felt this alive in years."

I pulled my jacket up around my neck as I watched her raise her arms toward the sky and twirl on her toes like a ballerina. She'd dropped the light wrap covering her shoulders, the gauzy material of her dress becoming almost transparent in the rain. Though she didn't seem to care, I draped my jacket around her.

"It's December," I said. "We'll both have a cold in the morning."

"Screw the cold," she said, grabbing my hand. "I want to see the other side of the square."

She was all smiles as we hurried past the Cabildo, the cathedral and the Presbytere. By now, her long red hair was wet and clinging to her head and neck. I grabbed her waist, wheeling her around.

"I'll bring you back when the rain stops," I said. "It's coming down so hard, you can't see anything anyway."

"What about the lights across the street."

"Café du Monde," I said. "Best coffee and beignets in the world. We're too wet to go there tonight. I'll bring you back, I promise."

Handing me the keys to Mama's Sprite, she put up little resistance as we hurried across the street.

We weren't far from her hotel, and I knew the entrance to the underground parking. The valet took the keys, gave me a parking stub, and pointed us toward the elevator. We were the only two people in it, as we continued up to her room. Once her hotel door was open, I got a surprise.

Adela tossed my jacket to me and then let her soaked dress drop from her shoulders to the carpet. Giving me a silly grin when I reacted to her nudity, she hurried away to the bathroom. Drying her hair with a towel, she returned draped in a plush terrycloth robe.

"There are more robes in the bathroom," she said. "Get out of those wet clothes."

"I probably need to go," I said.

"No way! I have questions for you, and they won't wait until tomorrow."

Adela had drunk a bottle of chardonnay by herself at the Riverfront. I realized now that she was a tad more than tipsy.

"I've got no dry clothes to change back into. I'll have to put on these wet ones before I go. I don't live far from here. I'll leave Mama's car parked overnight."

"Don't go. This hotel is old, and there's a radiator in the bathroom. Hang your clothes over a chair. They'll be dry when it's time to leave."

"Uncle," I said. "You're the boss, Miss Adela."

"That's what I like to hear," she said.

When I exited the bathroom, I saw Adela had dialed for room service. She'd already poured herself a glass of wine and had lemonade waiting for me. A single candle cast flickering shadows on the white tablecloth of the serving cart.

"Thanks," I said. "Now, what's so important that it can't wait until tomorrow?"

"I need to tell you something I haven't told anyone, not even Taj."

"Sounds ominous."

The room was dim, only a corner light and the candle casting dancing shadows on the wall. Adela had pulled the curtains on the window, thunder rumbling and rain pounding against the glass. She fumbled with a small leather purse on the table.

"Do you smoke dope?" she asked.

"Go ahead without me. I'm not offended."

She lit the crooked joint and took a puff.

"I have something important to tell you. I need to knock the edge off all the wine I drank."

Her logic or lack thereof, made me smile. "Then why did you order another bottle?"

"Because I need both the pot and the wine. Does that make sense?"

"Not really," I said.

"What I have to tell you is very serious to me. I need you to take a toke with me. Please?"

"Mama would kill me if I smoked dope with a client," I said.

"Mama's not here."

"Doesn't matter. She has a way of finding things out."

Adela took another puff and let her robe drop to the carpet. Sitting in my lap, she draped her arms around my neck and drew so close I could feel the dampness of her hair against my face.

"You know I like you. I didn't tell you that I feel as though I've known you forever."

"Maybe in another lifetime," I said. "You're a person I'd never forget."

A tingle raced up my spine when she nibbled my earlobe and then blew in my ear. I flinched when a clap of thunder rattled the window.

"Have you ever had a shotgun?" she asked.

"I have no idea what you're talking about."

Without explaining, she placed the lighted end of the joint into her mouth and blew a potent stream of smoke up my nose. The effect of the smoke was almost instantaneous. I felt my eyes cross. When I finally stopped coughing from the harsh smoke that had invaded my nostrils and lungs, I was already stoned.

"Am I making you nervous?" she asked.

She smiled when I said, "I don't think you have to ask."

"Maybe I better sit over there before I forget what it is I need to tell you."

She was naked when she returned to the chair beside the table. After taking another puff, she handed the joint to me. My mind had already slowed into tranquil numbness. After a long draw, I returned it to her.

"You'd better tell me this story while I'm still halfway cognizant."

"Let's get rid of this light."

Adela turned out the lamp in the corner, leaving only the single candle to light the room. As my eyes began adjusting to the dimness, I heard a haunting tune from a single violin coming from somewhere.

"Angel music," she said. "And there's something hallucinogenic in the pot."

Not knowing what I had smoked, I would have started to panic if the numbing effect of the drug hadn't prevented me from doing so. Adela poured a second glass of chardonnay and gave it to me. I touched the wine to my lips, savoring a delicate flavor I hadn't tasted in years.

Thunder sounded outside the building, lightning causing the curtains to oscillate like a strobe light when it flashed. Rain continued drumming the window. Even though it was shut, the curtain was flapping in a non-existent breeze. The fury of the storm had dimmed in my mind, replaced by music of the lone violin and numbness that had swept over me.

"Talk," I said.

Adela's story began as a husky whisper. "Do you believe there are people with special powers?"

"Yes," I said.

"I'm different than other people. I've known it since I was a little girl. I have powers I've never revealed to anyone."

"What powers?" I asked.

Adela concentrated her gaze on the candle burning on the table. The flame flared, wax melting into fat drops that hardened on the tablecloth. The candle began bending toward Adela's gaze until she turned away, looking to see my reaction.

"I could set this room on fire if I wanted to," she said.

Numbed by the wine and spiked pot, I must have seemed less than impressed because her eyes grew darker in the muted light of the candle.

"What else?" I asked.

Refilling my wine glass, she held it toward me. It left her hand, floating slowly across the room until I'd clutched it.

"I can do things that are beyond belief," she said. "I don't know why I have the power, or where I got it. I do know I can open and close doors with my mind and make objects levitate. I can levitate," she said.

As I watched, she floated slowly upward, her damp hair touching the high ceiling of the old hotel room before she descended.

"I'm drunk," I said.

"You don't believe your own eyes?"

"When on a bender, I've seen white elephants. I don't know if my eyes are lying, my brain, or both."

"Neither," she said. "What you see is real."

"Right now, I'm not sure what I see, or what I believe."

"Believe this. There's an evil room in this hotel, and I must visit it. Will you come with me?"

"Now?"

"Yes."

"How will you find it?"

"I sense evil the same way other people smell a foul odor."

"Won't the room be locked?"

"You witnessed only some of my powers. Are you ready for more?"

Chapter 10

As Adela took my arm, we floated off the carpet, my altered reality suddenly wrapped in a Kodachrome dream. When I blinked, I was in a different place and a different time.

Adela was gone. It took a moment for me to realize I was in a church, dressed in a white tuxedo, a white carnation in my buttonhole. The person beside me was someone I hadn't seen in years: Russell Bender, the best man at my wedding, looking as if he hadn't aged a day since the last time I'd seen him. I also saw Betty, my former mother-in-law.

Betty was smiling at me, as she sat alone on the first pew in the crowded church. When the music began, she turned away to look at my bride, walking down the aisle toward me. When Adela jostled my shoulder, I had little time to ponder the scene.

"Don't be frightened," she said. "We're going on a trip."

The candle in the room flickered and died as we floated toward the window, passing through curtains and glass as if they weren't there. When I glanced down, streetlights flickered up at us. What I was experiencing felt like a dream, or maybe a nightmare. I wanted to scream. A hoarse whisper was all I could muster.

"Don't let go of me," I said.

Adela squeezed my elbow tighter, probably the only thing about the situation that seemed even halfway real. Lightning flashed on the horizon. As we soared above the French Quarter, floating through damp clouds, my mind switched gears, and I was again in a church.

Betty, My former mother-in-law, had once again invaded my dream. This time, she looked older than before, and we were in a different church, this one much darker.

Betty stood beside me, grimacing as we stared into my ex-wife, Mimsy's open coffin. Mimsy's lifeless eyes stared back at us.

"Oh, Wyatt," Betty said. "I don't think I can handle this."

I awoke in Adela's grasp. Only the faintest whisper issued from my throat as I tried again to scream. I wanted to pull free from her grip, the reptilian part of my brain screaming for me to do so. We soared over Bourbon Street, a snippet of jazz issuing from an open door.

"Put me down," I said. "I don't want to be here."

Adela circled higher. We flew over the river, so high the boats below looked like flickering points of light. I felt as if I was gazing out the window of an airplane, except there was no window and no plane. When she let go of my arm, I slipped into another nightmare.

I was falling to my death, tumbling and not soaring. The scene morphed into another memory. I watched as Dauphine, the twin sister of Desire, the woman I'd loved, jumped to her death off the Crescent City Connection Bridge. She was staring at me, her arm outstretched as she fell. Adela was laughing, the nightmare fading when she grasped my elbow, halting my rapid descent.

I had only a moment to catch my breath as we circled Hotel Montalba and then floated upward to the darkened window of the thirteenth floor. As we passed through the closed window, into a dark room, a feeling of doom swept over me. At least my bare feet felt something solid beneath them when I touched the floor. I was dizzy, almost falling on my face, as I took a step.

Adela produced a candle, its flickering glow illuminating the interior of a hotel suite decorated as if from another era. I smelled an odor I vaguely recognized, and I recoiled when I stepped into something sticky.

"Blood," Adela said.

The blood had begun oozing between my toes as Adela directed me to follow her into another room of the large suite.

Because of strong drugs, insane dreams, or maybe both, reality had deserted me. Dark walls pulsated, the decorative wallpaper from another era making me woozy. The bedcovers on the old four-poster bed were in disarray and warm to the touch. I sensed someone, or something, wasn't far from us.

Hazy light radiated through the open bathroom door. Someone was splashing water in a tub. When Adela pressed against me, the voodoo veve on her chest began glowing red. Behind her, a shadow loomed. I wanted to run. I could not.

Steam wafted across the floor in a damp wave, the room warm with humidity. A woman was in the bathtub. Someone, or something else, was in the bathroom with her. A piercing scream caused Adela to straighten. I wanted to race out the door. Instead, she grabbed my wrist and pulled me toward the bathroom.

An antique tub dominated much of the room. Water, the color of blood, overflowed on the tile, the headless body of a woman flapping her arms as if she were still alive. I couldn't take my eyes off the bloody scene.

Adela and I watched until the body sank beneath the tub's steamy surface. Bloody water washed over my feet as something behind us made a noise. I sensed it was the woman's killer.

My first instinct was to run. I could not because a throbbing demon, stinking to high heavens, was blocking our escape. Globules of slime dripped off the apparition that began to transform into a creature from hell as we watched.

Adela and I backed away, not stopping until we touched the warm porcelain of the tub. My hand came out red when I accidentally dipped it into the hot water. The creature was now fully transformed and moving toward us. Worse, it held a woman's decapitated head in its appendage.

The eyes of the disembodied head had rolled back in their sockets as the creature dragged it across the tile. Though the head was waxen, I recognized the red tresses the creature was holding. It was Adela's hair.

The body in the tub had floated to the surface and was rising out of the water. When Adela slipped on the bloody tile, I grabbed her shoulders, pulling her to her feet.

By now, the gaseous demon was glowing red, its body, eyes and everything about it was red, even the fangs in its open mouth that had begun spewing slime and an odor so foul it almost made me gag. When Adela grabbed my elbow and began to levitate, the demon's roar echoed across the little bathroom.

"I will have you, Aisling."

Using her magic, Adela flew us over the demon's head. I held my breath as we passed through the wall and flew back outside into what had become a driving rainstorm.

Chapter 11

Mama and Taj waited on the sidewalk, beneath the awning in front of the Riverfront, until a cab appeared. When the cabbie saw Taj hold up a twenty, he slid to a halt and backed up to the curb. He hurried out of the car and opened the backdoor, Mama, and Taj both laughing after racing the short distance to the cab and piling in.

"Where to?" the cabbie asked.

"Musique Azul in the Warehouse District," Mama said.

"Sounds exotic," Taj said.

"It is. Like the blues?"

"Love the blues," he said. "I played ball for a season in Memphis. Some of the best blues music in America."

"Musique Azul's as good as the clubs on Beale Street. I think you'll like it," she said.

"Then it's not on Bourbon Street?"

"Not even in the French Quarter. It is part of the old industrial area we call the CBD—Central Business District. Entrepreneurs have converted many of the old brick structures and warehouses into expensive condos, rib joints, art galleries, and chic cafes."

"How big is this area?"

"Within walking distance of everything a person might need."

"I'm looking for a place to live," Taj said. "Are the condos nice?"

Mama laughed. "You kidding? They're so expensive, most of them are owned either by movie stars or professional athletes. You'd fit right in."

"Will you help me pick one out?"

Mama laughed again. "Honey Babe, I already know just the one you need."

"You're buying one?"

"I wish," she said. "The price tag has too many zeros on the end for a Tulane English professor to afford."

"English professor? I thought you were a voodoo mambo."

"Can't you be both?" she asked.

It was Taj's turn to laugh. "Do I need to start calling you professor, or doctor?"

"Either would be nice, though just Mama will do," she said.

"Where did you go to school?" he asked.

"University of South Carolina. You?"

"U.C.L.A., at least for a year. I was a one and done."

"Don't apologize," she said."

"When you climbed into the cab, I couldn't help but notice your great legs. Were you an athlete in college?"

"Track and field. Relays and 400 meters."

"Pro runners make lots of money."

"I could have gone pro," she said. "When I tore an ACL and missed the Olympics, my perspectives changed."

"Was that the only reason?"

"No," she said. "I was madly in love with my agent, a former world-class runner. When he dumped me for a sprinter from Jamaica, I decided to take a deep breath and think about the situation while I finished my education. When I finally did, I was too old to compete against the world's best."

"I'm impressed," Taj said. "Have you ever looked back and thought you may have made the wrong decision?"

"Have you?"

"Touché!" he said. "I'm so happy Sam gave me your name."

Before Mama had time to quiz Taj about Sam, the cab pulled up in front of an old brick building. It was easy to see from the floor to ceiling windows that someone had lovingly renovated it. Mama waited beneath the canopy over the front door until Taj had paid the cabbie and then hurried to join her.

"Does it ever quit raining around here?" he asked as they entered the bistro.

"Most places have sunshine punctuated by a day or so of rain. New Orleans is the opposite."

"Ever thought about moving to Florida or California?" he asked.

"Though I love both places, I'd never leave New Orleans. This is my home."

A woman in a colorful, floor-length dress met Mama with a hug when they entered Musique Azul.

"Mama," she said. "Where you been?"

"Busy semester," Mama said. "Sarah, this is Taj. . ."

"Davis," Sarah said releasing her grip on Mama and shaking Taj's hand. "The most handsome man in the NBA."

"I'll take handsome, though I wish it were the most valuable player in the NBA. Are you two sisters?"

Sarah was as tall as Mama, her hair just as long. They could have passed as sisters except. . .

"Sarah's my daughter," Mama said. "I had her

when I was ten."

"Well, Sarah's just as beautiful as you are," Taj said.

"Flattery will get you everywhere," Mama said. "We're here for the music, and we also need to talk. Do you have a table away from the stage?"

Sarah's long hair flowed when she shook her head. "Even with the rain, it's more crowded tonight than usual. People in town to see the Pels. There are a couple of seats at the bar, and that's about it."

"Even for your mother?" Mama said.

"Sorry, Mom," Sarah said, giving her mother another hug. "You taught me never to kick someone out in the rain."

Sarah grinned and shook her head when Mama said, "You could make an exception, you know."

"Have fun, you two."

Music aficionados packed the main room, the tattooed blues guitarist crashing out a powerful solo as the smiling drummer and shirtless bass player watched. The music grew fainter when they reached an adjacent area of the remodeled old warehouse.

"Sarah is lovely," Taj said.

"Guess I shouldn't have been so tough on her when she was growing up," Mama said.

"I don't believe a word of it," Taj said.

Though the inside of the old warehouse had undergone an extensive renovation, its high ceilings, plank floors, exposed brick, and massive I-beams remained and added to its charm. The antique bar was around the corner from the main stage. Though they could still hear the performance, it was muffled enough to allow for conversation. The people occupying the half-dozen tables were doing just that. Mama took a stool at the bar as the young bartender gave her a wink.

"Why Professor Mulate, it's so good to see you again. Are you here for the music, or to hear some of my poetry?"

Seeing the young man, Mama reached across the bar and gave him an enthusiastic hug.

"Cray Toussaint. When did you start bartending here?"

The handsome young man was dressed in black pleated pants and a black silk shirt. Someone had skillfully braided his dark hair into cornrows, the copper bands on his wrists his only concession to jewelry.

"This past summer," he said.

"Good Lord, has it been that long since I've been here?"

"Sarah said you've only been in once since last spring."

"You know Sarah?"

"We're dating."

Mama's mouth gaped open. Her smile returned when she remembered she was with Taj.

"Cray Toussaint, I'd like you to meet Taj Davis."

Cray beamed as he reached across the bar to shake Taj's hand.

"I can't believe this," he said. "I've looked up to you ever since I played college ball at Tulane."

"Glad to meet you, Cray," Taj said. "Any friend of Mama's is a friend of mine. Just let me know if you ever need tickets to a game."

"You mean it?"

"I wouldn't have said it if I didn't," Taj said.

"I'm so starstruck I forgot I'm your bartender. I know what Mama wants. What can I get you, Mr. Davis?"

"You can't get Mr. Davis anything. Taj will take a glass of cabernet."

"You bet, Taj," Cray said.

Cray mixed Mama's martini and waited for her

reaction. "Wonderful," she said. "You're still one of the best bartenders in town."

"I thought you'd like it. I have a special bottle of cabernet in back, Taj. I'll get it for you."

"What a nice young man," Taj said when they were alone.

"Yes, he is."

"You don't look particularly happy."

"How would you like it if your son was dating one of your exes?"

"You shitting me?" he said. "I've never been married, and I have no children. Is Cray an ex?"

"More like a short fling," Mama said. "I don't usually date men that much younger than me."

"Hey, I'm not judging you," Taj said. "I've dated younger women."

When Cray returned, he opened the wine and made a production of pouring it for Taj. The band had resumed, as had the noise of the appreciative audience in the other part of the old building. Mama was still not smiling as she sipped her martini.

"Does Sarah know we dated?" she finally asked.

"We began dating before I knew who she was. I told her about us as soon as I learned she was your daughter."

"And?"

"She wasn't happy about it, and neither am I. We were enamored with each other long before either of us knew the situation."

"Then you two are serious?"

"Very," he said.

Mama's smile returned, and she leaned across the bar, giving Cray a kiss.

"I'm happy for you. My daughter couldn't have picked a nicer, smarter, and harder-working man than you. I'd be jealous if you weren't so damn young."

"Thank you, Mama. You can't imagine how long I've been dreading this moment."

"Dread no longer. I'm okay with it. That table in the corner is empty, now. Taj and I have some things to discuss in private. Do you mind if we sit over there?"

"Heavens no," he said. "Go have a seat and I'll bring your drinks. I'll keep them coming as the tab tonight is on me."

Mama was still glum after Cray had brought her martini and Taj's bottle of wine. Taj topped up his wine glass.

"Earth to Mama," he finally said.

"I'm sorry," she said. "This is just so awkward."

"Not for me it isn't," he said, reaching across the little table and resting his big hand on hers. "Your daughter and that young man make a handsome couple. What could be wrong?"

"Just that I never intended to sleep with my future son-in-law. I feel like a pervert."

When Mama glanced up into Taj's smiling face, her own smile returned.

"I already know you're not a pervert or even close. Things always find a way of working out. They always do. Let's finish our drinks and go someplace else where you'll feel more comfortable."

"You're a sweetheart," she said. "I'm so sorry you got involved in something so personal. It certainly wasn't my intention."

"That young man didn't seem to mind, and apparently neither does your beautiful daughter. I feel something special for you right now. Please don't let this little blip in our relationship affect it."

Mama sipped her martini. "We're only supposed to be having a business conversation."

"Is that all it is?" Taj asked.

"For now, even though I'm strongly attracted to you, that's all it can be. Unless you want me to return your retainer."

"No way. Sam said you were the person who can help me. Now that I've met you, I know he was telling the truth. Attraction or not, I intend for you to earn that money."

"You mentioned Sam again," Mama said. "I've been to St. Louis Cemetery No. 1 many times. I don't recall ever seeing a caretaker named Sam."

"He was there, I promise you. It was pouring rain, and he called me into the little building where he lived."

"What did he look like?" Mama asked.

"Short, five foot eight, or so. The little building had no electricity, our only light coming from the candles he was burning. Didn't seem to matter to him because he had a pair of dark glasses he kept perched on his forehead."

"Then he wasn't wearing a hat?"

"No, but there was a top hat on the rack by the door."

"Was he smoking a cigar?" Mama asked.

"Yes, he was. Then you do know him."

"There's someplace else we need to visit."

"Another Warehouse District hot spot?"

"No," she said. "We're going to see Sam."

They were halfway out the door when Mama hurried back to the table and grabbed the half-empty bottle of wine.

"Still thirsty?" he asked.

"Trust me," she said. "We'll need this before the night is over."

Chapter 12

The rain had stopped as Mama and Taj left the Musique Azul. Even at this late hour, cabs were lined up on the sidewalk to transport happy music fans back to wherever they had come from. Lightning crackled across the darkened sky, signaling the possible return of more wet weather. Taj clutched Mama's hand as he tapped on the window of a cab.

"Where you going?" the cabbie asked.

"The entrance to St. Louis Cemetery No. 1," Mama said.

"It ain't open this time of night."

"Don't worry your pretty little head about it and just take us there," she said.

The driver wasn't used to being chastised by a woman. He saw Taj when he turned to see who he was dealing with.

"You're Taj Davis," he said.

"I am," Taj said, shaking the driver's hand.

"I'm Wink. Take one of my cards. Lots of people on the team call me when they need a ride. I got the best cab in town."

Wink was probably fifty-something with thinning hair, bushy gray sideburns, and a caterpillar mustache. He had the stub of a pencil resting on his ear which he used to write something in the notepad he kept in the front passenger seat.

"Pleased to meet you, Wink," Taj said. "This beautiful lady with me is Mama Mulate."

Wink smiled and nodded in Mama's direction. "You're new to the Big Easy. Sure you want me to take you to the cemetery this time of night?"

"Let's hail another cab," Mama said. "This man apparently has more important things to do than take us to where we want to go."

Wink started the cab and pulled away from the curb before Mama could open the door.

"Yes ma'am, sorry ma'am," he said.

Mama smiled as she crossed her arms and leaned back into the seat.

"What do you expect to see at the cemetery that won't be there tomorrow morning?" Taj asked.

"Spirits of the night," Mama said.

"Robbers, murderers, and rapists are more like it," Taj said.

"If you're frightened, I can have Wink, your new buddy, drop you off at your hotel."

"I don't like it," he said. "Where you go, I go. By the way, he's not my buddy."

"I was hoping you would say that. Spirits don't frighten me. Robbers, murderers, and rapists do. I'll feel much better with a strong man beside me."

"The gate will be locked," Taj said. "How will we get in?"

"I'll get us in. I need to talk with this man, Sam."

"He's probably not awake. Even if he is, what do you expect him to tell you?"

"Maybe a bunch."

"Who do you think he is?"

"In Vodoun, we call our deities loa. It's possible Sam is a loa named Baron Samedi. And Taj, don't tell me you think voodoo is a bunch of crap. If you do, I'm going to give you your money back and then get out and walk."

"If you believe in voodoo, so do I," he said.

"Good answer."

"What if Sam isn't Baron Samedi?"

"Then at least we'll know. Do you carry a gun?"

"No," he said.

"Good. Firearms scare me to death."

"I'll do my best to protect us. I'm not a boxer, but I can brawl with the best of them."

Mama rested her head on Taj's big shoulder and patted his knee. "You saw a demon your first night in town and dealt with it. I already know you are a brave man. One thing I don't know about you. Have you ever seen a ghost?"

"Can't say as I have."

"Then prepare yourself. Cemeteries are rife with spirits, especially at night. Like the other cities of the dead in New Orleans, the St. Louis Cemetery No. 1 is no ordinary cemetery."

It wasn't far from the Warehouse District to the cemetery. Wink pulled the cab to a stop in front of the iron gate marking its entrance. Unlike the Musique Azul, Wink stayed in the car behind the wheel, refusing to get out and open the door for them. Taj handed him a twenty through the window and told him to keep the change.

"Will you wait for us until we return?" he asked.

"Are you crazy?" Wink said. "We shouldn't even be here."

"Maybe this will change your mind," Taj said, producing a hundred dollar bill.

"I don't like it, and I don't have bullet-proof windows," Wink said. "But I'll be waiting."

"Good," Taj said. "If you're still here when we return, I'll have another one of those for you. If you aren't, I'm going to check the address on the card you gave me, look you up and kick your ass."

"Yes sir," Wink said with a smart salute.

A single streetlamp illuminated the entrance to the cemetery. Taj watched as Mama fumbled with the lock of the old iron gate. When it opened with a metallic clunk, she slipped into the walled cemetery. Taj followed her.

"How did you do that?" he asked.

"Magic," she said. "Would you really kick his ass if he leaves us here?"

"I'm a baller, and I don't make idle threats. What now?"

"Wait a moment until our eyes adjust to the darkness."

"I have pretty good eyes, but I'm not a cat," he said.

"Like I said, just wait a moment."

Mama was correct. Electricity wasn't needed, as their eyes began dilating. Bioluminescence lighted the ornate crypts and sparks danced over their heads. Taj did a doubletake.

"Amazing. I can see more detail now than I did the day I was here. Where does the light come from?"

"I'm sure that scientists have some formal explanation, though I can tell you some of it is caused by spirits of the dead."

"How do you know?"

"Check out those glowing orbs moving around us. It's what spirit investigators call paranormal activity. Believe me, when I tell you, there are spirits all around us at this very moment. They are as curious about us as we are of them."

"You're scaring me," he said.

"Don't be frightened. Unlike your demon the other night, most spirits are benevolent."

The dancing lights had coalesced around Taj, illuminating him for a moment. When he brushed his arms, a thousand tiny points of light moved away from him like sparkling fairy dust. When he took a step, the lights moved with him.

"I hope you're right about that. This place is beginning to spook me."

"Don't panic, they're just checking you out. Forget about the lights and take me to where you met Sam."

"I could have sworn it was right here, though I don't see his little building anywhere."

"Sure it wasn't around the corner? St. Louis Cemetery No. 1 is quite large."

"We had barely moved from the entrance when it started to rain. Sam's little house was here. He stuck his head out the door and invited me in. I swear this is where it was."

"What you saw wasn't real. He's here because Baron Samedi is the keeper of souls and cemeteries."

"Funny, because when we met, that's what he called himself," Taj said.

"There you have it," Mama said.

"Was what I saw just an illusion?"

"Not at all. When you met Sam, you and he were at a spiritual crossroads. To recreate the crossroads we must summon him," Mama said. "Can you chant?"

"What is it you want me to chant?"

"Papa Legba," she said. "You must do it with passion and rhythm, or it won't work."

"Show me," he said.

"Pa-pa Leg-ba, Pa-pa Leg-ba. Try it."

Taj felt a bit self-conscious as he began chanting, Pa-pa Leg-ba, Pa-pa Leg-ba. As he got into the performance, his deep voice began resonating through the cemetery, echoing off the old crypts and exciting the dancing lights that started moving to the rhythmic chant. Mama began to dance.

"Don't stop," she said.

Taj lost track of time and grew excited as Mama's dance became even more sensuous.

The dancing lights had grown brighter, his vision dimmer. Finally, he began to see a faint shadow bordered by a bright aura. The shadow moved closer to Mama. When it was no more than a few feet away, it transformed into a short man wearing a dark cape and top hat. The stub of a cigar in his mouth glowed red, reflected by the dark glasses he wore. Taj could see it was Sam.

"Why you summon Baron Samedi, mambo?"

"We have questions for you and pray you will answer them for us."

"Then show proper respect and dance for me."

Mama's reaction was instant as she began swaying, as if to a musical accompaniment. Her movement was sultry, a thin film of sweat, despite the December chill, coating her forehead and neck. Taj began chanting again. He noticed the bottle of wine in Mama's hand.

As Mama's movements became increasingly frenetic, she touched herself in a totally sexual manner and danced ever closer to Baron Samedi, rubbing herself against him, chest to chest and nose to nose, licking his neck with her tongue and fondling the crotch of his baggy pants

Backing away from him, she grasped the blouse of her dress with both hands and tore it open, exposing her naked breasts. Dropping to her knees, she drizzled wine down her chest, red droplets hanging from her nipples. When she arose and moved again toward Baron Samedi, he licked her from her waist to her neck with an inhumanly long tongue. Taj continued to chant until Mama stopped dancing and prostrated herself in front of the loa.

"What question do you have for me, Mambo Mulate?" he asked.

Mama rose to her knees, not bothering to cover her naked breasts wet from wine, sweat, and Baron Samedi's saliva.

"Who summoned Taj to New Orleans, and to what purpose?" she asked.

"Your answers lie in a courtyard garden in the French Quarter."

"There are many gardens in the French Quarter," Mama said.

"Only one is still cloaked in forbidden darkness."

Baron Samedi's image glimmered and grew dimmer. Once again a shadow with a flickering aura, it began moving away from her.

"Wait," Mama said. "That's not enough. Can't you tell us more?"

"Ask the Irish witch," Baron Samedi's fading image said.

"Please," she said as Baron Samedi's image began to fade away.

"There's someone who needs your help," Baron Samedi said.

"Who?" Mama asked.

"Aisling, the red-haired Irish girl."

When Baron Samedi's image faded into darkness, Taj put his arms around Mama and hugged her, feeling her warmth and the beating of her heart against his own. She was trembling.

"Are you okay?" he asked.

"Even mambos don't often converse with Vodoun loa. I'm a bit shaken."

Taj removed his long leather coat and draped it around her shoulders.

"It's a shame to put you through all of this and still not get the answers we needed."

Mama grabbed his face with both hands and kissed him.

"Oh, but we did, even if we don't know right this moment what it means."

"What now?" Taj asked.

"Wyatt texted me. He left my car in the parking lot of your hotel. If the cabbie is still waiting, we'll have him take us there."

Wink, glad to see them when they reached the cab, quickly opened the backdoor for them. Taj rewarded him with the promised hundred.

"Where to now?" he asked. "Charity Hospital?"

Mama let the sarcastic reference to the old hospital, abandoned since Hurricane Katrina, pass without comment.

"The Hotel Montalba in the Quarter," she said.

Mama was still shivering as they headed back toward the lights of the French Quarter. Taj put his big arms around her.

"I'm confused," he said.

"About what?"

"If you were trying to summon Baron Samedi, then why was I chanting Papa Legba? Who is Papa Legba?"

"Papa Legba guards the spiritual crossroads that separates humans from loa. When someone summons a loa, Papa Legba is the deity that either denies or accepts the request. He accepted our plea, and that is why we were able to communicate with Baron Samedi."

"Is it that rare to be able to talk directly with a loa?"

"Extremely so. My religion believes in possession. The only times I've seen a loa was when they had possessed a human's body."

"Then what made you think Baron Samedi would see us tonight?"

"Because of you. Sam was the actual Baron Samedi and not a human possessed by the loa. He met you in the cemetery for a reason. Apparently, an important reason."

Chapter 13

Wink dropped Mama and Taj in front of the Hotel Montalba, and they made their way to the parking garage. Wyatt had left instructions with the attendant to let Mama Mulate have the Bugeye Sprite when she arrived. Taj eyed the little vehicle.

"I don't think I could fit into your car if I tried," he said.

"That's why we took a cab. I'm worried about Wyatt. He's not answering my texts."

"Let's see if Adela knows where he is. We can take the elevator to the room from here."

Though Mama had lived in New Orleans for years, she'd never been inside the Hotel Montalba.

"I can't believe how ornate this old lady is," she said. "They don't construct buildings like this anymore."

"Demons seem to like it."

When Taj reached for his electronic key to open the door, Mama grabbed his hand.

"Are you okay with all the strangeness you witnessed tonight?"

"You kidding me? I watched a gorgeous woman perform one of the most sensual dances I could have ever imagined. It was worth it having spirits of the dead light me up like a candle. How in the world did you become a voodoo mambo?"

"Long story," she said.

"I've got lots of time. I'd love to hear it."

"And I'd love to tell it to you. Do you like gumbo?"

From the face Taj made, Mama could tell he didn't.

"It's not that I don't like gumbo. I've never tried it. Guess I'm more of a steak and potatoes man."

Mama was grinning when she said, "Though I'm trying very hard to like you, I'm not sure we're orbiting the same planet."

"Invite me for gumbo. I promise I'll try it. Even if I don't like it, I'll do my best acting job and never let you know."

Mama still had hold of Taj's hand. Though she was tall, she had to stand on her tiptoes to kiss him. Their smiles disappeared when they turned on the lights in the hotel suite and went into the bedroom.

※

The sudden glare of the overhead light awoke me from a fitful dream. I sat up in a strange bed, Mama Mulate, and Taj Davis, standing at the foot staring down at me. Both of them were frowning.

Someone moved beneath the covers, red hair mussed and makeup smudged when her head popped out from the sheets. It was Adela.

"What the hell!" she said. "Can't a girl get a little privacy around here when she's trying to sleep?"

Not waiting for an answer, she tossed off the covers and strolled naked to the bathroom, slamming the door behind her. With arms folded in a rebuke, Mama continued glaring at me.

"I think you have some explaining to do," she said.

One of the robes Adela and I had donned after coming in from the rain lay in a disheveled pile on a nearby chair. Rising to a sitting position, I pointed.

"Can you throw me that robe?" I asked.

Mama slung it at me. I climbed out of bed, covering my own nudity as best I could from the condemning eyes of Taj and Mama.

"Taj and I have been working diligently on his case, and we find you here, in bed with one of your clients."

"It's not what you think," I said.

"No? Then how is it?"

"I have a reasonable explanation. I'm not going to talk to you about it in front of Mr. Davis."

"You've betrayed us," Mama said. "I think you owe both of us an apology."

My eyes were caked and burning, the top of my head feeling as it were about to cleave off and explode. Mama's lecture was more than I could take. Wheeling around, I faced them both.

"I said I have an explanation. If you're too damn bullheaded to listen, then screw you. Right now I feel like hell and don't have time for your happy horseshit."

When Adela came out of the bathroom in a bathrobe, I took the opportunity to take her place, slamming the door behind me for effect. Adela had turned off the light. As I fumbled for the switch, I hoped like hell I'd find my clothes. If they weren't there, I would have to slink back into the bedroom to continue my search. I felt a moment of relief when I found them in a pile on the floor.

Mama and Taj were waiting for me when I came out of the bathroom. Adela was sitting in a chair, sipping wine from the bottle on the service cart. Mama's hands were on her hips, the frown still on her face, as I headed for the door.

"Where the hell do you think you're going?" she asked.

"My apartment," I said.

"It's raining out there," she said.

"I won't melt. I'll get dry when I get home."

I started away, down the long corridor, the sound of my heels echoing against the hotel's old walls. Mama came running after me.

"Stop," she said. "You have some explaining to do."

I punched the down button on the elevator. "I have a story to tell. If you want to hear it, I'll be in the bar at Bertram's."

"Wait, I'll drive you."

"Forget it. I'm walking."

I regretted my rash decision the moment I exited the front door of the Hotel Montalba onto Royal Street. Within seconds, I was drenched to the bone. Bertram's bar on Rue Chartres was close, but I didn't need to hurry. It really didn't matter. Except for the Cajun bartender himself, Bertram's was empty when I reached it.

"Well, look what the cat drug in," he said. You gonna tell me where you been?"

I was dripping water on the floor from my soaked clothes.

"Not until I dry off and change into something warm," I said.

I hurried upstairs to my second-floor apartment overlooking Chartres. My cat, Kisses, was waiting for me. I opened a packet of food for her before shedding my wet clothes. I always kept the door to my balcony cracked so she could come in and out. The floor was wet from rain, a cold breeze blowing through the opening. I shut the door and threw some towels on the damp floor before doffing my wet clothes and dressing in something dry and warm.

"You okay, little girl?" I said, lifting Kisses off the floor and giving her a few full-body strokes.

When I put her on my bed, she curled up against the pillow and went to sleep. I had no clue what time it was, though I already knew the curious Cajun would be waiting downstairs for me. Bertram was mopping the floor when I returned to the bar.

"Didn't your mama teach you better than to track water through the house?"

"Sorry about that. It was too wet to sleep on the street."

Bertram had a pot of coffee brewing. Its enticing aroma, coming from the kitchen, drew me to the bar. When Bertram finished mopping, he poured me a cup.

"Figured you might need some coffee," he said.

"How about a couple of aspirins?"

"Got a headache?"

"A headache, stomachache, you name it."

"Want to tell me about it?"

"I have a feeling Mama Mulate is going to join us before long. If you can wait until then, I'll tell you both at the same time."

"I got all night," he said. "What there's left of it."

"What's the story on Eddie's restaurant?"

"Let me pour a shot first, and then I'll tell you."

"You bet," I said.

I waited as Bertram laced his coffee with a shot of Cuervo. He took a sip before continuing.

"Looks like a no-win situation to me. The island is vacant except for two strange dudes. The restaurant is as old as the hills and needs lots of work. It's also huge and, like I said, there ain't no paying customers within twenty miles of the place. I did have a good bowl of oyster chowder and a mug or two of the best rum I ever tasted."

"Oh yeah? Where'd you get that?"

"Frankie's caretaker is also the keeper of the lighthouse. It was pouring down rain, and he invited us for dinner and a place to hang out until the rain slacked up."

"I thought you said he was strange."

"Just because he was hospitable, don't mean he wasn't strange. The little guy is an ex-Navy man with a big ol' pit bull named Brutus."

"What makes him so strange?" I asked.

"Just seemed like he has lots of secrets, and he and his buddy were a little too anxious to have Eddie take over the restaurant."

"What's his name?"

"Jack Wiesinski. His partner is a big Indian, and I do mean big. Had a funny name for an Indian."

"Funny ha ha?"

"Funny peculiar," he said.

"Such as?"

"Grogan La Tortue. I never heard of his tribe. Jack said they once was cannibals."

"Interesting," I said. "Seems I've heard the name La Tortue before, though I can't remember where."

"Too bad you don't drink anymore, because Jack give me a bottle of the rum I told you is the best I ever tasted," Bertram said.

"What brand?"

"From the Dominican Republic. The bottle he give me ain't got no label. I dug this empty one out of his kitchen trash when he wasn't looking."

Bertram pulled an empty bottle from beneath the counter to show me.

"Bottled in 1929. Other than its age, what makes it so valuable?"

"Dominican rum is like Cuban cigars; the best in the world. I got no idea where Jack come up with this bottle. I can't imagine he don't know how much it's worth, or why he would serve it with oyster chowder to two people he just met."

"Does sound strange," I said. "What's your take on it?"

"Something fishy if you ask me."

"I am asking you."

"The big Indian acted as if he didn't know we was going to be there. He'd brought a folder with him. I got a look at it when no one was looking."

"You playing amateur detective again?" I asked.

Bertram grinned. "It was a packet of maps and charts of the Gulf."

"So what?"

"Don't know," he said.

I wrote down the two names on my notepad, along with the information on the empty rum bottle.

"I'll check it out," I said. "Did Eddie tell you what he intends to do?"

"He's taking a cab out to Frankie Castellano's mansion on Lake Pontchartrain later on this morning. I imagine he's going to tell Frankie he's gonna pass on his offer. Knowing Eddie, you never know."

"Eddie was valedictorian in his law class at the University of Virginia," I said. "I'm sure whatever he decides to do will be well thought out."

"Eddie's smart except when it comes to women. Then he lets his little head do all his thinking."

"He'll figure it out. Right now, I have problems of my own."

"Like what?"

Without answering his question, I nodded at the door. Mama Mulate was coming in out of the rain. She didn't look happy. After reaching across the counter and giving Bertram a kiss, she sat on the stool next to me.

"You got here just in time," Bertram said.

"In time for what?" Mama asked.

"You like rum?"

"Nothing I like much better than Jamaican rum."

"Then prepare yourself for a treat," he said, filling a shot glass and handing it to her.

Mama's frown disappeared when she sipped the rum. "Good God, Bertram. I have to have a bottle of this. What is it?"

"Rum from the Dominican Republic, vintage 1929."

"Get the hell out of here," she said. "I've never tasted better rum. Where did you get it?"

"The Oyster Island lighthouse keeper give it to me."

"You mean down by the Gulf, not far from Mississippi? What were you doing there?"

"Tell you later," he said. "Wyatt has a story, and he's been waiting for you to get here so we could both hear it together."

"Well?" she said, looking at me for the first time.

"Better put on another pot of coffee and keep that bottle of prized rum handy. This could take a while."

Chapter 14

After his visit to Oyster Island, Eddie had all but decided to decline Frankie Castellano's offer to run the restaurant there. On their ride back to New Orleans, Bertram Picou had done nothing to dissuade him. Eddie was still undecided as he took a cab to Frankie's palatial estate on Lake Pontchartrain.

Frankie's estate occupied twenty acres on a spit of land jutting out into the blue water of Lake Pontchartrain. A fence of iron and white stone encircled the green lawn surrounding a two-storied mansion at the end of a long, one-lane road. Like everything else that Frankie owned, the southern-plantation-styled mansion was nothing less than spectacular. The cabbie dropped him off by the veranda encircling the house. Adele, Frankie's adoring wife, met him at the front door.

"Come in this house," she said in her Italian-flavored Metairie accent.

Adele was middle-aged gorgeous with big dark eyes. She'd trimmed her long hair since the last time Eddie had seen her. Now it was shorter, just over her ears and the top of her neck. She hugged him the moment he stepped through the door.

"You get more beautiful every time I see you. Why don't you leave that husband of yours and run away with me?" Eddie said, holding her at arm's length.

She was grinning when she said, "You are so full of shit. Frankie had business in town this morning and will be home soon. Let's go to the den. I'll fix us a cup of coffee."

"I've already had a pot of chicory-laced coffee. What I need now is a scotch to get rid of the buzz."

"Eddie, Eddie," she said. "You never change, do you?"

"You know you wouldn't like me any other way."

"Josie would."

Talk of Eddie's former fiancee and Adele's step-daughter momentarily wiped the smile off his face, as he followed her into the main living area of the large house. Frankie's den was more spacious than many small houses, the centerpiece leather couch situated in such a way as to take full advantage of the large windows overlooking the sailboats breaking the whitecaps on Lake Pontchartrain.

"The view is spectacular," he said.

"You never been here before?"

"Nope, today's my first visit."

"Well, I hope it won't be the last. I never saw Frankie so distraught as when he learned Josie wasn't going through with the wedding. He'd planned to have it out there on the lawn. Full orchestra, party tent, everyone in gowns and tuxedos. It would have been fabulous."

"It could still happen," Eddie said. "Josie might change her mind."

"Don't know," Adele said. "She's got a hard head, just like her papa."

Eddie was on his second scotch, he and Adele still talking, when they heard the jet engine of Frankie 's helicopter fly overhead.

"Is that him?" Eddie asked.

"Frankie has a chopper pad out back. It has

got to where he takes that noisy monstrosity everywhere. I better get his scotch. Guess I'm the only one still drinking coffee."

It wasn't long before Frankie Castellano, dressed in a blue pin-striped suit that probably cost more than all the suits Eddie owned, came bounding into the room. After tossing his coat onto the back of a chair and loosening his tie, he grabbed Adele and kissed her so overtly, it almost embarrassed Eddie.

Frankie wasn't a handsome man, though people were drawn to him by his smile and his strong personality. He shook Eddie's hand in a powerful grip and then gave him a demonstrative hug.

"How's my future son-in-law?" he asked.

"You might want to check with Josie for the answer to that," Eddie said.

"She'll come around," Frankie said, kissing Adele again when she handed him his scotch. "What did you think about Oyster Island?"

"It's too big, too secluded and doesn't have a snowball's chance in hell of succeeding," Eddie said. "That's why I'm going to pass on your proposal."

Frankie sipped his scotch. "That's what I like about you, Eddie. You don't beat around the bush."

"I speak the truth, though I'm sure you've already figured it out. I know you want the best for Josie and me. You don't have to manufacture an unworkable situation just to try and keep me around."

"Is that what you think I'm doing?"

"Isn't it?"

"You apparently don't know me as well as you think you do. Frankie Castellano never launches a project that has no chance of succeeding."

"Then maybe you better explain to me how

you're going to make this project work because I just don't see it."

Frankie pulled his cell phone out of his back pocket. "Johnny, get the Oyster Island presentation ready to show in the conference room." After returning the phone to his pocket, he said, "Prepare to be impressed."

"Trust me," Eddie said. "Nothing would please me more."

Frankie put his arms around Adele's waist and kissed her forehead. "Come with us, beautiful woman. This is something you also need to see."

Adele and Eddie followed Frankie down a long hallway to a room with an ornate conference table and comfortable leather chairs. Atop the conference table was a miniature diorama. Eddie recognized the restaurant and could see it was a rendering of the Oyster Island projected development.

"This is what I expect Oyster Island to look like in six months to a year," Frankie said.

"Great," Eddie said. "That still doesn't explain where the customers are going to come from."

An overweight man in a rumpled sports coat entered the door.

"Here's the remote, boss. Just touch the top button when you're ready."

"Thanks, Johnny," Frankie said.

"Just call if you need anything else," Johnny said as he hurried out of the room.

When Frankie touched the top button on the remote, a wall opened up revealing a small theater complete with a large screen and reclining leather chairs.

"Grab a seat and prepare to be amazed," Frankie said.

As the back panel closed and the lights grew dim, Eddie said, "I'm impressed. Bet you guys don't spend much money on movie tickets."

"You kidding?" Frankie said. "I usually get the new movies before they're available in the theaters."

"How do you do that?" Eddie asked.

"Tell him, Baby," Frankie said.

"Connections," Adele said. "My man here knows more Hollywood producers than Brad Pitt."

They watched as the professionally filmed and edited presentation explained Frankie's grand scheme for bringing commerce and customers to Oyster Island. The short film ended with credits and a burst of original violin music. Eddie clapped when the lights came back on.

"Wonderful," he said. "I know you're rich, though I doubt even you have enough money to finance such a grandiose scheme."

"You're right about that. Doesn't matter because I always prefer using OPM for risky investments. I've already raised a billion dollars if I need it."

"OPM?" Adele said.

"Other people's money, Doll," he said. "Everyone's looking for a dream. I'm here to supply them one."

"The movie was slick," Eddie said. "Maybe a little too slick. I'd like to hear about the development in your own words."

"Glad I never had you prosecuting me, Mr. federal D.A."

"Though I'm glad I'll never have to, I still need your personal assessment of the project."

"Let's go back to the den," Eddie said. "Our bottle of scotch is running low."

Adele let them walk ahead. "It's almost lunchtime. I'll go fix something up for us and bring it to the den."

"You got yourself a prize there, Frankie," Eddie said.

"Don't I know it. Best woman in the world."

"Better than your mother?"

"You were wonderful, Mama, God bless your soul, but Adele has edged you out, though not by much," Frankie said.

"Amen to that," Eddie said.

Frankie topped up their drinks from a fresh bottle of scotch retrieved from the wet bar.

"The Oyster Island project starts with infrastructure. I had an engineering and geological study done to determine the best place to put a two-lane bridge from the mainland to the island. I plan to develop the island into a world-class resort; a destination location."

"The world is rife with world-class resorts. Why will people suddenly be drawn to Oyster Island?"

"Water and location," Frankie said. "There's fresh water at only a thousand feet below the ground. I plan to put in a health resort and then market the hell out of it."

"And location?" Eddie asked.

"Let me give you an economics lesson. How much do you think a sack of cement is worth?"

"I don't know. A couple of bucks, I guess."

"The answer is, it depends on where you live. If your home is in Oklahoma City, a place surrounded by limestone quarries, the price is low. If you live in New Orleans, where there are no quarries, the price is at least twice as much because of transportation costs."

"So what you need is a limestone quarry near New Orleans," Eddie said.

"If you owned one here, you could make a fortune. I don't have a limestone quarry. What I do have is the closest vacation destination to New Orleans. A place where harried execs can go for the weekend and be rested and back on the job by Monday. A place with all the amenities."

"Such as?" Eddie said.

"Endless beaches, a championship-caliber golf

course, 5-star hotels, health spas featuring heated mineral water baths, casinos, live entertainment, and restaurants. What do you think?"

"You're persuasive, Frankie. I still don't know if it'll work."

"Then give it a try. You don't have anything else going right now. All you stand to lose is time. Right now, you have plenty of that on your hands."

"Maybe so. I'll need to pack my apartment first."

"No, you don't," Frankie said. "My boys are taking care of that little problem as we speak. You're already set. I can warm up the chopper and take you to Oyster Island now."

"Not so fast, boys," Adele said, appearing in the doorway with a tray of food in her hand. "No one's going anywhere until they eat their cannolis and Italian pasta salad."

✥

Eddie and Frankie were soon flying high above Lake Pontchartrain, heading southeast toward the Gulf of Mexico. Frankie poured them both a glass of scotch.

"I have to hand it to you, Frankie. You really know how to travel."

"Jet helicopter; the only way to fly," Frankie said. "I'm starting a first-class chopper service out of New Orleans. First stop, Oyster Island."

"How many people can afford that?" Eddie asked.

"Lots more than you think. The kind of people we want to visit the new resort, and then come home to New Orleans and tell their rich friends."

"You won't be able to taxi enough people onto the island by chopper. The existing two-lane blacktop is only safe for four-wheel drives and military vehicles."

"I got friends in Baton Rouge. Money has already been earmarked to widen and improve the roads."

"How did you pull that off?" Eddie asked. "There aren't enough taxpayers in this part of the parish to justify any road improvement expense."

"Neither a Democrat nor Republican be," Frankie said with a grin. "You'd be surprised what a campaign contribution can turn in to."

"I doubt it. I'm an ex-government prosecutor if you haven't forgotten."

"Tell me about it," Frankie said. "You've put some of my best connections in jail. I'm glad you're on my side now."

"Me too. Just don't ever ask me to do anything illegal. Capisci?"

Frankie smiled as he saluted Eddie with his glass of scotch. "Wouldn't have it any other way."

They were soon flying over the Gulf, following the coastline. Eddie could see how erosion had begun exacting its toll on the landscape.

"Louisiana's dissolving into the sea," Eddie said. "What's your plan for preventing Oyster Island from disappearing in the next twenty years or so?"

"Erosion will get it, though not in our lifetimes," Frankie said. "And not because of anything I did."

"Why then?" Eddie asked.

"Geologic luck. Unlike most of coastal Louisiana, Oyster Island is growing rather than shrinking."

"How so?"

"According to the report I paid dearly for, the island is sitting atop a structural scarp, protected by strategic barrier islands and situated in a perfect place to receive sediment from drainage into the Gulf. The center of the island is ten feet above sea level. There's a stand of old-growth hardwood trees that have never suffered seawater encroachment. It's the perfect seafront property, and I bought it for a song and a dance."

"Who'd you have to kill?" Eddie said.

"Don't ask," Frankie said.

"What's the story on Jack and the big Indian?"

"When it comes to Jack, what you see is what you get. He's a little nuts, but he is also reliable and intelligent. If he says he's going to do something, then you can pretty much count on it."

"And the Chief?"

"One strange duck. Don't know much about him except he owns twenty or so acres on top of the hill and wouldn't sell it to me. Not for any amount of money. He lives in a teepee."

"You have to be kidding," Eddie said.

"Nope, it's true."

By now, they had reached their destination and were circling over the island.

"It's bigger than I thought," Eddie said.

"Almost twenty square miles," Frankie said. "Some of it is a swamp, or too low to develop. The rest is perfect for what I want to do."

"Remind me again," Eddie said.

"Decades ago there were places away from the city where people went to escape the heat, noise, and bustle. Such places featured fine restaurants, bandstands with lots of entertainment, places to swim, bathe, gamble and cavort. I'm going to bring all that back, and you're just the man to help me do it."

"When do we start?" Eddie asked.

"When Jack called and told me he thought you liked the place, I sent a crew of carpenters, painters, and artisans to put the restaurant back to the way it was during Prohibition. Welcome to Oyster Island, Eddie. You're gonna love it here."

Chapter 15

When Eddie arrived, the restaurant was a beehive of activity. The workers had started with the suite of rooms where he would call home. His clothes and belongings were already waiting for him, the refrigerator in the kitchen freshly stocked, as was the large larder.

As he sat on the veranda overlooking the cove, all the workers had gone home for the day. Yesterday's rain had finally moved north, a hazy moon peeking through the cloudy sky. Not wanting to fire up the stove and cook a meal, he was eating crackers and drinking scotch instead, his feet propped up on the railing surrounding the deck.

Eddie's suite, in the center of the building and on its highest level, afforded him a wonderful view of the beach. The past few days had been stressful, and he'd gone without much sleep. He was about to nod off in the chair when a cool breeze blowing in from the Gulf caused him to open his eyes.

As he started back into the building to get a sweater, he saw something down by the beach. The faint glow of a campfire cut through the darkness. He decided to investigate.

The old restaurant had no elevator, new lighting and electricity yet to be installed. A commercial generator on the roof electrified

Eddie's suite. He used a flashlight to make his way down the stairs, the odor of mildew almost overpowering. He also sensed something else.

During a late night visit to the Charity Hospital in New Orleans, abandoned after Hurricane Katrina, Eddie had seen ghosts. Though he saw none now, he could feel their presence. It caused him to wonder how many people had died in the old restaurant, and how many spirits resided there. He let the thought pass as he ambled across the covered walkway to shore.

Though the rain had passed, a cold mist hung in the air as Eddie shuffled across the sand toward the beach. For the first time since arriving on the island, he smelled the salty air and heard the sound of waves crashing into the shore. Someone had pitched a small tent away from the beach. A fire was burning, and there was no one to watch it.

A large backpack mounted on an aluminum frame sat near the tent. The camper had spread an old red blanket on the sand in front of the tent, a speargun cocked and loaded lying atop it. The front flap of the tent was zipped shut. As Eddie watched from the shadows, someone emerged from the water and walked toward the fire.

The person dressed in a black wetsuit was small, no taller than five feet. When they dropped their mask, Eddie saw it was a young woman. When she pulled off the rubber piece protecting her head from the cold, her long blond hair cascaded in tight curls to her shoulders.

Consumed by voyeuristic attraction, Eddie remained locked in place as the young woman sat on the blanket and wrestled off her rubber pants to reveal a tiny, blue bikini bottom. When she removed the rubber top, he saw she was wearing nothing at all. A branch cracked when he stepped backward. He had little time to react as she dived for the speargun on the towel beside her.

"I see you, and you're about to get skewered. Step out into the light."

With his hands held high over his head, Eddie did as the woman directed.

"Don't shoot me," he said. "I give up."

"Stop right there. You get your eyes full?"

Eddie couldn't help but grin as the woman pointing the menacing speargun at him hadn't bothered covering her half-nude body.

"If I didn't, I am now," he said. "Why don't you put that fish sticker down before you hurt somebody?"

"You'd like that, wouldn't you?" she said.

"I'm not a mad rapist if that's what you think. I moved into the restaurant earlier today and saw the light of your fire from my window. I came down to investigate."

"No one lives in that old building except ghosts," she said.

"Well, they do now. You didn't see all the workmen here earlier?"

Eddie's question seemed to puzzle the young woman.

"I wasn't here earlier," she said. "I have no clue what you're talking about."

"Frankie Castellano is remodeling the restaurant. I'm running it for him. I've never touched another soul in anger my whole life. Can I lower my arms now?"

The woman pulled the trigger on the speargun, the spear burying into the sand beside her. She dropped the weapon and patted the knife sheathed on her tiny waist.

"My knife is sharp as a razor. Make one false move, and I'll cut your balls off."

"Whoa!" Eddie said, lowering his arms. "I'm a good guy. Ask Jack Wiesinski, or Chief if you don't believe me."

"You know Jack and Chief?"

"Yes, I do. They'll vouch for me."

The woman took her hand off the hilt of the knife. "Who are you?"

"Eddie Toledo, and you?"

"Odette Bellefleur."

"Pleased to meet you, Odette. Are you Cajun?"

"What was your first clue?" she asked.

"Your accent and now your name."

"You got that right," she said. "Cajun born and bred. Where you from?"

"New Jersey originally, though I've lived in New Orleans for the past several years."

"Doing what?" she asked.

"I was a government prosecutor."

"Figures," she said. "Every lawyer I ever met was kind of kinky."

"Why do you think I'm kinky?" he asked.

"You were standing in the shadows peeping on me. I'd call that kinky. You some kind of peeping tom?"

"I may have my foibles, but so do you. You haven't bothered covering your tits. Are you an exhibitionist?"

Odette had a smile on her pretty face when she said, "Well played."

Odette's long blond hair was beginning to dry into tight curls. It didn't exactly go with her dark eyes and Cajun sass. Reaching into the backpack, she removed a tee shirt that said L.S.U. and pulled it over her head. If at all possible, the effect of her protruding nipples poking through the white cotton fabric provided an even more erotic effect than her former nudity. Her eyes narrowed when she saw he was staring.

"What the hell are you looking at?" she asked.

"Sorry," he said. "It's not every night I see a beautiful half-naked girl emerge from the sea. Good thing for you I'm not a rapist."

"If you were, your balls would be rolling in the

sand right about now."

"Uncle," he said. "Sorry, I'm staring. What I need is a shot of scotch to get my mind back on track. Wouldn't happen to have one, would you?"

Odette reached into her duffel again, tossing a silver flask to him she'd fished out.

"You're a ballsy sort, even for a lawyer. This isn't scotch, but it's all I have."

Eddie unscrewed the cap of the flask and took a drink.

"Bet I know where you got this," he said.

"Bet you don't," she said.

"From Jack Wiesinski. I've never tasted better rum."

"Might have come from the same liquor store," she said.

Good prosecutors always seemed to know when someone was lying. Eddie wasn't just good, he'd been among the best. Odette was lying. He decided not to worry about it.

"That's a mighty big backpack for a little bitty girl," he said.

"Everything I own in the world," she said.

"Where did you park your car?"

"I don't own a car."

"Then how did you get here?"

"Walked and hitchhiked. I may be little. I'm not weak."

Goosebumps had begun popping up on Odette's arms and legs. Once again rummaging through the backpack, she fished out a pair of sweatpants, sweatshirt and down jacket. After pulling off her bikini bottoms without bothering to turn around, she slipped on the sweatpants, then the sweatshirt and finally the jacket.

"Sorry for staring," Eddie said. "I'm not used to having attractive females I just met taking their clothes off in front of me."

"Sorry about that. It's become a habit. I was a

stripper on Bourbon Street for a while. So many men have seen me naked, I don't even think about it."

"Hey, I'm not complaining," he said. "You from New Orleans?"

"Breaux Bridge," she said. "I lived in New Orleans for the past two years. Until yesterday."

"You're not on vacation?"

"Nope, this is my home now."

Before Eddie could speak, something inside the tent began scratching on the canvas, trying to get out. Odette unzipped the door, grabbed a scrawny puppy with a wagging tail to her breast and squeezed it. Eddie moved closer and rubbed the small dog's head.

"What a cute little dog. What's her name?"

"I call her Mudbug because I found her in a ditch, sealed in a plastic bag. She'd managed to tear a hole in the plastic, or else she would have smothered to death."

"Good grief!" Eddie said. "The things people are capable of doing to helpless creatures never ceases to amaze me."

"I know."

"Mudbug, huh? Good name for the dog of a Cajun girl. How do you intend to live here? There are no toilets and no running water."

"Yes, there is. This was a public beach in the thirties. The WPA drilled a well and installed a bathhouse about a hundred yards from here. The well still works, and so does the bathrooms. No hot water, but there are even working shower stalls."

"You're welcome to use mine anytime you want," Eddie said. "What about food? You'll get tired of a steady diet of fish after a while."

"I have enough freeze-dried food for a week, though I didn't account for Mudbug."

"I just got here today myself. Someone had stocked my pantry and refrigerator with more food than I can ever eat. Come up to the restaurant with me. I'll fill a shopping bag for you." Odette didn't bother replying. "Well?" he said.

"I just met you. I'm still not sure about your intentions."

"My intentions, I assure you, are honorable. And Mudbug looks hungry."

"Sorry. Even a sack of food isn't worth taking a risk for."

"I didn't know I look so predatory," Eddie said. "I'll run to the restaurant and bring a sack of supplies with me when I return."

"You don't have to do that."

"I'll be back," he said, heading into the darkness, toward the restaurant.

As Eddie walked up the stairs to his new digs, he wondered about his decision to take on a new way of life. Outside, the wind had begun blowing, creating all manner of creepy noises in the old building. He tried not to worry about it as he opened the door to his new abode and went straight to the cupboard.

A half-hour had passed before Eddie returned to the blanket on the beach. Odette had gathered a stack of driftwood, her little fire glowing brightly. He found her lying on her back on the blanket, playing with her new puppy. She stiffened when she heard him approaching.

"Didn't mean to scare you," he said.

"Not scared, just startled."

"Whatever. I brought you two bags of food. I kept finding things I thought you'd like."

"Anything for Mudbug?"

"Little Miss Mudbug hit the jackpot. Whoever stocked my cupboard threw in a little of everything, including both cat and dog food. Hard, dry, moist and soft. Take your pick. I was hungry myself, so I made us a couple of bologna sandwiches."

Mudbugs little belly was soon full, and she fell asleep in Odette's lap. Odette smacked her lips and whisked away non-existent crumbs off her hands.

"Thank you," she said. "You didn't have to do that for us."

"I've only been here one day, and I've already learned how lonely that old building is. Sure you and Mudbug won't accept my offer of a room for the night?"

"Sorry. I'm starting to like you. I still don't trust you. You'll have to deal with your loneliness on your own."

Eddie sipped rum from Odette's flask. "You were in the water when I came to the beach. What were you doing out there in the dark?"

"Looking for something," she said.

"Couldn't it have waited until tomorrow?"

"You find things out there after a storm. There's another storm coming tomorrow. I wanted to get into the water before then."

"What did you expect to find?"

The object Odette pulled from her pocket glimmered in the light of the fire.

"This," she said.

Odette's open hand revealed what looked like a piece of a Spanish doubloon. Eddie took it from her, trying to catch the light as he turned it in his palm.

"This has to be gold," he said. "Where did you find it?"

"In about ten feet of water, just beyond the breakers. Last night's storm stirred up the sand and uncovered this piece of Spanish gold."

"Is there more out there like this?"

"Probably, though that's not what I'm looking for."

"What exactly are you looking for?" Eddie asked.

"A sunken Spanish treasure ship laden with a fortune in gold and emeralds."

"What makes you think such a shipwreck exists near here?" Eddie asked.

"It's late, and I've already told you too much," Odette said. "Mudbug and I are headed for the tent before it starts raining again. Thanks for the supplies and we'll see you later, Eddie."

Chapter 16

Mama's irritated glare remained as Bertram poured himself another shot of rum and waited for me to begin.

"No matter what it looked like, I would never try to bed one of my clients. Though I don't remember how I ended up there, I do remember why."

"Then don't keep us in suspense," Mama said.

"My story is going to sound incredulous. I'm not sure it isn't a dream."

"Tell the damn story and let me and Mama figure it out," Bertram said.

"Adela was quite drunk when we left the Riverfront. She fell in love with your little car and wanted to drive it. I agreed because I figured she was a better driver than I am."

"Wait a minute," Bertram said. "Who's Adela? Bring me up to speed here."

"Mama and I met new clients. They gave us front row seats to see the Pels and then treated us to dinner at the Riverfront."

"Sweet," Bertram said.

"Taj Davis is one of our new clients and Adela the other," Mama said. "They both just arrived in New Orleans. They wanted to talk with Wyatt and me because we have the knowledge they seek."

"Like what?" Bertram asked.

"They had just met and learned that both have identical voodoo veves on their chests. Someone told Taj I could answer his questions."

"Taj Davis, the basketball player?"

"Yes," I said.

"Think he can get me some tickets?" Bertram asked.

"That's not what we're here to discuss," Mama said before turning her attention back to me. "You let Adela drive my car?"

"Sorry. It was pouring rain when we drove past Jackson Square. Adela was enthralled and insisted on parking and getting out. We were wringing wet by the time we made it back to the car."

"I can't believe you," Mama said. "The seats got so wet, I don't know if she'll ever be the same."

"I said I'm sorry."

Bertram poured Mama another shot of rum. "Go on with the story," he said.

"Adela and I were both in the same condition as your car when we reached her room. It was then I got my first real surprise of the night."

"Like what?" Bertram asked.

"She stripped off her clothes in front of me and insisted I stay."

"Whoa!" Bertram said. "A nice surprise."

"It put me in a compromising position I didn't want to be in," I said.

Mama wasn't smiling. "And you just stood there ogling the poor girl when you could tell she was drunk? Why didn't you just leave?"

"Because she informed me I worked for her, and we had more business to discuss."

"She was naked, and you just stood there, dripping on the carpet?"

"Shut up, Bertram," I said. "You're not helping matters."

"What did you do?" Mama asked.

"Adela was only naked for a moment before going to the bathroom and changing into a bathrobe. I tried again to leave. She said she had something very important to tell me. Something she'd never told anyone."

"And you just kept standing there, dripping wet?" Mama said.

"I removed my clothes in the bathroom, draping them over a chair to dry. Adela had ordered a bottle of wine while I was in the bathroom. She offered me a glass when I returned."

"You fell off the wagon?" Bertram said.

"No, at least not at that moment."

"Then you got drunk, just like you used to, and took advantage of our client," Mama said.

I'd maintained my sobriety for some years, and Mama's reprimand was like a slap in the face.

"No, I didn't. Stop with your accusations and let me finish."

"What were you wearing?" Bertram asked.

"I wasn't naked if that's what you're getting at. I found a robe in the bathroom, and it covered me quite nicely, thank you. I declined the glass of wine, but. . ."

"But what?" Mama said.

"Adela had marijuana and offered me a puff. When I declined she let her robe drop to the floor, sat in my lap and began blowing in my ear."

"Good God Almighty!" Bertram said. "What does this woman look like?"

"Shut up, Bertram," Mama said, smiling for the first time. "So you're saying she seduced you and not the other way around?"

"I'm not a saint, and I probably wouldn't have had the wherewithal to put on my wet clothes and go. I never found out because she used a shotgun on me."

"What the hell?" Bertram said.

"She put the lit end of the joint in her mouth and blew smoke up my nose. It wasn't only pot she was smoking. There was something hallucinogenic in the joint as well. That's when I started drinking wine."

"Damn!" Bertram said. "We may run out of this great rum before you finish this story."

"I think we've heard enough," Mama said. "You succumbed to your baser instincts and bedded our client."

"No, I didn't," I said. "There's lots more to this story if you'll just shut the hell up and let me finish telling it."

Mama looked no happier when she flicked her wrist and eyed her empty glass. Bertram shook his head and poured her more rum. Outside, the winter storm had returned with a vengeance, rain pelleting the window. Bertram refilled my lemonade glass.

"Don't want you to get so dry you can't finish talking," he said.

"Adela told me she has powers."

Suddenly attentive, Mama turned on her stool until our knees were touching.

"What kind of powers?"

"Magic," I said.

"Magic, or just illusion?" Mama asked.

"Real magic. At least as best I could tell. Keep in mind I was under the influence of some psychotropic drug and wasn't sure what I was witnessing. I'm still not sure."

"Tell us what you think you saw," she said.

"Adela used mind control to cause the candle on the serving tray to melt down. She also made objects levitate off the table. Then she began to levitate and float around the room."

"Was she still naked?" Bertram asked.

"When was the last time you had a date?"

Mama said.

"Just asking a simple question," Bertram said.

"The answer is yes," I said. "Adela was definitely naked."

"A naked woman was floating around the room? You making this shit up?" Bertram asked.

"I'm just telling you what happened. It could have been an induced fantasy. I don't know. What I do know is, it's not where the fantasy ended, and it only got darker from that moment on."

"I'm listening," Mama said.

"Adela took my hand. We levitated and then flew through the window. As we hovered over New Orleans, I realized we were both naked."

"Wait a minute," Bertram said. "You flew through a closed window?"

"We passed through the glass as if it wasn't there."

"Man, you were more screwed up than I thought you was," he said.

"It didn't feel like a dream. I was cold, and when we floated through a damp cloud, I got a chill. And that's not to mention a sudden fear of heights had kicked in, and I was terrified I was going to fall to my death."

"You right," Bertram said. "You were smoking something bad."

"Real bad. We finally returned to the hotel but not to the room we had left from. It was on the thirteenth floor and smelled of dust and mold. The sheets on the bed were mussed and warm. The bathroom door was open. I could hear someone splashing water in the tub. We went in to see."

"Another naked woman?" Bertram said.

"A naked woman with a missing head, jerking around as if she were still alive and with blood spewing out of her neck. The body sank into the water as Adela and I watched. It was then we realized the killer was standing behind us in the little bathroom."

A clap of thunder shook the windows and Bertram jumped. Filling his glass, he drained it in a single swallow. Mama reached for the bottle and poured herself another.

"Go on," she said.

"A demon was blocking the bathroom door. I don't know if it was the same demon Taj told us about or a nightmare induced by memories of his story. Adela grabbed my wrist and levitated us over him, out the bathroom door and then back outside. It was the last thing I remember until you and Taj found us in bed. Except. . ."

"Except for what?" Mama said.

"The demon spoke to us as we were leaving."

"I'll bite. What the hell did it say?" Bertram said.

"The demon had the head of the disembodied woman, holding it by its long red hair and dragging it across the tile. It was Adela's head."

"Get out of here," Bertram said.

"What did the demon say?" Mama asked.

"I will have you, Aisling."

"Who the hell is Aisling?" Bertram asked.

"An Irish witch," Mama said before I could answer. Bertram and I both stared at Mama, waiting for her to explain. "Taj and I also had a paranormal experience tonight."

Bertram tipped the bottle of rum, watching as the last drop dribbled into his glass.

"Damn!" he said. "Guess I'm going back to Cuervo."

"Then will you make me a martini?" Mama asked.

When Bertram went behind the bar to find Mama's favorite vodka, Mama handed me an envelope from her purse.

"I was going to keep the entire retainer and tell you I was no longer your business partner. Your story convinced me you did nothing out of line. Deposit this in your bank and then write me a check for my half."

"Twenty grand is a lot of money," I said.

"I tried to give it back. Taj was having none of it. He even offered to give us more."

"Sounds like my kind of client."

Bertram returned as I was stuffing the envelope into the pocket of my jacket. He made a production of handing Mama a chilled glass with an olive in the vodka.

"Voila. Guess you know who mixes the finest martinis in the Quarter."

Mama smiled after sipping the concoction. "I can't argue with that, Bertram. Your martini is definitely the best in all of New Orleans."

"Good, now let's hear your story."

"The reason Taj came to me was the cemetery keeper at St. Louis Cemetery No. 1 gave him my name. From the way Taj described the man, I was suspicious. We took a cab to the cemetery to talk to him."

"After dark?" Bertram asked.

"Just a few hours ago," Mama said.

"You about a brave one," Bertram said. "That's a good way to get your throat cut."

"Taj was with me, and he's a giant of a man. As I had thought, there was no ground's keeper living on the premises. I used my powers to summon Baron Samedi, the keeper of souls and cemeteries."

"The real Baron Samedi?" Bertram asked.

"Not someone possessed by the Baron. It was the real Baron Samedi, the person Taj had met who had given him my name."

"Isn't it unusual to encounter an actual voodoo deity?" I asked.

"It's never happened to me before, and I've never heard of it ever happening to anyone else,"

Mama said. "He appeared to us because Taj is somehow a person of interest to the powers that be in the realm of Vodoun. I asked him who had summoned Taj to New Orleans, and for what purpose?"

"And?"

"He said my answers lie in a courtyard garden in the French Quarter. A garden still cloaked in forbidden darkness. A garden known to a red-haired Irish witch named Aisling."

"Adela," I said. "We need to talk to her about this."

Thunder rattled the windows as someone opened the door to Bertram's bar and entered. It was Taj Davis.

"I thought I'd find you here," he said.

Chapter 17

Taj Davis reached the bar in three long strides. Grabbing my jacket by the neck, he lifted me off the bar stool. Before I could react, he punched me in the face. It was the last thing Taj remembered for awhile because Bertram tapped him on the back of his head with the weighted club he kept for security purposes under the bar.

"Are you okay?" Mama asked as I massaged my jaw.

Bertram handed me a bar rag to staunch the blood dripping down my chin.

"I'll live. I'm not so sure about our new client."

Taj was out cold on the floor. "You didn't have to kill him, Bertram," Mama said.

"He ain't dead," the Cajun bartender said. "He might wish he was when he comes to."

"Should I call an ambulance?" Mama asked.

"Why hell no," Bertram said. "He's taken worse hits than that playing basketball."

Bertram was correct. As we watched, Taj blinked his eyes and pushed himself up into a sitting position. Bertram's club made a sharp cracking noise when he slapped it against the bar.

"You need to get your ass out of here," he said. "I don't allow fighting in my bar. I also don't like bullies, and I might just hit you again for general principles if you don't hightail it."

Taj was still sitting on the floor. "Mama, you're not going to let this man get away with this, are you?"

Mama's reaction was a surprise to the big basketball player. She reached into my jacket, pulled out the envelope containing the retainer and tossed it at him.

"I thought you were a gentleman. You're not. On top of it all, you're a fool. Bertram told you to get the hell out of here. Take your money and go."

"That man tried to rape Adela," Taj said, pointing an accusing finger at me.

"No, he didn't," Mama said.

"I know what Adela told me," Taj said.

"How long have you known that woman?" Mama asked.

"Long enough," Taj said.

"Then you're also an idiot," Mama said. "I don't work for idiots."

Bertram rapped the bar again with the weighted club. "Pick the envelope off the floor and then get the hell out of here before I call the police."

"Wait just a minute," Taj said. "If you know something I don't know then please let me in on it."

"You can't come in here like a common street thug and start throwing punches," Mama said. "I won't tolerate it."

"You're saying he didn't rape Adela?"

"You don't deserve an answer," Mama said. "Do like Bertram told you and go."

Taj got to his feet, brushed himself off and started for the door as he gave Bertram a glance.

"I can't believe you people. Doesn't it matter to you that he drugged and raped Adela?"

"You stop right there, Taj Davis," Mama said. "Wyatt didn't drug or rape anyone."

"Adela said he did."

"I can't let you leave thinking that. You need to

listen to Wyatt's side of the story. Get back in here. Sit on this stool, keep your mouth shut, your hands to yourself and listen."

"And if I don't?"

"Then forget about ever learning the truth, and accept the consequences of your actions."

"All right, but tell the crazy Cajun to put away his billy club."

Bertram returned the club to its spot beneath the bar. "I'm Bertram," he said. "If your money's good, I'll even fix you a drink."

Taj pulled up a stool next to Mama as morning light began peeking through the windows.

"Glass of cabernet," he said.

Taj wouldn't look me in the eyes as he sipped his wine. Before my story was half told, I had his full attention. When I concluded, he finished his wine and motioned Bertram for another.

"Well?" Mama asked.

"I owe you all an apology," he said. "As much as I hate to admit it, Wyatt is telling the truth."

"You sure about that?" Bertram said.

"I'm positive," Taj said. "He was either in the same room on the thirteenth floor of the Hotel Montalba as I was, or else he's a mind reader."

With my hand, I rotated my sore chin. "Wish you'd known that before throwing your punch," I said,

"I'm truly sorry. I don't usually go around hitting people," Taj said, pulling the envelope out of his coat pocket and pushing it across the bar toward Mama. "Please take back your retainer. I need you two even more than I realized."

"You sure about that?" she said.

"As sure as I am about anything," he said. Leaning over the bar, he extended his hand. "Bertram, I apologize for causing a disturbance in your fine establishment. I promise it won't happen again. Wyatt, I'm so sorry about hitting you."

"Already forgotten," I said. "Now that the air has cleared, we need to talk about Adela."

"Is she the answer to your questions or the root of your problem," Mama said. "More importantly, what does she know about the Irish witch named Aisling that the demon and Baron Samedi both mentioned

"Since Adela is claiming I raped her, I should probably bow out of this investigation," I said.

"Maybe I stretched the truth a bit," Taj said. "Adela told me someone had spiked her drink and that's why she wound up in bed with you. If she had any memory of the story you just told, she kept it to herself. Again, I'm so sorry for jumping to the wrong conclusion."

"Can you call Adela?" Mama said. "Ask her to join us?"

"Now?" Taj asked.

"The sooner we get a handle on this, the better," she said.

Taj punched in a number on his cell phone and was soon talking to Adela. After disconnecting, he said, "I'm starved. Think we have time to get some breakfast?"

"Wyatt, take them to your booth in the back," Bertram said. "I'll cook something up and bring it to you before my customers start getting here."

There was an empty booth in a secluded corner of Bertram's bar I used for meeting new clients. We grabbed our drinks and convened to the booth. Morning customers had begun pouring into the bar, and Bertram didn't join us after bringing our breakfast on a tray. I was just finishing the last bite of my oyster and shrimp omelet when Adela arrived.

"Smells wonderful," she said. "Hope you saved some for me."

Bertram must have known she would be hungry and appeared shortly with more omelets and a fresh pot of Cajun coffee. Mama and I were full. Adela attacked hers with gusto. Taj had no problem eating what Mama and I didn't want. Adela had slid into the booth next to me, not acting as if I had drugged or accosted her. Mama and Taj both noticed.

"Why are you two staring at me?" she finally asked.

"We just thought you might be upset with Wyatt after last night," Mama said.

Adela turned her head and glanced at me. "Why? What did he do?"

"Taj said you told him someone had spiked your drink," Mama said.

"My head felt like it was about to split when I awoke. I think it was the bottle of wine I ordered when we returned to the room. You know what they say: beer on whiskey, mighty risky."

"And Wyatt?" Mama said.

Adela smiled and squeezed my thigh. "He was a doll. The thunder had me spooked, and I didn't want to be alone. I may have coerced him a bit to stay with me and not leave. Hope you're not mad at me," she said, squeezing my thigh again.

Bertram showed up with a tray of fresh drinks and a bloody mary for Adela.

After sipping the concoction, she grinned and gave Bertram a wink. "This is wonderful," she said.

"Nothing cures a hangover better than one of Bertram's bloody marys with my secret ingredient," he said.

"Thank you so much, Bertram. What is your secret ingredient?"

Bertram returned her wink. "If I told you it wouldn't be a secret, now would it?"

"Guess you met Bertram already," I said after our Cajun bartender had left the table.

"He introduced himself when I came in. Asked me what I was drinking and showed me where you were. He's a doll."

"Bertram knows no strangers," I said.

"Why is everyone looking at me?" Adela asked as she sipped her bloody mary.

"Wyatt told us a story when I got here," Taj said. "It got my attention."

Adela glanced around the table. "What story?"

"Wyatt, would you mind telling it one more time?" Mama asked.

Adela sat mesmerized as I told the story for the third time that morning.

"Well?" Taj asked when I'd finished.

"Well, what?" Adela said.

"You were a major participant in the story," Mama said. "We were hoping you might shed some light on the room, the demon and the murdered woman."

Adela laughed. "Apparently, Wyatt was more screwed up than I was. He was either dreaming or having a nightmare," she said.

"A nightmare you were no part of?" Mama said.

"Of course not. Surely you don't believe anything about his absolutely wild-ass tale is true, do you?"

"Don't know," Taj said. "Is it?"

"I have no clue what the three of you have been smoking. I'd like to have a puff."

"I don't think it was a dream," I said.

"What else could it be?" she asked.

"I've had lucid dreams before that I've remembered parts of, though nothing like last night. I remember every vivid detail. I was cold. When I touched, you were real, and I'll never forget the stench of the demon."

"The same foul odor I smelled when the demon confronted me," Taj said. "I know I wasn't dreaming and Wyatt described the room perfectly. How would he have known if he hadn't been there?"

Adela looked at Mama. "There must be a reason. Do you know?"

"Wyatt is a sensitive, so it's possible I guess," Mama said.

"What's a sensitive?" Taj asked.

"A person with special insight and who can see things that others can't. It's possible Wyatt became so enthralled with your story, he got into your mind, and his dream is no more than a case of transference."

"We're not talking transference here," I said. "What I saw was through my own eyes, not Taj's."

"What you saw, or thought you saw has nothing to do with me," Adela said. "I saw no demon or headless woman. I certainly can't levitate, much less fly. I can understand Wyatt being confused by a vivid dream. I don't understand why you and Mama are taking his story seriously."

"Because Mama and I also had a strange experience last night," Taj said. "Have you ever heard of a voodoo deity named Baron Samedi?"

"I know almost nothing about voodoo," Adela said. "What happened?"

"I think that's a story best left for another time," Mama said. "I need to discuss something with Wyatt. Do you two mind waiting here without us while we have a few moments alone at the bar?"

"Fine with me," Adela said. "At least if you ask Bertram to bring me another bloody mary."

"Consider it done," Mama said.

I followed Mama to the bar where she ordered the bloody mary for Adela.

"What?" I said.

"Either Adela has no memory of your experience, or else she's lying through her teeth. There's also a third explanation."

"Which is?"

"You were hallucinating on some psychodelic

drug."

"Then how would I have been able to describe the room in such detail?"

"Transference, as I said in the booth."

"I don't think so."

"We need to find out. You need to find out," Mama said.

"And how do you suggest I do that?"

"Take her to see Madeline. If anyone can tell if Adela is a witch, it will be another witch."

"Great idea," I said.

"I think you should do this alone," Mama said. "Taj and I would just get in the way."

"How will you explain this to Taj?"

"I'll take care of it," she said.

When we returned to the booth, Taj was nibbling on the crumbs left on his breakfast plate, and Adela was drinking her bloody mary. I slid in beside her while Mama remained standing.

"Taj, you wanted me to show you some expensive condos. Let's go now. Wyatt can escort Adela back to the hotel."

Taj started to say something when he noticed Mama's same stern expression as when he'd punched me.

"Will you be okay?" he asked Adela before heading to the bar to clear the tab with Bertram.

"Of course I will. Wyatt tried to show me Jackson Square last night. It was raining so hard we both got drenched long before we saw anything. I want to see all of New Orleans, and he'll make the perfect tour guide."

"Good," Mama said. "Have fun."

Chapter 18

Tourists and regulars had begun filling Bertram's bar as we finished the last of our drinks. Bertram stopped us before we reached the front door.

"Mighty happy to meet you, Miss Adela," he said.

Adela hugged him. "The pleasure is all mine."

"Hope Taj's theatrics this morning didn't upset you too much," I said.

"You kidding? He picked up the whole tab and give me a hundred dollar tip. He's my new best customer," Bertram said.

"Glad to hear it. Adela and I are going on a foot tour of the Quarter."

"Watch your step with that one, Miss Adela," he said as we walked out the door.

The rain had moved north leaving the streets and sidewalks wet and the sky a dismal shade of gray. The morning gloom did nothing to negate Adela's smile as she pulled her coat up around her neck.

"Cold?" I asked.

"Feels like springtime compared to the weather they're having in Michigan. Hope you didn't mind me volunteering you to take me on a sightseeing trip."

"Nothing I'd rather do," I said. "Jackson Square is just up the street. Looks as if we may even get a break from the rain."

After days of persistent stormy weather, the Quarter was abuzz with tourists on both sides of the old street. Adela was looking in the other direction.

"This neighborhood seems so familiar to me. Were you really serious about the story you told us?"

"It seemed so real, I'm having trouble not believing it actually happened."

"You were dreaming," Adela said.

"Then why did we wake up naked in bed?"

Adela laughed. "Is that a rhetorical question?"

"I'm serious. If what I told you was only a dream then why don't I remember getting naked and into bed with you? How did I get drunk or drugged?"

"Because part of your story actually happened. I ordered a bottle of wine while you were in the bathroom. You wouldn't drink any until I offered you a puff of pot."

"Was there something in the pot other than marijuana?"

"Just Mary Jane is all," she said. "You got a little frisky and passed out soon as we got in bed. I let you sleep. I can't control your dreams."

"How do you explain to me knowing what the room with the demon looked like?"

"I have no idea," she said. "What street is this?"

"Chartres Street."

"What's the next street over?"

"Royal."

"Let's go to Royal," she said.

"If we do, we'll miss Jackson Square."

"There'll be time for Jackson Square later. I want to see what's on Royal Street."

"Shops, bistros, art galleries and street musicians," I said. "Everything that exemplifies the French Quarter."

"Then that's where I want to go," she said.

"I'm right behind you," I said.

More tourists, browsing shop windows and strolling along the sidewalks, occupied Royal Street when we reached it. As if greeting an old friend, Adela drew a deep breath.

"I love the narrow streets and wrought iron balconies," she said. "So many different colors: yellows, pale blues and three different shades of beige. The colors are all different and even on this gloomy day they bring the old buildings to life."

"And you can always count on the green shutters."

"They tie the buildings together. Is this French architecture?"

"More like a mixture of French and Spanish. People around here just call it Creole."

"I like this street. Do you mind if we follow it for a while?"

"Not at all," I said.

We passed a young man, a guitar in his arms, sitting on the sidewalk beside his open guitar case. A small black dog lay beside him on an old throw rug. Adela tossed a handful of dollar bills into the case and blew the young man a kiss. After passing Pirate's Alley, we took a moment to check out the artwork of a street artist who had hung his paintings on the fence surrounding the back of St. Louis Cathedral.

We passed art galleries, quaint cafes, and souvenir shops. The businesses gradually began to thin as we reached a part of Royal which was mostly houses. Adela showed no signs of turning around.

"Am I wearing you out?" she asked.

"I needed a good walk to work off some of

Bertram's breakfast. This part of Royal is more residential. We can go over a block to Bourbon Street and then work our way back toward Bertram's."

"Let's go a little further," she said.

Before I could reply, Adela touched her forehead and sank to her knees on the cracked sidewalk. I quickly knelt beside her, grabbing her arm to keep her from falling and hitting her head.

"Are you okay?" I asked.

"My head is splitting," she said. "Please help me up."

When I pulled her to her feet, she clutched her arms around me.

"I'll call a cab," I said.

"I can't wait for that. Help me back the way we came. Please hurry."

I was half-carrying her down the sidewalk when a passing couple asked if they could help.

"Could you please call a cab for us?" I said without stopping.

The man and woman were staring at us as we walked away. The man quickly got on his cell phone, leaving me to wonder if he was calling a cab or the cops. I had little time to worry about it as Adela leaned heavily on my shoulder.

A hundred yards from where Adela had her fainting spell, she returned to normal. When a cab pulled to the curb, I had a hard time convincing her we needed to get in.

"Where to?" the cabbie asked.

"Madeline's Magic Potions," I said. "Know where it is?"

"You bet," he said.

"Are you feeling better?" I asked Adela.

"I'm okay."

"What happened back there?"

"I don't know," she said. "Where are we going?"

"There's someone I want you to meet. Her

place isn't far from Bertram's."

Madeline's Magic Potions was on Royal, near the intersection with Toulouse. We'd walked past it earlier. The door was locked, and I rang the bell. A woman soon opened it a crack and peered out. I could see her smile when she saw me.

"Come in. I somehow had a feeling I would have a special visitor today."

Madeline Romanov had dark hair sprinkled with ample gray. She had blue eyes, a dark complexion, a hooked nose and a slight accent indicative of her Romanian heritage.

Adela glanced at me, waiting for an introduction.

"Madeline Romanov, this is Adela Kowalski."

After placing the closed sign on the door, Madeline embraced Adela as if she'd known her all her life.

"I'm so happy to meet you, Adela. Let's cut through the shop. I'll fix tea, and we can sit in the courtyard."

We followed Madeline through her dimly lit shop which was a hodgepodge of esoteric items ranging from aromatic soap, crystal specimens, and souvenir tarot cards, to an ancient suit of armor in the corner. The old fan sitting on a display cabinet did its best to spread the aroma of peppermint incense and cover the odor of the old building's must. A Gregorian chant emanated from a broken speaker hidden somewhere in the rafters.

"I love your shop," Adela said.

"So do the tourists," Madeline said. "My sales pay the bills, though it isn't my primary source of income."

"Which is?" Adela said.

"I do seances, read tarot cards, and occasionally use my grandmother's crystal ball to tell the future."

Adela's attention was suddenly rapt. "You can

do that?"

"Yes, dear. Like my Romanian mother and grandmother, I was born with the gift, though sometimes it proves more a punishment."

"Will you tell my future?" Adela asked.

Madeline stopped in her tracks and clutched Adela's hand.

"More often than not the future is best left untold. I only use the crystal ball on rare occasions and then only after determining there is indeed a life or death reason to do so."

Adela didn't reply as a black cat bounded off one of the display cabinets and joined us. Adela picked up Madeline's cat and stroked it.

"What's your kitty's name?"

"Jinx," Madeline said. "She usually doesn't like being held. I can see you're a special person."

Madeline's cat, purring like a throaty kitten, was indeed enjoying his time in her arms. Interpreting Adela's silence as declining to have her future read, she continued to the backdoor. Adela released Jinx and rushed past Madeline as she exited into the courtyard.

"I love your patio," Adela said. "It's like a fairy tale come to life."

Madeline's tiny courtyard was picturesque, complete with slate paving stones, stuccoed walls, and a central fountain filling the area with the soothing melody of dripping water. Wind chimes and hanging plants hung from the second-story balconies surrounding the courtyard. The chimes rustled in a gentle breeze, performing a symphony, along with the fountain.

"You should see it in the spring and summer when the plants are lush, and my geraniums are in full bloom," Madeline said. "At least the surrounding walls keep in some of the heat during our cold snaps. Make yourself comfortable, and I'll get tea."

Jinx jumped back into Adela's lap when she and I sat on the park bench near the edge of the courtyard.

"Can Madeline really tell the future?" she asked.

"I can attest to it. She once used tarot cards to tell mine."

"And?"

"Unfortunately, she had it nailed."

"Unfortunately?"

"Like Madeline said, the future is usually best left untold. What I wish she could tell us is more about your past than your future."

"I know all about my past," she said.

"Do you?"

"I'm Adela Kowalski from Michigan."

"And you're sure about that?"

"Pretty sure."

"Have you ever been hypnotized?" I said.

"Why do you ask?"

"A professional might be able to regress you, see if you really are Adela Kowalski."

"That's crazy talk. Who else would I be?"

"Someone who has a voodoo veve on her chest and doesn't have a clue how it got there."

"You think I know more about the dream you had last night than I'm letting on," she said.

"Something like that."

Before we could finish our conversation, Madeline returned with a tray.

"Such intense discussion," she said. "Were you two arguing?"

"Just talking," I said.

Madeline set the tray on a table and filled our cups.

"Hot tea is what we all need on such a gloomy day," she said.

Madeline was correct, Adela displaying her first smile in many minutes as she cradled the steaming cup in her palms.

"Jinx is here. Where's Calpurnia?" I asked.

"That gorgeous bird loves dreary weather and is probably soaring among the clouds high over the river right about now."

"Who is Calpurnia?" Adela asked.

"A regal raven with feathers as black as the depths of a Romanian coal mine."

"And she's a talker," I said.

"Your raven talks?" Adela asked.

"Oh yes," Madeline said. "Ravens are among the most intelligent birds in the world."

As if on cue, we heard the flapping wings of a bird circling the courtyard. As we watched, a large black bird descended quickly and landed on an ornate perch.

"Calpurnia," Madeline said. "You must have heard us talking about you."

"She's beautiful," Adela said.

Calpurnia reacted instantly when she heard Adela's voice. Flying from her perch, she landed on Adela's shoulder, pecking her lips with her burnished beak. From the way her tail was moving and feathers fluffing, it was apparent she was excited.

"Aisling, Aisling," the big raven kept repeating.

Chapter 19

Eddie awoke to the sound of hammers and saws working at the restaurant. His cell phone told him it was only six A.M. and still dark outside.

"No rest for the wicked," he muttered beneath his breath as he crawled out of bed and got dressed.

He had no trouble traversing the steep steps from his apartment because powerful beams of light flooded the main ballroom. The carpenters had stirred a layer of dust and it hung in the air along with the odor of sawdust and sweat. Eddie smelled something else: the aroma of bacon and eggs coming from the restaurant's kitchen. Realizing how hungry he was, he hurried to investigate. What he found was a surprise.

Clad in sweatpants and her blue bikini bra, Odette was cooking eggs, sausage, bacon, and flipping pancakes on the grill of a stove. One at a time, the workers approached plates in hand, awaiting their share of the hearty breakfast she was cooking. Odette didn't disappoint, heaping their plates with the efficiency of a seasoned line cook. Odette jumped when Eddie tapped her shoulder.

"Hope you don't mind," she said. "I was on my way to wake you when I heard one of the men complaining about missing breakfast because they have to leave home so early to get here by six. I decided to fix breakfast for everyone. As you can see, no one's complaining."

"I'm impressed," Eddie said. "Where did you learn how to feed thirty people?"

"Put on an apron and help me," she said. "I'm starting to fall behind. When the rush is over, I'll tell you all about it."

"Yes, ma'am," Eddie said with a salute.

Eddie was soon cracking eggs and mixing pancake batter. When they'd fed the last worker, Odette scooped what was left into two plates, handed them to Eddie and pointed to a table in the corner of the kitchen.

"I'll join you soon as I clean the grill," she said.

Odette brought a fresh carafe of coffee with her when she joined him.

"Like I said, where'd you learn to cook for thirty people?"

"Since I wasn't born with a silver spoon in my mouth I've had to work my whole life for whatever I have. I had a partial scholarship at L.S.U. and worked as a cook to make ends meet. My dad was a roughneck on offshore rigs. During summer breaks, I worked as a cook on the jack-ups. We fed hungry crews twenty-four hours a day."

"This food is great. What's a college graduate doing working in a strip joint on Bourbon Street?"

"I didn't graduate. My dad was killed in a gas explosion on an offshore drilling rig my senior year. I had to drop out to help Mom make ends meet. The strip joint was the easiest place to make the most money. When my mom finally got her insurance settlement, I began looking for something else."

"I'm so sorry," Eddie said. "I didn't mean to pry. Where's Mudbug?"

"Right behind you," she said.

Odette had turned a box and some old rags into a dog bed. The young dog, situated near a radiator, was sleeping soundly.

"Why didn't you re-enroll in college?"

"I only lacked a few hours to graduate. A required course I need isn't offered until next spring. Though I'd decided to keep stripping until then, the lifestyle finally got to me."

"I can't imagine an educated woman stripping for a living," Eddie said.

"Don't be such a prude. Lots of college girls strip to earn extra money. Strip joints aren't whorehouses, you know."

"Guess so," he said. "Tell me again why you came to Oyster Island?"

"Like I said, I was sick of stripping."

"So you just packed your stuff and hitched-hiked here?"

"Something like that," she said.

"What else can you cook besides breakfast?"

"My mom is the best Cajun cook on earth, and she taught me everything she knows. My major in college is restaurant management. I can cook Cajun, Creole, fusion, you name it, and I've taken all the business, management and accounting courses you need to run the biggest restaurant in New Orleans."

"I need a chef," Eddie said. "Sounds like you're well qualified to fill the position. You're hired if you want the job."

"You're just going to take my word about my qualifications?"

"If it doesn't work out, I can always fire you," Eddie said.

"You mean it?"

"Absolutely."

"I don't want a job if I'm just going to be somebody else's flunky," she said.

"You'll be the head honcho. When the restaurant is ready to open, you'll be responsible for hiring the cook staff. You'll be the boss. You're not afraid of the responsibility, are you?"

"I relish responsibility," she said. "How much does this gig pay?"

"Hell, I don't know," Eddie said. "I've never owned a restaurant before though I guarantee whatever I pay you will be equivalent to any head honcho."

"You're an idiot, you know? Nobody hires an ex-stripper to take on an important position."

"I just did," he said.

"Doesn't matter. I'm never going to sleep with you."

"Not even if I marry you?"

Odette grinned. "I'll take your job. When do I start?"

"You already did," he said. "Consider yourself on the payroll. Until we get the place rolling, you'll be the chief cook and bottle washer."

"Does that mean I do the dishes?"

"Quick learner," he said.

Odette reached across the table and kissed him. "Thank you," she said.

"I can't have my employee's living in a tent on the beach. Pick out one of the empty bungalows, and we'll put it on a contract-for-deed for you."

"You are an idiot," she said. "How do you know I'm not a serial killer?"

"I'll take my chances," he said.

Odette kissed him again. "Then I have to get to work. These men will be expecting lunch in a few hours, and I need to check the pantry and see what we have available."

The sun was coming up over the eastern horizon when Eddie left the restaurant. The first thing he saw was two people he knew. Jack and Chief were down by the marina looking at the trawler.

"What's up?" he asked.

"Just having a look at the old trawler," Jack Wiesinski said. "Chief and I were wondering if you'd let us take it out for a cruise."

"Where to?" Eddie asked.

"Not far. Chief wants to do some diving."

"Have an extra tank?" Eddie asked. "I haven't dived since I moved to Louisiana and I wouldn't mind going with you."

Jack and Chief exchanged a glance.

"You know how to dive?" Jack asked.

"I'm certified if that's what you mean," Eddie said.

"Sure," Jack said.

"When do you want to go?" Eddie said

Jack looked at the bank of clouds gathering from the south. "Now. There's another storm moving in later today."

"You wouldn't be looking for Spanish gold, would you?" Eddie said.

"What makes you ask?" Jack said.

"A girl was camping on the beach last night. She found a piece of a Spanish doubloon while snorkeling in the surf."

"Oh?" Jack said.

"She said it was kicked up by the last storm."

"There's no telling what you might find out there in the surf," Jack said.

"She said it was from a sunken Spanish treasure ship laden with gold and emeralds."

Jack and Chief exchanged knowing grins. "We've heard that one before," Jack said. "Who is this girl?"

"Odette Bellefleur. She says she knows you two."

"Never heard of her," Jack said.

Chief was shaking his head. "Yes, you have."

"Says who?" Jack said. "I don't remember no Odette Bellefleur."

"That's because you were so drunk you don't remember anything that happened that night."

"What the hell are you talking about?" Jack said.

"Our trip to New Orleans last month. You were trying to impress this little stripper in a bar on Bourbon Street by telling her about a sunken treasure ship off the island here."

"I did not," Jack said.

"You damn sure did," Chief said. "I had to practically drag you out of the place."

"So, there's no Spanish treasure ship out there?" Eddie asked.

"Why hell no," Jack said. "I hope you told her there's no camping on the beach and sent her packing."

"Actually, I hired her."

"You're opening a strip joint on the island?"

"I hired her as the head chef for the restaurant."

"You did what?" Jack said. "You hired a stripper to be your head chef? You gotta be kidding me."

"She's cooked professionally for years, and she's college educated. She was only a stripper for a short time."

"What's Mr. Castellano going to say about that?" Jack asked.

"Not your business what he says," Eddie said. "Forget about using my boat."

Eddie's quick rebuff caught Jack by surprise. Chief bumped the little man with his shoulder, as Jack stood there with his mouth open.

"Hey, I'm sorry," Jack said, recovering his composure. "I was out of line."

"Very much so," Eddie said.

"It won't happen again, I promise. We have an extra wet suit and tank and would love to have you go diving with us."

"Then you're not looking for a sunken galleon?"

Jack laughed. "There ain't no sunken Spanish treasure ship out there. I swear on a stack of Bibles."

"I'll accept your apology," Eddie said. "If you treat Odette with respect she deserves next time you see her."

"We would have anyway," Chief said. "Though Jack's a blithering idiot when he gets drunk and sticks his foot in his mouth occasionally when he's sober, he's usually a perfect gentleman."

Eddie decided to let the matter drop, and they were soon motoring out of the channel leading to the Gulf of Mexico. Jack was correct about the clouds moving in from the south, and Eddie wondered how far they'd get before the rain began falling again. Chief was somewhere on deck, Eddie in the wheelhouse with Jack.

"This boat is beautiful. You said it was a rumrunner. What's the rest of the story?" Eddie asked.

"This beautiful old lady's name is Argo. A rumrunner who lived part-time on Oyster Island owned her. Its original name was the Island Mistress because though the rumrunner had a wife and family in New York, he had a mistress who lived with him during the time he spent on the island."

"Interesting," Eddie said.

"The Argo was built in 1928. The decks are teak, the hull constructed of the finest Douglas fir. A 180-horsepower diesel engine propels it, and its dual 200-gallon fuel tanks are big enough to get you to the Bahamas."

"So the Argo was used to smuggle illegal alcohol?"

"She was registered as a fishing vessel. Her crew would pick up a load of hooch, store it in the hold, and top it with a load of fish. She's so slow the Coast Guard never suspected she carried illegal booze in her hold."

Eddie glanced around at the polished brass and woodwork in the cozy wheelhouse.

"Is that unusual?"

"Pretty much so. The Coast Guard had a fleet of fast boats armed with cannons. Most rumrunners, much faster than the Argo, were shot out of the water."

"Sounds like a dangerous profession," Eddie said.

"But lucrative. The man who owned the Argo lived like a king on Oyster Island."

"The Feds never caught him?"

Jack laughed. "No, but his jealous wife finally did. Shot his knee off and crippled him. Stopped his running around forever. She also made him change the name of the Island Mistress to Argo."

"The reason I've never been married," Eddie said. "Where are we heading?"

"A barrier bar just ahead. The water depth drops off pretty fast on the Gulf side. It's about fifty feet deep where you'll be diving, the water fairly clear."

Jack handed him a pair of binoculars. Eddie saw the barren, low-lying island that paralleled the shoreline.

"What do you expect to find?" Eddie asked.

"Ruined hulls of boats caught out beyond the barriers during unexpected storms."

"But not a Spanish treasure ship?"

"Just some old fishing boats which had no business motoring this far from shore," Jack said.

"Are we in any danger?" Eddie asked.

"The Argo is seaworthy and has traveled more than once all the way to Jamaica. In anything short of a hurricane, she's good to go."

"What happens if we get caught in a hurricane?" Eddie asked.

"A hundred years from now, divers would be motoring out to dive atop our remains," Jack said.

Chapter 20

A flock of brown pelicans lifted skyward as the Argo motored past the barrier island. Eddie watched as they headed north to avoid the approaching storm. A hundred yards on the seaward side of the island, Jack killed the engine, drifted to a stop and dropped anchor. Eddie followed him out of the wheelhouse and down the ladder to the main deck.

Chief was waiting for them, the diving tanks resting against the hull and wetsuits draped over the railing. A dull gray sky had only grown dimmer as Chief and Eddie pulled on their wetsuits and readied their equipment. Jack was polishing the railing with an old rag.

"You're not diving with us?" Eddie asked.

"Would if I could swim," Jack said.

"In the Navy for thirty years and can't swim. How'd you get away with that?"

"Wasn't easy."

"You wouldn't be pulling my leg, would you?"

"Nope, can't swim a lick."

"Being out on the water doesn't scare you?"

"Not anymore," Jack said. "At least until someone reminds me."

"Sorry about that," Eddie said. "What would you do if our boat started sinking?"

"Take the rubber life raft, or else go down with the ship," Jack said.

Chief had heard it all before and was shaking his head as he adjusted the air tank on his back.

"You ready?" he asked.

Eddie gave him the high sign. "Any special instructions?"

"Just follow me down," Chief said.

Chief did a backward splash into the blue water of the Gulf, and Eddie followed him off the side of the boat. The anxiety he'd had about diving in the Gulf disappeared as he sank beneath the surface. Chief was below him, bubbles from his regulator rising upward as he tracked the anchor line to the bottom.

Visibility was good, though the water was a hazy shade of bluish-green, ambient light fading as they reached the bottom. Bits of metal and other debris lay on the sandy floor, green and red organisms growing on top moving like slow motion dancers in the current. A school of groupers swam between them. Not far away, Eddie saw something else.

A jumble of old cars and boat hulls lay strewn on the sandy surface. Eels and tiny fishes swam among the cracks and crevasses, and Eddie realized why the large school of groupers had congregated at that particular spot. The old vehicles formed an artificial reef on the floor of the Gulf, and all manner of fish and vegetation had taken advantage.

Chief swam past the maze of old wrecks after giving the man-made reef a cursory inspection. Enthralled by the plethora of life that had assembled around the old wrecks, Eddie gave it a closer look. When he saw a glint of light reflecting off something rocking in the gentle current, he was glad he did. Scooping it up, he placed it in the pouch attached to his wetsuit.

Chief was looking for something else and moved around the vehicles in ever-widening circles. A large shark swam past them as he turned back toward the anchor. When they reached the line, Chief grabbed it, pointed toward the surface and started up. They got a surprise when they reached the surface.

The frontal edge of a storm was upon them, heavy rain rippling the Gulf's surface. Chief heaved his fins over the railing and started up the ladder to the deck of the Argo. Lightning lighted the dark sky, thunder sounding almost immediately as Eddie followed Chief up the ladder. Jack was in the wheelhouse and shouted to them as they hurried to remove their tanks.

"Get a move on and let's get the hell out of here. This old tub's too slow to outrun the storm, and we're about to catch hell."

Rain pummeled the deck as Chief and Eddie hurriedly stowed their gear and made for the ladder up to the wheelhouse. Waves were pouring over the deck, the old boat rocking as Chief reached the ladder. Missing a rung, he lost his footing, and his grip, and fell backward into Eddie's arms. Blinded by the tumult and the wildly rocking boat, he didn't see him coming.

Eddie tried to hold on and break his fall, but Chief was simply too big and too slippery. Even amid the fury of the storm, Eddie heard a crack when Chief hit the deck.

"You okay, Big Guy?" Eddie asked.

Chief struggled to get up. "I think I broke my arm," he said.

Eddie grabbed him around the waist, wrestling him into a sitting position.

"You gotta help me," Eddie said. "We need to get below before we get washed overboard."

Eddie pulled the big man to his feet. This time, they avoided the ladder and made their way around the deck to the door leading into the main cabin. Chief grimaced as Eddie managed to lay him on the bunk. Jack had raised the anchor, turned the old boat around and was making toward shore.

Chief was looking unwell and holding his arm. Finding a butcher knife in the galley, Eddie sliced the sleeve of the wetsuit to reveal the injury. The wound was more than just a break, The bone had pierced the skin and blood was soaking Chief's arm. Eddie found some rags, applied a tourniquet and compressed the wound as best he could to staunch the bleeding.

Chief nodded when Eddie asked, "Are you going to make it? Then hang tight a minute. I've got to tell Jack what happened."

Rain pelted Eddie's head as he exited the cabin door. He could barely keep his footing as he climbed the ladder to the wheelhouse. Bounding through the door, he forced it shut with some difficulty.

"What's going on down there?" Jack said.

"Chief fell and broke his arm."

"Bad?" Jack asked.

"Real bad. The bone splintered and punctured the skin. I got the bleeding stopped, but we need to get him to a doctor."

"There's a hospital about twenty miles up the road from the island. I'll call for an ambulance. With a little luck, it'll be waiting for us when we reach port."

"Are we going to make it?" Eddie asked.

"Made in the shade," Jack said. "We were safe once we passed through to the lee side of the barrier islands. Go take care of Chief."

"He's in a lot of pain," Eddie said. "Got anything to help him?"

Jack tossed him a flask. "Give him some of this. Hell! Give it all to him."

The rain continued falling in waves as Eddie exited the wheelhouse. At least the boat was no longer rocking nor waves crashing the deck. Chief hadn't moved from the bunk where Eddie had left him.

"You okay?" Eddie asked.

Chief's eyes were half closed, and he was chanting in some language Eddie didn't understand. After loosening the tourniquet and checking the bandage to make sure the bleeding had stopped, he opened the flask and held it to Chief's lips. After the initial sip, Chief quickly slurped the rest of it down.

"Thank you," he said in a whispered voice.

"There'll be an ambulance waiting when we reach the marina. Jack says it isn't far to a hospital. You'll be okay."

The ambulance was waiting as they motored into the little harbor, docking with a precise thud. EMTs hurried aboard, removing Chief on a stretcher and taking him to the awaiting ambulance.

"I'm going with him," Jack said.

Dressed in a rain slicker, Odette grabbed Eddie's wrist.

"What happened?" she asked.

"Chief took a tumble and broke his arm."

They watched as the ambulance raced away, its siren blaring.

"Come inside," Odette said. "Let's get you warmed up and something to eat.

The building was dark. Odette had a flashlight and led the way. When they reached the restaurant, candles lighted the gloom.

"Where is everybody?" Eddie asked.

"The squall knocked out the power, and the workmen all went home early. Lucky for us there are plenty of storm candles."

"I've got to get out of this wetsuit," Eddie said.

Odette handed him the flashlight. "Be careful going up the stairs. Good thing we have gas because I have a pot of gumbo simmering on the stove."

Feeling safe and warm for the first time in many hours, Eddie returned dressed in chinos and monsoon sweater, the aroma of spicy gumbo easily leading him to the kitchen.

"Grab a chair at the table. I'll get you a bowl," Odette said.

Spotting him from her bed beside the stove, Mudbug came running. Eddie picked her up and put her in his lap.

"Did you miss me, girl?" he said.

Mudbug's wagging tail told him she had. Odette was smiling when she placed a steaming bowl of gumbo and dish of rice on the table.

"She likes you," she said.

"What's not to like?"

Eddie's long hair was still damp, and Odette began drying it with a bar rag.

"You'll catch your death running around in this weather with wet hair," she said. "Did you find what you were looking for out there?"

"You mean your Spanish treasure ship?"

"What else would I be talking about?" she said.

"All we found was a jumble of old wrecked cars and boats, though I now know where to go fishing."

"Artificial reefs," Odette said. "They're all over the Gulf. Did Chief and Jack tell you what they were looking for?"

"No, but it wasn't what we found. I didn't have a chance to talk to Jack about it though I could tell Chief wasn't a happy camper."

"Will he be okay?"

"I think so. He was in lots of pain, so I gave him some of Jack's rum. He'll have more than just an aching arm when he wakes up tomorrow."

When Odette finished cleaning the kitchen,

she sat down with Eddie. Eddie had found a bottle of scotch in the bar and was having a drink. The storm had stalled over the island, rain pelting the window panes. It didn't seem to matter as the scotch, along with the flickering candles, had begun lulling Eddie into a relaxing stupor.

"You okay?" Odette said, shaking his shoulder.

"Sorry," Eddie said. "I didn't get much sleep last night. This scotch and your wonderful gumbo have me more relaxed than I'd care to admit."

"Why don't you just go upstairs and get some sleep? Everyone's gone home, and there's nothing left to do here."

"Stay with me tonight," Eddie said. "The weather's too wild out there to risk sleeping in the tent."

"You're my employer. Good employees don't sleep with their bosses."

"I know. I've been fighting the urge to ask you since you met us at the dock," Eddie said.

"We just met last night. Though I may have worked in a strip joint, I've never been one to sleep around."

"There's a spare bedroom in my apartment. At least stay there for the night. I wouldn't get a wink of sleep if I knew you and Mudbug were out in the storm."

Odette grinned. "Sure you won't come sneaking into my room during the night?"

"There's a lock on the door," he said. "You'd have to want to let me in."

"What are we going to do, Eddie? You know I'm attracted to you. I want this job as restaurant manager more than I've wanted anything since I can remember. Please don't spoil it for me."

"I won't," he said. "I promise. Chief and Jack didn't find what they were looking for. I found something quite interesting."

"Spanish doubloon?"

"Wait here, and I'll show you," he said.

Eddie retraced his steps up the dark stairway to his apartment, returning with the pouch from his wetsuit. Opening it, he pulled out an ornate bottle of rum and set it on the table. Though the bottle was burnished by sand and the motion of currents, the seal was intact and still filled with dark rum, the same as the day it had been bottled.

"Where did you find this?" she asked.

"Among the wrecked cars in the man-made reef. I looked for more. This was the only one I found. It's what you really came to the island for, isn't it?"

"Yes," she said.

"Chief said Jack was drunk and making a fool of himself when he pulled him out of the bar."

"Jack was drunk. We were sitting together at the bar. He was trying to come on to me and hoping like hell I would respond."

"Where was Chief?"

"Sitting alone, watching the dancers on stage. Jack was buying me drinks, and I was only half-listening. Until. . ."

"Until what?"

"He started talking about sunken treasure. I was laughing at him, telling him I'd heard the story before. He staggered out to his truck and returned with a bottle of rum just like the one you found today and gave it to me."

"Did he say where he got it?"

"No, but he said it was worth its weight in gold, and there were lots more bottles on the island just like it. When Chief checked on him and realized how wasted he was, he carted him out of there."

"My friend Bertram says it's the best rum he's ever tasted."

"I took pictures of the bottle with my cell phone and researched it the next day at the Tulane library. It is from a distillery in the Dominican

Republic and was bottled during Prohibition. I sold it to a pawn dealer for five-hundred bucks, and he told me an unopened bottle would be worth at least three-thousand dollars."

"You drank the rum?" Eddie asked.

"It was only half full when Jack gave it to me. You had some of it last night."

"No wonder it tasted so good. Did you figure out how it got here on the island?"

"This island was once a haven for rumrunners and a major entry point for illegal booze coming into Louisiana. I'm betting somewhere out there, a sunken rumrunner, still loaded with crates of Dominican rum, is waiting for us to salvage it."

Chapter 21

Madeline and I watched in surprise as Adela hugged the large raven to her breast, kissing its beak and ruffling the feathers of its head with her chin. Calpurnia reveled in the attention. If birds could smile, she would have been smiling.

"You two know each other?" Madeline said.

Adela's face glowed with a satisfied smile. "Although I haven't the foggiest idea how it's possible, I feel as if we do. I've also enjoyed meeting you and visiting your shop and beautiful courtyard, though I'm not sure why Wyatt brought me here."

Calpurnia climbed back onto Adela's shoulder when she finally stopped caressing her. The bird continued rubbing her head against Adela's neck and calling her Aisling.

Madeline took the tea tray and pointed to the door of the building where she lived.

"Wyatt is a man who rarely does anything without a purpose. He brought you here because we have important things to discuss. It is getting chilly out on the patio. Please come with me to the house."

Calpurnia hopped on Adela's hand when she placed it near her shoulder. When she lifted her hand, Calpurnia flew into the air and began circling her head.

"Aisling," she said. "Aisling."

Madeline took our cups, and we followed her into the living area. She led us into a room with a dinner table that overlooked the courtyard through a large window.

"Sit," she said. "Now, I think Wyatt has something to tell me. Am I correct?"

"Something important I think you can help us with," I said.

"Then speak. Perhaps we can make some sense of how my majestic raven seems to know this beautiful young woman."

Madeline sipped her tea as I recounted last night's visit to the thirteenth floor of Hotel Montalba and our meeting with the demon. Even though Adela kept making faces, Madeline seemed taken by the story. When I'd finished, I waited for her to comment. Adela spoke before she had a chance.

"It was just a dream," Adela said. "None of Wyatt's story ever really happened. It's so preposterous I don't understand why anyone who hears it can't see through it."

Turning to Madeline, I said, "It does sound preposterous, even to me. Doesn't matter because it was as real to me as this teacup I'm holding in my hand."

"Lucid dreams often seem real," Madeline said.

"When I told the story to Taj and Mama, Taj told me I'd described the room and the demon just as he had seen it. If it were a lucid dream then how was I able to describe the exact room that Taj stayed in his first night in New Orleans? He wasn't dreaming and has a cut foot and bloody voodoo doll to prove it."

"I didn't say what you saw never happened. Perhaps you experienced the vision in a dream because of your special powers."

"What powers?" Adela asked.

"Wyatt is a Traveler," she said.

Madeline's declaration caught Adela's attention. "What's a Traveler?"

"A person who has lived many lives in many ages, and can physically traverse time. What Wyatt saw was an excerpt from your own thoughts. I cannot explain how but perhaps you somehow entered his dream. What Wyatt saw was quite possibly something you had experienced."

Adela gazed at me while sipping her tea as if she were seeing me for the first time.

"Impossible," she said. "Nothing like that has ever happened to me."

"That's not the entire story," I said. "Mama Mulate and Taj visited St. Louis Cemetery No. 1 last night on a hunch."

"A hunch?" Madeline said.

"The voodoo deity Baron Samedi had appeared to Taj earlier as a cemetery keeper at St. Louis Cemetery No. 1. When he told the story to Mama, she was suspicious because she knew of no such keeper at the cemetery. Taj's description of the man got her thinking something other than coincidence was involved."

"So they went to see?"

"Baron Samedi is the keeper of souls and cemeteries. When they got to St. Louis Cemetery No. 1, Mama summoned him, and he appeared. When she asked him about Taj's meeting with the demon, Baron Samedi told her the answer lies in a French Quarter Garden. She quizzed him further though all he would tell her was to ask the Irish witch named Aisling. Calpurnia called her Aisling. I think Adela is Aisling, the Irish witch."

Adela flashed a frown. "I've been called worse."

"There's nothing wrong with being a witch, my dear," Madeline said. "I am a witch myself, as was my mother and my grandmother. I assure you there is no shame in being a witch.”

"If I were a witch, don't you think I'd know it?" Adela said.

"Maybe you do know it and are hiding your abilities from us. If what Wyatt says is true, you can levitate and fly. No mere human can do either."

"Neither can I," Adela said. "Wyatt was dreaming. I have no control over what he dreams. I'm not a witch, and I have no special powers."

"That's not what you told me," I said. "I wasn't asleep when you said you had special powers and had known it since you were a little girl. I was wide awake when you levitated off the floor and floated across the room."

"I lied to you. The pot you smoked did have a hallucinogenic drug mixed with it," Adela said. "You were drugged. I'm sorry, but you're only describing what you think you saw and not what really happened."

Madeline refilled my teacup. "You smoked marijuana?" she said.

"I confess I did," I said. "Doesn't matter because my thinking was clear."

Adela was smiling and shaking her head. "I'd like to be a fly on the wall when you told your story to a judge. I'm pretty sure it wouldn't hold up in a court of law no matter how many stacks of Bibles you swore on."

She was right. For a moment, I began to doubt what I was certain I had seen. It didn't matter because Madeline didn't give me a chance to defend myself.

"Maybe Adela just does not know she is a witch," Madeline said.

"There's something else I haven't told you. Adela has a voodoo veve on her chest," I said. "An identical veve to one on Taj's chest. Though they had never met, Adela knew about Taj's veve."

Madeline glanced at me, and then back at

Adela. "Is that true?"

Adela nodded. "Yes."

"How does a girl from Michigan get a voodoo veve on her chest?"

"I have no recollection of where it came from," Adela said. "I've had it as long as I can remember."

"Is it a tattoo?" Madeline asked.

"See for yourself," Adela said, pulling up her sweatshirt.

Like a doctor examining a wound, Madeline drew closer for a better look.

After a moment, she said, "This is no tattoo nor does it look like a birthmark. No two veves are ever exactly alike. How is it possible for two people to have identical veves on their chests? More importantly, how did you know about Taj's veve?"

"Not by coincidence," I said.

"That's not so," Adela said. "Taj's shirt was open to his waist when I met him. I couldn't help but see the marking."

"All I know is Adela and Taj are inextricably connected. In my mind, the connection has something to do with the 13th floor of the Hotel Montalba."

"What else?" Madeline asked.

"Mama confirms deities rarely appear to humans in their real form."

"What do you mean by that?" Adela asked.

"They usually speak to humans through surrogates whose bodies they've possessed. The fact the actual Baron Samedi appeared to both Taj and Mama tells me whatever force of nature brought Taj to New Orleans is of prime importance to the Vodoun hierarchy."

"Like I've said before, I know nothing about voodoo. The only voodoo I ever heard about before coming to New Orleans was in some sleazy exploitation movie," Adela said.

"And your parents are Christians?" Madeline

asked.

"Of course they are."

"And you?"

Adela's face reddened. "Except for weddings or funerals, I haven't been inside a church since I was a teenager. That doesn't make me a witch."

"Nor does being religious preclude you from being a witch," Madeline said. "I was a Catholic nun. I still believe the dogma though I assure you I am truly a witch."

"Okay, say I am a witch. What are my motives for keeping that interesting bit of information secret?"

"If I knew, I would have the answer to your mystery. Calpurnia apparently knows you. She either knows you from the Quarter or perhaps another life."

"This is my first trip to Louisiana," Adela said. "You're raven is beautiful and intelligent. It doesn't matter because she mistook me for someone else."

"I do not think so," Madeline said.

"Maybe she knew Adela from the French Quarter courtyard Baron Samedi spoke of," I said.

"You are both insane," Adela said. "I'm from Michigan. My name is Adela Kowalski. I'm Polish, not Irish."

"You are here for a reason," Madeline said. "The veve on your chest is no coincidence. It is a voodoo veve. If Mama Mulate says she spoke last night with a voodoo deity, then I believe her. If you are a witch, why not just admit it. It makes no difference to Wyatt or me. We are only trying to help you."

"I know nothing about the French Quarter," Adela said. "If I'd lived here before, surely there would be things I'd remember."

"There's something else," I said. "I haven't mentioned it because it was very upsetting."

Madeline glanced at Adela. "What could

possibly upset Adela more than the things we've already discussed?"

"Trust me," I said.

"You tell me now, or I'm going to have to embarrass myself in front of Madeline by yanking your hair out."

"I don't think you'll like what I have to say," I said.

"I'll take my chances. Tell me."

"When the demon blocked our departure from the bathroom, he was dragging the head of the woman in the bathtub by its long red hair. The head was lifeless its blue eyes rolled up in a death stare. It was your head. You were the murdered woman in the bathtub."

Madeline's hand went to her mouth. "Are you sure of that?"

"As sure as I can possibly be."

My pronouncement failed to affect Adela. She was grinning as if I'd just told a joke.

"This is getting absolutely insane," she said. "I'm obviously not dead. How could it have been me?"

"According to the bellman who talked with Taj, the murder in the hotel happened centuries before you were even born. Though it couldn't have been you, I'm sure it was your doppelganger."

"Or someone you are incarnate of," Madeline said.

"What on earth would prompt me to return to the place where I was murdered?" Adela asked.

"Revenge," I said.

"I think you are both jumping to absolutely absurd conclusions," Adela said. "Any sane person would think you are both crazy."

"That doesn't explain how Calpurnia knows you, and you her?" I said.

"She's just a bird," Adela said.

"A bird that called you Aisling, the very same

name the demon used when confronting us. The same name Baron Samedi used. You can't just explain that away."

"I truly have no idea," Adela said.

"You were drawn to the city for a reason, or you would never have met Mr. Davis or learned you both have identical veves on your chests," Madeline said. "I have a notion you lived in the French Quarter during another lifetime, as did Mr. Davis."

"Yes," I said. "Before we came here, Adela and I did some exploring of the French Quarter. She seemed familiar with Royal Street and even told me as much. Her curiosity took us for a long walk up the street. When we reached the 1100th block of Royal, she grew faint and almost passed out. I thought I was going to have to call an ambulance."

"The Lalaurie Mansion," Madeline said. "It is located in the 1100th block of Rue Royal."

"Of course," I said. "I should have put two and two together."

"What is the significance of the Lalaurie Mansion?" Adela asked.

"It was a place of pure evil," Madeline said. "A house of unspeakable horrors."

Chapter 22

Calpurnia was waiting for us when we returned to the courtyard. Landing on Adela's shoulder, she continued acting as if she'd known her forever. Adela was all smiles when Madeline hugged her.

"I hope you find the answers you seek. If only Calpurnia could tell us. Alas, she can't, and I am sorry I couldn't help you myself."

"Yes you did," I said. "You've pointed us in the right direction."

Adela's mood darkened again as we exited to the French Quarter sidewalk. The sky had turned an angry shade of gray, though at least it had stopped raining.

"Now, where are you taking me?" Adela asked.

"You said you wanted a tour of the French Quarter. I'm giving you one."

"I seriously doubt any tourists have visited Madeline's courtyard."

"Bet you're right about that," I said. "Where we're going now is a neighborhood bar, on the edge of the French Quarter."

"You thirsty?"

"There's someone there who can tell us about the Lalaurie Mansion."

"If it's a tourist attraction, can't you just research it on the Web?"

"My friends at the bar will know things about the mansion which aren't common knowledge. Madam Toulouse used to work at the Notarial Archives."

"What's that?"

"A repository of knowledge. The city's founding fathers kept precise records of everything from marriages, property sales, building permits, the sale of slaves, to you name it. There isn't much about New Orleans Madam Toulouse doesn't know. And if she doesn't, her significant other Armand does."

"Armand?"

"An art and rare book dealer, especially as they pertain to New Orleans. The rich, famous, and powerful, value his expertise. No two people know more about this old town than Armand and Madam Toulouse."

"How much will you have to pay them?" Adela asked.

"They're friends."

"Must be, if they're as knowledgeable as you say and you expect them to help us for nothing."

"I'm taking them something they'll value more than money. We have to make a stop at a liquor store."

The little liquor store I was familiar with wasn't far away, and the owner knew me from when I was a drunk. Adela browsed the racks of wine as I found what I was looking for.

"A bottle of scotch?" Adela said. "Sounds kind of chintzy to me."

"This isn't just any scotch," I said. "It's Armand's favorite, rare and expensive. It'll get us the answers we want."

"If you say so," she said. "How do you know they'll be at the bar?"

"Because it's their office. Where their clients go to find them."

Adela glanced up at the cloudy sky. "Must be quite a bar."

"Just the opposite," I said. "It doesn't even have a sign in front."

"Then how does anyone know to go there?" Adela asked.

"People who matter all know where Allemands is located."

There are many great bars in New Orleans, most of which tourists never hear about. Allemands is a hole-in-the-wall bar situated on the edge of the French Quarter. Adela gave me an as if look when we reached the door.

"You sure this place is safe?" she asked.

"Safest place in town," I said, opening the door for her.

The bartender recognized me, saluting as we entered. The place reeked of stale beer and cigarette smoke. The patrons sitting at the bar didn't bother turning around. The place was dim, pool balls sounding as someone was breaking a rack. The couple we were looking for had a table of their own.

"Well, look here," Armand said.

"Brought you a present," I said, handing him the sack.

Armand beamed as he tore it open. He was from a different era, a quintessential beatnik if such a person still existed. His black hair had thinned even further since the last time I'd seen him. His cookie-duster mustache was also black, as were all his clothes. Even in December, he wore no socks with his sandals. His companion blew me a kiss.

Madam Toulouse's red leather miniskirt showed off her long legs. Her bouffant hair pointed toward the ceiling. As usual, she was sucking a sugary drink through a long red straw. Armand was grinning as he admired the bottle of scotch.

"Eighteen-year-old single malt Laphroaig," he said. "I ain't drank this good since the last time you dropped by for a visit."

"Adela, this is Madam Toulouse Joubert and Armand."

Armand had stepped out of the booth and motioned for us to slide in beside them.

"Sit on this side of me, baby," Madam Toulouse said to Adela. "I want to visit with both you and with Wyatt."

With Madam Toulouse sandwiched between us, we waited while Armand walked over to the bar to speak with the bartender.

"I didn't forget you," I said, handing Madam Toulouse a package.

"Oh my God!" she said when she saw the piece of jewelry I'd brought her. "Is this what I think it is?"

"A diamond encrusted fleur de lis necklace worn by my mom when Dad was King of Rex."

"I can't take it," Madam Toulouse said. "This piece of jewelry is priceless and needs to be in a museum."

"Leave it to the New Orleans Museum of Art when you die," I said. "Enjoy it until then. It's been in my dresser drawer far too long, and there's not a person on earth who will appreciate it as much as you."

Madam Toulouse was beaming when Armand returned to the booth.

"Armand, you're not going to believe what Wyatt gave me."

The little man in black leaned across the table and took a long look at the necklace.

"I keep forgetting your old man was once King of Rex," he said. "You know how much this piece is worth?"

"I don't want to know," I said. "I would never sell any of Mom's jewelry. I'm just so happy one of my very best friends in the world can enjoy and appreciate it."

The bartender, a man named Jake, arrived with a pitcher of lemonade for me, a bottle of champagne and three glasses. Despite the weather, Jake's shirt was sleeveless, probably to show off the multiple tattoos decorating his brawny shoulders. After placing the champagne and lemonade on the table, he removed the cigarette resting on his ear and lit it.

"We're celebrating and may need more than one bottle, my man," Armand said.

"You got it," Jake said. "Just give me the high sign."

Before leaving the table, Jake made a production of opening the champagne and then filling the glasses. Armand lifted his glass in a toast.

"Good friends and drink," he said.

After a couple of glasses of champagne, Adela's mood began to lighten. She was laughing and kibitzing with Madam Toulouse as more customers entered Allemands.

"Where are you from?" Madam Toulouse asked. "Your accent isn't one I recognize."

"Michigan. My ex-boyfriend and I decided to visit over semester break."

"And where is he?" Madam Toulouse asked.

"He ditched me," Adela said.

Madam Toulouse touched her hand. "Dear, I'm so sorry."

"It's okay. I wasn't in town for even a single day before strange things began happening."

"Such as?"

"I have a mark on my chest. It's been there for as long as I can remember. My boyfriend and I were taking a tour of St. Louis Cemetery No. 1. The only other person on the tour, though I didn't know it at the time, was a pro basketball player."

"Who was that?" Armand asked.

"Are you a basketball fan?" Adela asked.

"You kidding me?" he said. "Only bigger fan in town is Madam Toulouse."

"We've had season tickets for ten years now," Madam Toulouse said. "Tell us who it was?"

"Taj Davis. Heard of him?"

"No way! Every fan in town is wondering why the team traded Zee Ped for him. He's good but he ain't Zee Ped good."

"We think we know the reason," I said.

"Then tell us," Armand said.

They both looked amazed when I said, "Voodoo."

"You're making this up," Madam Toulouse said.

"Taj's shirt was open to his waist when I met him. Probably to show off his chiseled pecs and the gold chains he wears around his neck," Adela said. "I couldn't help but see he had a mark on his chest. It was just like the one on my chest."

"What kind of mark are you talking about?" Madam Toulouse asked.

Adela glanced around the dark bar to see if anyone was looking and then raised her sweatshirt to show Armand and Madam Toulouse the mark between her breasts."

Armand leaned closer for a better look. "Damn!" he said. "That's a voodoo veve. Where the hell did you get it?"

"Born with it," Adela said.

"Impossible," Madam Toulouse said, touching the symbol.

"Is it a tattoo?" Armand asked.

Madam Toulouse shook her head. "More like a birthmark."

"It's too damned detailed to be a birthmark," Armand said. "Surely, someone put it there."

"The mark on Taj's chest is larger, though identical to mine. We decided it was too much of a coincidence for us to have met in the way we did without something very powerful having caused it."

"Something like voodoo," I said. "That's how Mama Mulate and I got involved."

"It's a voodoo veve," Armand said. "It's not very detailed, and I'm wondering if the person who drew it was an amateur and not a mambo or houngan."

"Are you saying it's not an authentic voodoo veve?" I said.

"It's a veve, all right. A Baron Samedi veve. Each deity has a specific symbol though all are slightly different depending on the person drawing it. This one doesn't have all the flourishes a mambo might have used."

"Would it still work?" I asked.

"Don't see why not," he said.

"Interesting," I said. "That puts a strange little twist to things."

"How did you and Taj hear about Mama and Wyatt?" Madam Toulouse asked.

"A man who Taj met at the cemetery told him about Mama Mulate," Adela said.

"And Taj Davis, the professional basketball player, was taking a tour of St. Louis Cemetery No. 1 when you met him? Why the hell was he doing that?" Armand asked.

"He was staying at Hotel Montalba when a demon accosted him. He ended up with a cut foot and a bloody voodoo doll in his hand when he ran out into the hall," I said.

"This story gets stranger by the minute," Madam Toulouse said.

"Taj thought so too. He booked a tour of the cemetery at a voodoo shop because he was trying to make sense of the demon and the voodoo doll," Adela said.

"I know this is hard to believe, but the man he met at the cemetery was apparently Baron Samedi," I said.

"Unlikely," Armand said. "Voodoo deities never appear to mortals except through possession."

"Mama and Taj visited the cemetery last night. Mama summoned Samedi, and he appeared. Mama is convinced it was the actual voodoo deity and not someone possessed by him."

Adela was grinning. "What are you smiling at?" Madam Toulouse asked.

"Even though I have this mark on my chest, I still can't believe it has anything to do with voodoo, and people around here actually believe in it," she said.

"It's real in the Big Easy," Armand said. "I promise you."

"How do you know? Have you ever attended a voodoo ceremony?" Adela asked.

"There ain't much me and the Madam here haven't done or seen here in New Orleans," Armand said. "It's what we do."

"In this town, knowledge is power and power is money. You don't have one without the other, and there's always a price to pay for both," Madam Toulouse said.

"And the price is knowledge," Armand said. "Powerful people in this town pay big bucks for it."

Flashing me a look of exasperation, Adela reached for her handbag. Seeing her reaction, Madam Toulouse realized Adela had misinterpreted their boasts.

"He didn't mean you and Wyatt," Madam Toulouse said.

"Wyatt is family," Armand said. "Can't put a price on that."

Madam Toulouse's shoulders were wider than many of the linebackers playing for the Saints. She was smiling when she wrapped her arms around us.

"You're family now. Tell us how we can help you."

Chapter 23

Cold air filled the room when customers entered. The rain had returned, wetting the floor before the door had closed. Armand signaled Jake to bring us another bottle of champagne.

"Lots has happened since Taj hired Mama and me to help solve the mystery of the bloody voodoo doll," I said. We met Taj and Adela at the Riverfront last night. After dinner, Mama and Taj went to a jazz club, and I took Adela back to her hotel. That's when things began getting crazy."

Jake interrupted my story when he arrived with a fresh bottle of champagne. Adela's smile had disappeared.

"We're waiting," Madam Toulouse said.

Adela squirmed, slugging her champagne. "Before Wyatt starts, let me say his story is ridiculous. He was dreaming. The only part of his fairy-tale that's real is when he drinks wine and smokes marijuana."

As if on cue, Armand produced a joint, lit it, took a puff and then passed it to Adela. The recognizable odor of marijuana began wafting through the smoky little bar.

"Nothing goes better with champagne than a good toke," Armand said.

"Amen to that," Madam Toulouse said.

A puff of pot lifted Adela's mood. When Madam Toulouse attempted to pass the joint to me, I waved it off.

"Can't hold your pot, Cowboy?" Armand asked.

"I had too much last night," I said. "And yes, I drank some wine. Adela confessed to having powers she has possessed since she was old enough to know about them."

"Powers?" Madam Toulouse said.

"Adela can move objects with her mind, cause them to levitate. She can levitate. I saw her do it."

The gaze of Madam Toulouse and Armand's eyes turned to Adela.

"That's bullshit!" Adela said. "Wyatt was drunk and stoned and trying to get me into bed. When he did, he passed out and had a dream induced by pot and wine."

"Adela can also fly," I said. "She flew us to the same room where Taj saw the demon his first night in the city. We saw the demon, and something else."

"Like what," Armand said.

"The headless body of the woman in the bathtub."

"Bullshit!" Adela said.

"The demon was dragging a woman's head by its long, red hair. Adela's head."

"Damn, Cowboy! What you had was more than pot and wine. Sounds like an acid trip to me."

"Exactly," Adela said. "Nothing he's telling you is real."

"The specter spoke to us," I said.

"What did it say?" Madam Toulouse asked.

It said, "I will have you, Aisling."

"Who the hell is Aisling?" Armand said.

"Adela is Aisling," I said.

"Whoa, Cowboy. You're confusing me."

"Then let me explain. Adela and I visited

Madeline Romanov before coming here. Her raven Calpurnia repeatedly called her Aisling. That's not all. Baron Samedi told Mama Mulate a red-haired witch named Aisling can lead us to the French Quarter courtyard where our answers to this mystery lie. Whether she knows it or not, Adela is Aisling."

"Wyatt was high on LSD," Adela said. "The only part of his story that holds water is the color of my hair. Madeline's raven called me Aisling, but the demon and the voodoo deity in the cemetery are nothing more than drunken fantasies."

"I've never known Mama Mulate to tell a lie," Madam Toulouse said.

"Neither have I," Armand said. "How do you explain her meeting with Baron Samedi?"

By now, Adela's arms were folded tightly around her chest. "My name is Adela and not Aisling. I'm Polish and not Irish. I have no magical powers, and I'm certainly not a witch."

"Before our visit to Madeline's, we walked down Royal Street," I said. "When we passed the Lalaurie Mansion, Adela almost fainted. People have past lives. I believe Adela is the Irish witch Aisling, and the courtyard we are looking for is at the Lalaurie Mansion."

"Madeline's raven called you Aisling?" Madam Toulouse asked.

"Though Madeline's bird is adorable, it didn't live here centuries ago, and neither did I," Adela said.

"You seem a bit too sure about that," Madam Toulouse said.

"You think I'm lying?" Adela said. "You people believe in voodoo, magic, and reincarnation and seem amazed I don't agree with you."

"Suspend your disbelief for a moment," I said. "You certainly can't explain where your voodoo veve came from, or why Taj has an identical one on his chest."

"What you're suggesting is crazy," Adela said.

"Is it? I don't think you're lying. I think your memories of a past life are just repressed."

A clap of thunder sounded outside the bar. The front door opened slightly, wind and rain blowing through the crack. Jake was shaking his head as he brought us yet another bottle of champagne.

"Tell us how we can help," Madam Toulouse said.

"Two things," I said. "The unsolved murder that occurred years ago at the Hotel Montalba, and details about the atrocities that happened at the Lalaurie Mansion."

"Both events are real," Armand said.

"The murder in Room 1313 actually occurred?"

"Yes," Madam Toulouse said. "The murder took place in 1834, the very same year the Lalaurie Mansion burned."

"You know about it?" I asked.

Madam Toulouse nodded. "No one knows more about the murder in Room 1313 than I do, though I haven't thought about it in years."

The large woman became introspective, sipping her champagne and then giving Armand a pensive look. Armand reacted immediately, relighting the joint and handing it to her.

"Š'il te plait ne pleure pas mon amour," he said.

"I'm okay," she said.

"The murder must have profoundly affected you," I said.

"More than I care to elaborate," she said.

"Is it too painful for you to continue?" I asked.

"The murder in the hotel has nothing to do with me, though it mirrors something that happened to my family."

Madam Toulouse seemed comforted when

both Adela and Armand took her hands.

"Sorry, Cowboy," Armand said. "Talk of this murder has upset Madam Toulouse. I've got to cut this short."

"No, Armand," Madam Toulouse said. "I've carried this with me far too long and now's as good a time as any to get it off of my chest."

"You sure?" he said.

"I'm sure."

Though I had no clue why a murder that had happened more than one-hundred-eighty years ago should affect Madam Toulouse so profoundly, I waited for her to tell the story. Armand asked me to trade places with him. With Madam Toulouse between them, he and Adela clutched her hands as she began telling us about the murder at the Hotel Montalba.

"I came across old newspaper clippings when I worked at the Archives. To say the details of the killing caught my attention would be an understatement. I became obsessed with it, absorbing every scintilla of information I could find about the case.

"A chambermaid found the body of the deceased when she arrived to clean the room. The distraught woman went screaming into the hallway. Police found the nude body of a headless woman in the bathtub, the water red with blood and cold to the touch. The woman's head was never found."

"Did they identify the victim?" I asked.

"It was long before the discovery of DNA. It was the body of a female, her identity never determined."

"Who occupied the room?" I asked.

"Someone using a false name, though it doesn't matter because the clerk recognized the man and identified him to the police."

"Who was it?" I asked.

"Dr. Leonard Louis Nicolas Lalaurie, Delphine Lalaurie's third husband," Madam Toulouse said.

"Was the desk clerk sure about that?" I asked.

"Most likely," Armand said. "Rich folks in those days were local celebrities."

"Why in hell wasn't he charged with the murder?" I asked.

"Because the Lalaurie Mansion burned that very night," Madam Toulouse said. "Dr. Lalaurie disappeared, along with Madam Lalaurie, after the fire."

"Quite a coincidence," I said. "Are the murder and the fire connected?"

"They have to be," Madam Toulouse said.

"Who started the fire at the Lalaurie Mansion?" I asked.

"Some say the cook, though no one knows for sure," Armand said.

"What's the story on Dr. Lalaurie?" I asked.

"Madam Lalaurie's third husband and much younger than she was," Madam Toulouse said. "They had a son out of wedlock and got married shortly after."

"Why was he attracted to an older woman?"

Armand laughed. "Hot sex and rampant sadism, maybe?"

"Dr. and Madam Lalaurie disappeared the night of the fire and never resurfaced here in New Orleans."

"Do you remember anything in the records about a girl from Ireland?" I asked.

"No, though it wouldn't surprise me. Madam Lalaurie was Irish," Madam Toulouse said.

"You have to be kidding," I said. "I didn't know that."

"Delphine's maiden name was Macarty, her grandfather born in Ireland. They had the name shortened from MacCarthy. It was common for rich families to have indentured servants from

Europe."

Armand chimed in. "Her family was connected, her uncle the governor of Spanish-American provinces in Louisiana and Florida. One of her cousins was the Mayor of New Orleans."

"Some say the reported abuse and torture never occurred," I said.

"It happened. Slaves rescued from the fire had been horribly abused, and some tortured," Madam Toulouse said. "Abuse and torture had long been rumored. When actual proof arose, a mob formed, demanding justice."

"The slaves all survived the fire?"

"Miraculously, though a few passed away shortly after that."

"Baron Samedi said the answers to our questions lie in a French Quarter garden. Though I've never been inside the Lalaurie Mansion, it doesn't look as though it has a courtyard."

"The present house isn't where the torture occurred," Armand said. "Madam Lalaurie acquired the original house from Edmond Soniat Dufossat. That house burned in the fire. It's likely little of the original structure survived."

"The appearance of the original house was similar to the Soniat House on Chartres. That house exists to this day, and it definitely has a courtyard," Madam Toulouse said.

"The so-called house of horror you see today didn't even exist when Madam Lalaurie owned it. The present Lalaurie Mansion wasn't built until several years after the fire," Armand said.

"What else suggests torture occurred at the original house?" I asked.

"The Lalaurie Mansion was large. The Lalauries hosted many lavish parties. Even so, the couple had more slaves than they needed to serve a house even as large as theirs. Some say many slaves spent time at the house. Graves were found in the courtyard, and bodies in the well on the property," Armand said.

"While all of the Lalaurie's slaves were abused, not all were tortured," Madam Toulouse said. "For at least half of the slaves, torture was their only purpose."

"Was torture common in 1834?" I asked.

"Abuse was common though torture was rare," Madam Toulouse said.

"Why was that?" I said.

"Code Noir," Armand said. "A comprehensive law governing the rights of slaves. Slave owners could chain and beat their slaves. It was illegal to mutilate or kill them."

"Slaves were valuable assets, and most owners tended to treat them well to protect their value. Intercourse was encouraged and families discouraged," Madam Toulouse said.

"What kept the slaves from rebelling if they had the Lalaurie's outnumbered twelve or more to one?" I said.

"Whips, chains, intimidation, and one mean-as-hell enforcer," Madam Toulouse said.

"They had an enforcer?" I said.

"The Lalauries owned a large black man straight from Africa who had been captured far away from the usual slave trade. He had no tribal ties to the other slaves and capitulated to Madam Lalaurie's whims because it curried him special treatment from her."

"How big was he?" I asked.

"Tall enough to play in the NBA," Armand said.

Suddenly interested, Adela asked, "What was his name?"

"Strange though it may seem, his name was Taj," Madam Toulouse said.

Chapter 24

Mama was feeling guilty after spending the day, looking at upscale condominiums with Taj. Enthralled by the tall, handsome woman, Taj didn't immediately notice her frown. It finally became too apparent to overlook.

"What's the matter?" he asked.

"I'm such a heel," she said. "I berated poor Wyatt this morning for being unprofessional. I've had so much fun helping you shop for a condo, and I've done nothing at all on your case. I'm the one who should be tongue-lashed."

"It's okay. I don't know what I'd have done without your help."

"It's not okay," she said. "You hired Wyatt and me for a specific reason. I've become enamored with you. I've shirked my duty."

"I'm not complaining," he said. "You aren't the only one who's become enamored."

"It's affecting my judgment," she said. "We can't let our feelings go any further."

"Too late for that," Taj said.

"Then I'm going to give your money back."

"Nonsense," he said. "Let's go to the hotel and talk about it. After we work things out, I'll take you to the most expensive restaurant in town. You're a woman who needs to be wined and dined."

"No, I'm not. I'm a simple person. Let's go to my house. I'll fix you the best meal you've ever eaten. It's been forever since I was home and my cats will be missing me."

"You have cats?" Taj said.

"You don't like cats?

"Didn't say that," he said. "Just that I've never been around them much."

"No dog or cat when you were growing up?"

"A turtle is all," Taj said.

Mama grinned. "You're not allergic are you?"

"Not that I know of."

"If you are, I have a potion that will fix it," she said.

"You sure?" he said.

"Positive. Let's catch a cab."

Taj saluted and followed the handsome woman to the curb. Mama lived in an old neighborhood near the river. It worried Taj when he saw the car on blocks in the front yard of the house across the street.

"We're not going to get mugged, are we?" he asked.

"Don't worry, Baby," she said. "I'll protect you."

Neat and freshly painted, Mama's house stood out as the nicest home on the block. Despite December's lower temperatures, her front porch pansies were still blooming. Ferns hanging from the rafters swayed in a chill breeze as she fumbled for her keys in the darkness.

"Be it ever so humble. . ." Mama said as she unlocked the door and held it open.

Within seconds, three cats, meowing as their claws scraped across the bare wood floor, came running around the corner. The tailless cat in the lead jumped straight into Mama's awaiting arms.

"Oh, my gorgeous babies! Did you miss your mama?"

Taj had never particularly liked cats. Seeing the reaction between Mama and her three pets, he decided not to mention it. Mama led the three felines into the little kitchen of her Creole cottage, opened a can of cat food, and fed the hungry beggars. Taj watched, his arms tightly folded across his chest.

"My three babies Bushy, Cliffy, and Ninja. You don't like cats, do you?" she said.

Taj was quick to react, a smile replacing his solemn expression and his arms dropping to his sides.

"I've never been around cats. I know I'm going to like yours."

"How do you know that?" she asked.

"Because I like everything about you."

"Good answer," she said. "If you didn't like my babies, I'd have to call a cab and send you back to your hotel room alone."

"Please don't do that," he said.

Taj felt the warmth exuding from the cozy little house, and the welcoming though faint odor of herbal incense in the air. He glanced around, taking it all in.

"I love your house," he said, changing the subject.

"Creole cottage," Mama said. "I've done my best to restore it to the way it looked when it was built more than a century ago. I'll admit I've added a few things a bit more modern."

One of Mama's additions was obvious. She'd converted an entire wall into a built-in bookcase. From the number of books in the bookcase, Taj could see she was an avid reader.

"Nice," he said.

"Do you read?" she asked.

"The sports page," he said.

"No problem. I like you anyway."

"And I'm thankful for that," he said.

"It's a little chilly in here," Mama said. After adding wood to the pot-bellied stove in the corner of the kitchen, she made a production of lighting it. "It'll be warm in a few minutes."

"I didn't notice a chill," he said. "Guess I'm still used to the weather in Cleveland."

"Then let me take your coat," she said. "Grab that chair, and I'll get dinner started."

Not realizing how tired he was, Taj collapsed in the comfortable recliner. Connected to the kitchen, the living area was part of Mama's open floor plan.

"Love this chair," he said. "Never seen one quite this big."

"I must have had you in mind when I purchased it," she said. "Relax, I'll be a while."

Taj needed no convincing. He'd dozed off, his feet extended in the recliner when Mama returned from her bedroom dressed in a sexy turquoise-colored caftan. The creaking of the old wood floor beneath Mama's feet aroused him from his nap.

"I flat passed out," he said

"Neither of us got much sleep last night."

"That's a fact," he said. "I'm hoping we don't get much tonight, either."

"Oh ho!" she said. "This isn't Cleveland, and we do things differently here. You may not like me anymore after a few days. I don't know about you, but I intend to proceed carefully into this relationship."

"New Orleans is starting to grow on me. I don't believe I'll have a problem with either you or this beautiful and mysterious city."

Mama opened a bottle of wine and put a glass on the table beside the chair.

"Have some wine and continue with your nap," she said. "It'll be an hour or so before dinner is ready. I want you rested for later on tonight. Just in case I don't toss your ass out first."

Taj grinned and took a drink of Mama's wine before raising the handle on the recliner to prop up his feet.

"Why would you do that?" he asked.

"I don't see a ring on your finger. That doesn't mean you aren't married. Are you?"

"Never had the pleasure," he said.

"Steady girlfriend?"

"Been a while since I had a steady girlfriend," he said. "I've been completely single for quite some time now."

"Do you meet lots of chippies on your road trips?"

"Maybe when I was younger," he said.

"Now, I mostly have a good steak, a bottle of wine and then turn in early. What about you? You're the best-looking woman in New Orleans. Surely you have men knocking down your door."

"I wish," she said.

"What about Wyatt?"

"We're business associates," she said. "We've somehow managed to keep it that way. Go back to your nap. I have work to do in the kitchen."

Taj closed his eyes, falling fast asleep. He awoke to a wonderful aroma he didn't recognize that was wafting through the room. All three of Mama's cats were asleep and curled up on his large chest.

"They like you," she said. "I've never seen them take to a stranger as they have to you."

"What smells so good?" he asked.

"Tournedos Marchand de Vin," she said. "My version of one of Antoine's favorites. Hope you like steak done Creole style."

"I didn't know they did Creole-style steak here," Taj said.

"Get used to it. When it comes to good food, there's no better place in the world than New Orleans. You're going to love it here."

"You don't need to twist my arm," he said. "And my little nap did the trick. I haven't felt this alert in years."

"Maybe because I added a little magic to your wine," she said.

"It's not going to get me in trouble with the NBA if I have to take a piss test, will it?"

"One-hundred-percent safe and totally

herbal," she said.

"What if I like the results?"

"Then don't play around on Mama Mulate," she said. "I'm the only one who knows the formula."

"Yes, ma'am," he said.

Mama served dinner on a table lighted only by candles in a silver candelabrum. Taj had never tasted such a combination, the steak served with Creole cornbread, baked Acadian cushaw, and broccoli pie. Afterward, he was almost in tears.

"I have never eaten a finer meal," he said. "Home cooked, or otherwise."

"Don't get used to it," Mama said. "I don't cook this way every night."

"You kidding? I'm lucky to have experienced it once in a lifetime. What now?"

"Let's turn on some music. I'll join you in the recliner."

Mama put a Trombone Shorty album on her outdated stereo and then sat on Taj's lap. Barely a moment passed before they began acting like horny teens in the backseat of an old beater. Mama was the first to open her eyes.

"You can't be comfortable in your street clothes. There's a robe in the bathroom that may fit you," she said. "Try it on for size."

"Just the robe?"

"You won't need anything else," Mama said

"Does this mean I'm staying the night?" he asked.

"I'm leaning in that direction," Mama said.

"Grab the robe, and we'll talk about it."

Though the robe was a bit too small, neither Taj nor Mama noticed as they returned to the recliner. Flickering light from the candles in the kitchen revealed the veve on Taj's chest when she brushed the robe open with the back of her hand.

"What's the matter?" Taj asked. "Did I do something wrong?"

"Not at all. I'm looking at the veve and once again starting to feel guilty."

"It's okay. All that business can wait until tomorrow."

"Maybe not," Mama said. "We haven't heard from Wyatt and Adela all day."

"Call them if it'll make you feel better," Taj said.

Mama Mulate extracted herself from Taj's lap and returned to the kitchen table. After checking her phone for missed calls, she dialed Wyatt's cell phone.

"Now I am worried," Mama said. "The call went straight to Wyatt's voicemail."

Taj joined her at the kitchen table. "I'll call Adela." After a moment, he said, "Straight to voicemail."

"I'm wondering what this means," Mama said.

"Maybe they went to the movie and turned off their phones."

"Wyatt doesn't go to movies."

"They're adults and have taken care of themselves for years. They're fine."

"I'm sure you're right," Mama said.

Mama poured coffee from the pot warming

on the stove. Opening Taj's robe again, she rubbed the veve on his chest.

"Why don't we go back to the chair?" he said.

"Not right now," she said. "There's something about your veve. I should have noticed it before now."

"What about it?"

"It's a Baron Samedi veve. While all veves are different depending on the person drawing it, this one is simpler."

"What does it mean?" Taj said.

"Don't know," Mama said. "Maybe the person who drew it wasn't a practitioner of Vodoun. Maybe it was just put there by a tattoo artist who had no appreciation of what the veve is supposed to mean."

"Let's worry about it tomorrow," Taj said. "Your comfortable chair is calling my name."

"You're right," Mama said. "The answers we seek will probably be forthcoming when we've had time to sleep on it."

"That might be the day after tomorrow," Taj said.

"I think you're boasting," Mama said. "I'm a college professor and believe in proof, not boasts."

"Then prepare yourself, lovely woman. There's nothing I relish more than a friendly challenge."

Mama and Taj barely had time for a kiss when a knock on the door interrupted their ardor.

Chapter 25

A dreary day had turned even bleaker as Odette and Eddie sat in the restaurant's kitchen drinking coffee. All the workers had gone home for the day. They were alone with only Mudbug for company. Odette glanced out the window.

"There's a cab pulling up out front."

"Must be Jack and Chief," Eddie said.

"It's parked by the walkway. No one's getting out," Odette said.

Eddie headed for the door. "I'd better go see what's up.

"Wait," Odette said. "Take an umbrella. They're in the rack by the front door."

Eddie grabbed two umbrellas on his way out. Jack opened the rear window a crack.

"I forgot my wallet. Can you pay for the cab?"

"No problem. Here's an umbrella. Odette has coffee waiting in the kitchen.

Jack and Chief huddled beneath the umbrella and hurried toward the covered walkway as Eddie paid the cab driver. The cab pulled away and started up the rise to the one-lane bridge as lightning streaked across the horizon. Odette was draping a large blanket around Chief's shoulders as Eddie reached the kitchen.

"Making it, Chief?" Eddie asked.

"Thanks to you. The nurses said I'd have bled to death if you hadn't put the tourniquet on me."

"Jack did his part. I wouldn't have thought the old tub could go so fast."

"He's a pretty good babysitter," Chief said.

Chief was savoring his coffee, though Jack hadn't touched his. Board-straight in the chair, his arms were crossed and a frown on his face.

"Did I say something wrong?" Eddie said.

Odette had just placed steaming bowls of gumbo in front of them. Chief started eating. Jack continued to sit and scowl.

"It's not you," Odette said. "It's me. I'm sorry, Jack. I know you don't want to cut anyone in on the treasure you're looking for. Eddie and I can help you recover it. Why don't we bury the hatchet?"

"You wouldn't know anything about the treasure if I hadn't gotten drunk and opened my big mouth," Jack said. "Chief and I have been working on it for years. It's not fair to have to split it when we're this far along."

"Seems to me without our help you have about a snowball's chance in hell of finding your treasure," Eddie said. "Even if I help, you can keep my share. I can't speak for Odette."

"You don't even know what it is we're looking for," Jack said.

Odette reached behind a cabinet and retrieved the bottle of rum Eddie had found during the dive.

"You mean your 1929 Dominican rum?" she said.

"Where did you get that?" Jack asked.

"On our dive," Eddie said. "My guess is there are lots more where that came from."

"Did you find the sunken boat?" Jack asked.

"Just a single bottle," Eddie said.

Odette uncapped the rum and poured some in each of their coffee cups.

"You crazy, woman?" Jack said. "You don't add priceless rum to coffee. It's too good for that."

"There's more where that came from," she said.

"You know where the sunken boat is?" Jack asked.

"Eddie says you have the NOAA charts for this part of the Gulf. I majored in restaurant management. My minor was oceanography. Show me the charts, and I'll tell you the most likely place to find the sunken rum boat."

"It just ain't fair," Jack said.

"If the cache is as big as you think it is, it's worth a small fortune. You can't swim, and Chief's arm is broken. Seems to me you need us more than we need you," Eddie said.

"You can keep fifty percent," Chief said. "I'll cut Odette in out of my share."

"That's bullshit, and you know it," Jack said.

"One hundred percent of zero is still zero," Eddie said.

"Pigs get fat, and hogs get slaughtered," Chief said.

Jack grabbed his cup and drank some of it. "Uncle," he said. "You and the girl help us recover the rum, and we do a four-way split."

"Girl?" Odette said. "I'm a woman, and my name is Odette. "Unless you start treating me as an equal, I'm not going to tell you where the treasure is."

"I'm sorry," Jack said.

"I'm sorry, what?" Odette said.

"I'm sorry, ma'am," Jack said.

"Call me by my name," Odette said.

"I'm sorry . . . Odette," Jack said.

Odette extended her hand. "Shake on it?"

Jack, Chief, Odette, and Eddie exchanged handshakes.

Chief had finished his gumbo and was licking his lips. "That's the best gumbo I've ever eaten, Odette. Jack needs to take a few lessons from you."

"You've never complained about my chow before," Jack said.

"And I'm not now," Chief said. "When it comes to cooking, you're as good as they come. Just try a bite of the gumbo."

Jack took a bite, pretended he was going to spit it out, and then began to grin. "The big Indian's right. This is the best gumbo I've ever eaten. Can I get the recipe from you?"

"You know Cajuns don't use recipes," Odette said. "There's a large pot simmering on the stove. Don't be shy. I'm used to cooking for thirty at a time."

The storm continued outside the restaurant as Jack and Chief worked on seconds, and then third bowls of gumbo. The Dominican rum was also getting low.

"The NOAA packet is at Chief's teepee," Jack said.

"Too nasty out there," Eddie said. "I'll put you up here for the night. We can have a look tomorrow."

"No can do," Jack said. "I've been away all day. I need to feed Brutus."

"You'll drown going up the hill," Eddie said.

"Not if you let us use the ATV," Jack said.

"Didn't know I had an all-terrain vehicle," Eddie said. "Where is it?"

"In the metal building at the end of the pier," Jack said.

"Unless it has a roof, you'll still drown," Eddie said.

"It's got four-wheel-drive, a ninety-horse motor, and a canvas top and sides. Seats four and there's no place on the island, no matter what the weather, it won't go,."

"Fine," Odette said. "Then we'll all go. We need to be in the water at first light, the moment the storm ends."

"Sounds to me as if Odette is the smartest one here," Chief said.

"I second that," Eddie said.

"I've got no problem with that," Jack said. "We've been looking for the sunken boat now for five years. If Odette can tell us where it is, I'm ready to kiss her ass."

Chief laughed. "You've been ready to do that since the night we met her in New Orleans."

"I meant no disrespect," Jack said.

"None taken," Odette said. "Let's clean up, get Brutus, and then have a look at those charts. With all this pressure on me, I just hope I'm able to perform."

When they left the restaurant, they were wearing storm slickers. Odette had tucked Mudbug beneath hers. Jack fumbled with the keys when they reached the metal building.

"Hurry up before we drown," Chief said.

"Hold your horses," Jack said. "It's dark, and I can barely see."

The metal door soon creaked open, the stale air inside gushing out. Jack fumbled for the lights. When they came on, Eddie was amazed at how big the building was. They not only saw the ATV, but also the black Range Rover that went with the restaurant.

"Hope this metal bucket has a lightning rod," Chief said.

Illuminated by fluorescent lighting, Eddie could see the stacks of wooden crates that filled the large metal building almost to the ceiling.

"What's in all these crates?" Eddie asked.

"Who the hell knows?" Jack said. "Most everything in here has been stored since the original owners shut this development down some seventy years ago. One thing for sure, everything in this building is yours. Mr. Castellano told me so."

"Is there a manifest anywhere that catalogs the contents of the boxes?" Eddie asked.

"None I've ever seen," Jack said.

"The boxes are marked with different symbols. Surely, there's a meaning," Eddie said.

"Could be," Jack said. "Right now, we better get moving. We can worry about these boxes at any time."

Jack started to get behind the wheel. Odette stopped him.

"I've always wanted to drive one of these things," she said.

Jack moved out of the way. "Be careful. It has more power than you think. Don't let it get away from you."

Odette patted Jack on the butt. "Don't worry. I'll get us to where we're going in one piece."

"Yes ma'am," he said, climbing into the front passenger seat.

Jack was holding Mudbug in his lap, Eddie, and Chief holding on for dear life in the backseat as Odette powered up the hill to the lighthouse. When she slid up to the front door, Jack handed Mudbug to her and then ran inside to get Brutus. Jack returned with the dog and two bottles of rum.

"Someone needs to direct me to Chief's teepee," Odette said.

"Might help if you'd turn on the headlights," Jack said.

"You could have told me this bucket of bolts has headlights," Odette said. "How do you turn them on?"

Jack reached across her and turned on the lights.

"Down the hill," Chief said. "I'll give you directions as we go."

With Chief's help, Odette followed the beach until he tapped her left shoulder.

"Left?" she said.

"Straight up the hill. Watch out for the trees. You'll go straight to it," Chief said.

They found Chief's teepee at the top of the hill, in a grove of old-growth oaks. Odette pulled up to the front flap, and they all piled out, following Chief into the teepee. Chief sat on an Indian rug and used flint to start a fire in the center of the teepee.

"I could have lent you a match," Eddie said.

"It's important to honor the old ways," Chief said. "Jack, can you feed my animals?"

"Sure," Jack said.

"You have animals?" Odette asked.

"You kidding?" Jack said. "Chief here's a rancher. He's got horses, cattle, cats, stray dogs. Why hell, you just name it, Chief's got them."

"I'll help you," Odette said. "I love animals."

The fire in the center of the teepee had warmed the large structure when Odette and Jack returned from feeding Chief's animals.

"You have a llama?" Odette asked.

"She keeps the coyotes away," Chief said.

"Is that a still in the back of the teepee?" Odette said.

"Are you a government agent?"

"No," she said.

"I can't always trust Jack to supply my alcoholic needs," Chief said.

"The Chief here makes some of the best moonshine in the parish," Jack said.

"I've never tasted moonshine," Odette said.

Jack glanced at the top of the teepee where the smoke from the fire was exiting, and said, "Good Lord, have mercy!"

Chief hefted a ceramic jug over his shoulder, took a swig, and then handed it to Odette.

"Watch it, Missy. It kicks like a mule, and it'll knock you on your ass quicker than you can say scat," Chief said.

"Whoa!" Odette said after drinking a healthy slug. "What's the alcohol content of this shine?"

"You don't even want to know," Jack said. "Take a gander at these charts before you drink anymore. If you don't, you'll be out for about eight hours."

Odette passed the jug to Eddie, and he took a healthy swig. Jack grinned as he watched Eddie's eyes cross.

"Damn!" Eddie said. "That burned all the way down. This shit's potent."

"Moderate," Chief said. "You just don't know how potent. Sometimes Jack and I use it, instead of peyote, in my sweat lodge."

"You have a sweat lodge?" Odette said.

"Yes ma'am, I do," Chief said.

"I want to try it," she said.

"It's for men only," Chief said.

"Are we partners or not?" Odette said.

"Hell, Chief," Jack said. "We ain't never seen any spirits yet, and I'm pretty sure your sweat lodge don't work. What will it hurt?"

Chief glanced at the escaping smoke as nearby thunder shook the teepee. "What the hell," he said. "While you're studying the charts, I'll go crank up the sweat lodge. Maybe it's time for divine intervention."

Chapter 26

Morning found Odette, Eddie, and Jack in Chief's sweat lodge. Despite the rain that continued to fall, temperatures inside the small teepee had reached triple digits. Stoked by Chief's moonshine, singing, and one-handed drumming of his tom-tom, they hadn't really noticed.

Before the ceremony had begun, they'd stripped off their clothes. Dressed only in breechcloths and ceremonial paint, they'd taken to the native ritual with enthusiasm. A bucket of cold water in Eddie's face awoke him from his stupor. Cold water also rudely awakened Odette and Jack.

"Everyone up," Chief said. "The ceremony ends with a ritual bath at Dripping Springs."

They followed Chief down a path through thick trees that led to a clear pool created by the damming of a small creek. Impermeable clay formed the bottom of the pool. Water from the previous night's rain poured over the little dam. Jack stuck his toe in the water.

"I'll pass," he said. "Too damn cold for this old sailor."

"It won't kill you," Chief said.

Jack reluctantly followed Odette and Eddie into the water. Chief threw them sponges.

"Wash off the paint and reflect on your moments in the sweat lodge."

Eddie was rubbing his temples. "Remind me to never drink moonshine again. That stuff will kill you."

"Tell me about it," Odette said. "This cold dip is starting to revive me."

"Dripping Springs mineral water," Jack said. "There was a spa on the island in the thirties. People paid big bucks to bathe here."

Eddie dipped his head beneath the water then used his hands to squeeze the liquid out of his long hair.

"I'm starting to feel a little better," he said.

Chief tossed them towels when they exited the pool, and they wrapped themselves in them on their walk back to the teepee. After dressing, they returned to the restaurant in the ATV.

"You didn't tell us much last night after looking at the charts," Jack said.

"Tell you the truth, I don't remember much of anything about last night," Odette said. "Let's go to the kitchen. I'll cook breakfast, and then study the charts."

"I have a better idea," Jack said. "I'll cook breakfast. From the look of the clouds, I'd say this little patch of clear weather is going to be short-lived."

Except for Jack, they were soon sitting around the old plank table, drinking coffee, and eating bacon and eggs, as Odette studied the charts. The workers had already arrived, and Jack was busy cooking and feeding them. When the last worker had eaten, he joined the others at the table.

"Any idea where the boat went down?" Odette asked.

Jack pointed to a spot on one of the charts. "The barrier islands form a natural levee around Oyster Island. Problem is, some of the islands don't protrude out of the water much or else lie a few feet below the surface. They pose a danger to large boats riding low in the water."

"Even with bottom finders?" Odette asked.

"The locals didn't need bottom finders. The Coast Guard boats were too big to get into the harbor except by way of the main channel. If a rumrunner could make it through an opening, they could usually escape their pursuers. The night the Coast Guard blew the Island Star out of the water, that wasn't the case."

"Are you sure this is where the boat went down?" Odette asked.

"It's where the Coast Guard reported the sinking."

"Too bad they didn't make it to the lee side of the barriers."

"Not really," Jack said. "If they had, they'd have already salvaged the rum. As it is, there's still a chance for us to find the sunken boat."

"What do you think?" Eddie asked.

"The prevailing current is from east to west. The energy of the current will carry its load until the energy dissipates. When it does, it drops its load," Odette said.

"Such as?" Eddie said.

"At the mouth of a river, for example," Odette said.

"I have the geological and engineering study for Oyster Island which Mr. Castellano had commissioned. Will it help?"

"Don't know," Odette said. "Get it and let's have a look."

When Eddie returned with the report, Odette opened it and began pouring through the maps.

"Bingo!" she finally said.

Jack, Chief, and Eddie were quickly all ears. "What do you see?" Jack asked.

"There's a structural ridge underlying the

island. It's the reason for the rolling hills and artesian spring. The subsurface ridge runs transverse to the coastline and extends into the Gulf." Odette pointed to a spit of land protruding into the Gulf. "The current makes an abrupt turn right here. The water's one-hundred feet deep. At least twenty feet deeper than the average water depth this far from shore."

"And your conclusion? Eddie said.

"Unless I miss my guess, we'll find the wreck in the deep water just off this point."

It wasn't long before the Argo was motoring out of the harbor on its way to the spit of land labeled Devil's Arch on the navigation charts. It crossed Eddie's mind there might be some reason for the scary name. He let the thought pass as he stood in the wheelhouse beside Jack.

"You think Odette knows what she's talking about," Eddie asked.

"I got no idea," Jack said. "She sounded knowledgeable. Then again, bullshitters always do."

"She has no reason to bullshit us," Eddie said. "She gains nothing unless we find the sunken boat."

"That's why I'm driving this crate instead of bitching," Jack said. "Have you ever made a hundred-foot dive?"

"Can't say I have," Eddie said.

"What about the girl?"

"I haven't talked to her about it," Eddie said.

"There's a dangerous rip current down there."

"How do you know?" Eddie asked.

"Divers steer clear of Devil's Arch. Get sucked up in one of those currents, and your body won't surface until you're halfway to Texas."

"I'll keep it in mind," Eddie said. "I'm going on deck and help Chief and Odette."

With his broken arm in a sling, Chief was little

help to Odette as she readied the tanks for the dive. Eddie pulled her aside.

"Have you ever made a dive this deep before?" he asked.

"About a thousand times," she said. "My dad took me diving when I was ten. I've dived on every man-made reef in the Gulf."

"Jack says there's a rip current where we're going."

"He's half right," Odette said. "Rip currents are found at the surface. What we'll be dealing with is a deep-water current. Just as dangerous, if you get caught in it, and harder to escape."

"How do you know where it's at?" Eddie asked.

"Sea creatures avoid it like the plague. Hopefully, we'll see the turbulence."

"And if we don't?"

"Deep currents are narrow, usually no more than twenty meters wide. It's hard but not impossible to escape a current. Sometimes, you have to go with the flow and conserve your strength until there's a change in energy."

"That doesn't sound encouraging," Eddie said.

"We'll be attached by a long rope. If one of us gets sucked in by the current, maybe the other's weight will be enough to leverage the other out of it," Odette said.

"And if it isn't?" Eddie asked.

Odette tapped the knife belted at her side. "Cut yourself loose. No use both of us drowning."

"Sounds grim," Eddie said.

"The boat won't be in the current, though it could be close to it," Odette said. "We just need to be cautious."

When Odette glanced up at the wheelhouse and gave Jack thumbs up, he cut the engine and dropped anchor. She and Eddie had donned their wetsuits and scuba gear.

"You okay?" she asked.

"A little scared. What about you?"

"I'd be lying if I said I wasn't," she said. "Stay behind me the length of the rope. If we're careful, the current will be no problem."

Odette dived over the side of the boat. Eddie waited a few seconds and then followed her. Something was roiling the water. He became concerned when he found the visibility much less than during his first dive. He continued downward, following Odette's bubbles as they floated past him.

In addition to the limited visibility, there were no fish or sea creatures around. He remembered Odette's words, "they avoid currents like the plague." He tried not to think about it as he continued to descend deeper than he'd ever dived.

Eddie was near the bottom when he saw Odette swimming ahead. She must have spotted something because he was as far away from her as the rope would go.

Odette could see the broken hull of a boat in the murky water. From its size and shape, it could be the wreck of the rumrunner. Swimming forward, she ignored the tug on her rope. When she reached the boat, a sudden yank left no doubt Eddie had swum into a current.

As the current pulled Odette across the top of the sunken boat, she looked for something to grab. She was quickly approaching a broken piece of iron protruding from the railing and knew it was her only hope.

Odette clutched the bar, the current too strong, and her grip too tenuous to hold on to it for long. It gave her just enough time to jam her fins against the railing, creating slack in the rope. She began looping the rope around the misshapen piece of iron bar, continuing until Eddie's listless body floated toward her through the gloomy water.

Eddie had swallowed water, but his regulator

was still in his mouth. After detaching the rope and holding on to Eddie, Odette began following her bubbles to the surface. They were at least a hundred feet from the boat when their heads popped out of the water.

Chief spotted the two and signaled Jack to raise the anchor. Odette was doing her best to revive Eddie when the boat reached them, and Chief tossed them a line. They were soon on the deck of the Argo, Odette performing mouth-to-mouth as Jack pumped Eddie's chest and Chief watched.

Chief was searching for a pulse when Eddie began belching seawater. In a moment, his eyes popped open. Jack turned him over, lifting him by the waist until all the water had cleared from his lungs. After a coughing jag lasting five minutes, Chief put an oxygen mask on him, leaving it there until his ashen complexion became normal. When Eddie removed the mask, Odette kissed him.

"Oh my God!" she said. "I thought you were dead down there."

"I would have been if you hadn't saved me. The current sucked me in. I was powerless to get out of it," Eddie said.

"Did you see the boat?" Jack asked.

"The rumrunner's down there," Odette said. "I saw the name on the hull. I'm going back."

"No, you're not," Eddie said.

"I've dived around currents before. I want to know right now if there's rum aboard the wreck."

"I won't allow it," Eddie said.

"I know what I'm doing. Do you have a fresh tank, Chief?"

Jack, Chief, and Eddie watched as Odette disappeared over the side of the boat.

"She'll be fine," Chief said. "She knows more about diving than I do."

Eddie wasn't so sure. When Odette's head

finally broke the surface, he was more relieved than he could ever remember.

"Anything down there?" Jack asked as they helped her aboard.

"Something at the end of the rope," she said.

They watched in anticipation as Eddie reeled in the rope. What popped to the surface was a wooden crate. Jack helped him haul it onto the deck. Chief handed Jack a crowbar, and he soon had the top popped off revealing four bottles of Dominican rum.

"Is there more of this down there?" Jack asked.

"That's all there was," Odette said.

"You sure about that?" Jack said.

"Nothing in the hold. I found that crate in the galley," Odette said.

"Dammit!" Jack said.

"At least there are four bottles," Chief said. "One for each of us."

"Very funny," Jack said. "Five years of work down the proverbial drain."

"Maybe not," Eddie said.

"What?" Jack said.

"The outside of this crate has a bottle branded on it. Seems like I saw lots of crates in the metal storage building branded with that exact symbol."

"You sure about that?" Jack said.

"The only thing I'm sure about right now is we're all alive. Let's crack open one of those bottles of expensive rum and celebrate."

Having consumed a bottle of the Dominican rum, the four treasure hunters were feeling little pain when Jack landed the Argo at the marina. The boat had barely touched the dock when Eddie jumped to the walkway and sprinted toward the metal building. Odette, Chief, and he were waiting at the door when Jack arrived with the keys and a crowbar in his hands.

Eddie grabbed the crowbar and headed for the

nearest crate with a bottle marking on it. Odette stood with her eyes closed and her fingers crossed as Eddie ripped off the wooden top of the crate.

"Pay dirt," he said as he produced a bottle of Dominican rum.

Chief and Odette were exchanging high fives. Jack was frowning.

"Aren't you excited?" Eddie asked. "There are several dozen crates of rum in here."

"And it's all yours," Jack said.

"Huh?" Eddie said.

"I'm sure it won't take you long to figure out you own it all and don't have to cut us in," Jack said.

"You think I'd do that?" Eddie asked.

"You're a lawyer, aren't you?" Jack said.

"Forget that shit!" Eddie said. "We're partners. There's a quarter here for each of us. You have my word on it."

Chapter 27

The sky had grown dark, only remnants of a winter sun dying on the horizon as Adela and I left Allemands. Despite the pot she'd smoked, and champagne she'd drunk, she wasn't in a good mood.

"Where are we going now?" she asked.

"To the hotel to see Mama and Taj."

"That's not where they are," Adela said.

"How do you know?" I asked.

"Madeline called you a sensitive. Maybe you don't have the gift she thinks you do."

"And you do? I thought you said you have no special powers."

"You don't believe your own eyes?" she said.

"Are you confessing?"

"I'm mocking you. You've told your story about me flying so many times I think you're actually starting to believe it."

"I know what I saw," I said.

"Do you? What about this?"

A blaze ignited when Adela held up her palm. Putting the fire to her lips, she sucked it in and then blew flames from her mouth.

"Magic," she said.

"Now, you're playing games."

Adela's blue eyes sparkled in the flashing

neon of a nearby sign. Instead of answering, she disappeared. She was smiling when I wheeled around, sensing her presence behind me.

"I like games," she said. "Don't you?"

"Not when someone is playing them on me. Let me in on your game," I said.

"So you want to play with magic?"

"Is that what we're doing?"

"Maybe," she said. "Let's walk down Bourbon Street."

Adela didn't wait for an answer, heading for a shortcut to the most famous street in the world.

"Hold up," I said. "How do you know where you're going?"

Adela clutched my hand, pulling me toward the music and lights coming from the clubs and shops on Bourbon.

"Catch up, slowpoke."

We were only a block away and found the atmosphere on Bourbon Street electric. People wandered along the old byway and the sidewalks bounding it. The rain, leaving only a damp chill in the air, had moved north. A barker standing in the doorway of a strip club whistled when he saw Adela.

"Get in here, gorgeous," he said. "We got naked girls, cold beer, and the best drinks in town. Only twenty bucks cover charge each, and that includes your first drink."

The barker's eyes grew large when Adela raised her arms, her clothes disappearing as she pirouetted. As the strip club barker and dozens of tourists stopped to get a glimpse of the naked young woman, Adela pirouetted again. The gathered crowd turned away, not believing their eyes, as Adela's clothes reappeared.

"Are you getting your rocks off?" I said.

"Shut up, or I'll make your clothes disappear."

We worked our way through the slow-moving

masses, often stopping to peer into the lighted windows of the many souvenir shops, music venues, and half-opened strip club doors. One tee shirt shop had a live, mannequin model in the window.

"Will you buy me a tee shirt like the one she's wearing?" she asked.

"You bet I will," I said. "It'll look great on you."

Bells tinkled as we entered the little tee shirt and souvenir shop. Rows of tee shirts filled the well-lighted room that reeked of incense and spilled beer. Finding the cheap tee shirt she wanted, Adela pulled it from the hanger and tossed it to me. A purple and gold fleur de lis decorated the front of the gaudy green tee shirt.

"Sure it'll fit?" I asked.

"Want to see?" she said.

I quickly turned away, reaching for my wallet as I headed for the checkout counter. I handed Adela the sack containing the tee shirt, and we returned to the cacophony of Bourbon Street.

"What now?" I asked.

"Buy me a Hurricane?" she said.

Half the people around us were carrying alcoholic beverages purchased from kiosks and street vendors. One Bourbon Street establishment had a window open to the sidewalk that served drinks to the passing customers.

"There's a place," I said.

"Not there. I want a real Hurricane, from Pat O'Brien's."

"Why not?" I said. "We aren't far away."

A raucous crowd waited on the sidewalk outside the venerable French Quarter nightclub. Music poured from the open door as we entered the carriageway. We followed the slate floors to the courtyard bar and sat at a table near the flaming fountain. A waiter quickly found us.

"Two Hurricanes, one real and one Shirley

Temple." Adela was glancing around the lush courtyard, her former morose expression having returned. "What's the matter?" I asked.

"Something about this place makes me sad."

"You kidding? Strong booze, dim lights, hanging plants and a flaming fountain? How can this beautiful French Quarter courtyard make you sad?"

Adela didn't answer as the smiling waiter returned with our Hurricanes.

"Don't drink them too fast," he said.

Sounds of laughter and music surrounded us as Adela sipped her icy pink concoction through red straws. I took a sip of my own and quickly pushed it away.

"That's the real deal. Our waiter must have given you the Shirley Temple," I said.

"Trust me," she said. "This one isn't a Shirley Temple either. Give me yours. I'll drink them both."

"And I'll be carrying you back to the hotel."

"I can handle my booze, thank you."

"It's your hangover," I said.

I drank the water the waiter had also brought as I watched Adela continue to gawk at our surroundings.

"Have you been here before?" I asked.

"No," she said. "It reminds me of someplace."

"Where?"

"I remember a courtyard like this from my dreams, nightmares really. I've had them since I was a little girl."

"Hangover maybe. That's the only thing this courtyard has caused. Not nightmares."

"The courtyard in my dreams didn't cause my nightmares. It was the evil that went on there."

"Please explain," I said.

Adela's head drooped for a moment. "I don't remember. The images always melted away when I opened my eyes. They always left me with a feeling of utter helplessness that would sometimes stay with me for hours. I feel that way now."

"Are you playing games again or is this for real?"

"No games. I'm suddenly as depressed as hell."

"Do you want to go?"

"Not yet. Maybe I'll feel better when I finish this drink."

"Trust me," I said. "You'll feel lots better."

After finishing her first Hurricane and then starting on mine, Adela's smile returned. Neither of us talked as we listened to the soothing sound of water dripping from the flaming fountain shaped like a giant champagne glass. Laughter pealed around us as patrons in the main bar sang along with the piano player. Despite her smile, Adela's demeanor remained glum.

"Sorry, I'm not much company," she said.

"This courtyard must remind you of the one at the Lalaurie Mansion," I said.

"I'm not convinced I was ever there," she said. "I'm Adela Kowalski from Michigan. This is my first visit to New Orleans."

"What about what Baron Samedi said, and your fainting spell when we walked past the Lalaurie Mansion? That doesn't include the voodoo veve on your chest and the fact you met a complete stranger with an exact veve on his chest. That's a lot of coincidences."

Adela shook the ice in her nearly empty glass and drank the last drops. When she plucked a cherry from the glass and used her teeth to separate the sugary fruit from its stem, a rush of erotic desire surged up my loins. Adela had other things on her mind and didn't notice my wanton stare.

"What about the demon in the hotel and the dead woman both you and Taj claimed to see," she said. "What does that have to do with anything?"

"That's what Taj hired Mama and me to find out."

"What difference does it make? Will it end my nightmares?"

"Taj is right to try and find answers to this puzzle. I don't know if knowledge will end your nightmares." I said. "They might even get worse."

"Whatever you do, please don't make that happen."

The courtyard bar was beginning to fill up as I motioned for the waiter to bring our tab. A block from Bourbon Street, darkness and solitude began engulfing us. Persistent humidity had formed a hazy umbra around the moon.

"Today is the first day of winter," I said.

"Winter solstice," Adela said. "The shortest day and longest night of the year."

"It looks like the moon is full."

Adela squeezed my hand. "Almost. It won't be full until tomorrow."

"Are you a calendar checker?"

"I'm a witch, remember? I don't need a calendar to know when it's a full moon," Adela said. "Want to make love?"

"No can do," I said. "You're still my client, and Mama almost killed me for that very reason last night."

"Mama Mulate has no room to talk," Adela said.

"Maybe you'd better explain."

"She and Taj are a number now. I don't know if they've consummated the relationship yet. What I do know is they soon will."

"How can you be so sure?" I asked.

"I'm a witch. At least that's what you've been telling everyone."

"A beautiful witch," I said. "Even if what you say is true, it doesn't change the fact I probably shouldn't have sex with you. As it is, I'm already compromised enough."

"But you want to, don't you?"

"I'd be lying if I said I didn't."

I closed my eyes for a moment as the moon began to dim. When I opened them again, I was in bed with Adela at the hotel. We were both naked. I had my arms around her and my hands on her breasts.

"I'm neither drunk nor stoned. Either I'm dreaming, or else this is real," I said.

"I'm very real, and your nearness is exciting you as much as it is me," Adela said.

Adela's body was warm and soft and didn't feel like a dream.

"Is this another game you're playing on me?"

"We aren't playing anymore," she said.

Scooting away from her, I said, "Game or not, this isn't a good idea. If I don't get the hell out of here right now, I won't be able to."

Adela ignored my feeble protests as she crawled on top of me. Her sexual ardor had gone much too far for me to resist. My desire had grown red hot when her body suddenly stiffened, and she rolled off me. Her arms, locked across her bosom, red eyes, and the tears on her cheeks quickly poured cold water on my lust. She laughed through her tears when I finally managed to speak.

"That's a record for me," I said. "The fastest I've ever been rejected."

Adela's body remained rigid as she uncrossed her arms. Grasping my hand, she rested it on her breast.

"Take me," she said. "I won't resist you."

"I can't."

"Please do it."

"I've never forced myself on anyone."

"Am I going to have to get you drunk and stoned again," she asked.

"You're the problem and not me."

Adela's arms crossed her chest and began sobbing again.

"I thought I could make love to you. I want to make love to you. I just can't. Perhaps I never will."

"Are you. . . ?"

"A virgin?"

"You aren't, are you?"

Adela's tears had begun flowing freely, and she buried her face in the pillow. When I got out of bed and began searching for my clothes, she stopped crying.

"Please don't leave me. I don't want to be alone tonight."

"Then get dressed. We're both leaving."

"Where are we going?" she said.

"Mama Mulate's house. We need her help."

Chapter 28

Neither Adela nor I spoke during the cab ride to Mama Mulate's house. Except for Mama's beckoning porch light, the neighborhood was dark. The short respite from the rain we'd enjoyed most of the day, ended as we exited the cab.

The sky darkened, opening into a deluge as we rushed to Mama's covered porch. Someone turned on a light in the entryway. Mama came to the door, opening it a crack.

"Who is it?" she said.

"Wyatt and Adela. Let us in, we're drowning out here."

Mama pulled us inside. "Come in this house," she said. "You weren't answering your phone. I was worried."

As we followed Mama into her den, I gave Adela a quizzical glance. "You wouldn't have anything to do with that, would you?"

"Maybe," she said.

Mama grabbed towels from her linen closet and tossed them to us. "It's raining cats and dogs out there. I have warm robes in the bathroom. Get out of those clothes and put them on. You won't be going anywhere for a while."

I waited in the hallway until Adela emerged

from the little bathroom dressed in a fluffy bathrobe. When I joined them, I found Adela, Mama, and Taj waiting at the kitchen table.

"A slumber party," Adela said. "I love it."

Mama ignored Adela's frivolity when she saw me staring at Taj. "I won't even try to explain. You have every right to be angry with me after the way I treated you this morning."

"No explanation or apology required. I already knew about you and Taj."

"And how is that?" Mama asked.

"I told him," Adela said.

"What else do you know?"

"Maybe the reason Adela and Taj are in New Orleans," I said.

Mama went into the kitchen, smiling again when she returned with a pot of coffee. "If you don't like coffee this late at night, I have other beverages."

"I'd rather have what Taj is having," Adela said. "Or, maybe even something stronger."

"Not a bad idea," Mama said. "Coffee will do nothing except keep us awake. I have a bottle of vodka chilling in the freezer."

"Sounds lovely," Adela said.

"Hungry?" Mama asked. "I have Tournedos Marchand de Vin that's still warming on the stove."

"Not for me," Adela said. "Don't want to ruin my buzz."

"I'll have some," I said. "We haven't eaten since this morning. I'm starving."

Mama's cats awoke when a nearby clap of thunder shook Mama's little Creole cottage. They scurried into the room to satisfy their curiosity, all three soon crawling in Adela's lap. Adela, hugging and stroking the cats, didn't seem to mind. Mama shook her head when she returned with the tournedos and bottle of vodka.

"Hope you're not allergic to cats."

"No problems with allergies and I love cats."

"Then you're a cat person?"

"I had a few when I was growing up," Adela said.

"I can tell," Mama said. "So can my babies."

Mama shooed the cats back into the kitchen as we gathered around the table, everyone except me drinking wine or vodka. I made do with a large mug of Mama's strong Cajun coffee and a tasty plate of her tournedos. Mama replaced a Trombone Shorty CD with soothing background music from a string quartet.

After lowering the volume, she said, "I'm thinking seriously of returning Taj's retainer. I did nothing today to help solve the mystery."

Before Taj could protest, I said, "That's what partners are for. Adela and I learned a lot. I still have questions. I also have a few answers."

"Not another story about flying naked over the Mississippi River," Mama said.

"No one will do much flying out there in the storm. If you're skeptical about what I have to tell you, maybe I'll just eat your wonderful tournedos and forget about telling you what we learned today."

"Mama was just kidding," Taj said, topping up his wine from the bottle on the table. "I'm sure she didn't mean it the way it sounded."

"I wouldn't want to waste my breath," I said.

"I'm sorry," Mama said. "I had no place to comment. Please finish your tournedos and tell us what you know. I'll refrain from further snide comments."

"Sorry," I said. "I haven't had much sleep in the last two days."

"Welcome to the club," Taj said.

Mama topped up my coffee. "The pot's on the stove. I'll make more when you drink what's left."

I glanced at Adela to check on her demeanor. She looked as if she was about to sit through a boring movie for the third time.

"After Adela and I left Bertram's this morning we took a stroll down Royal Street. We went all the way to the LaLaurie Mansion. When we reached it, something strange happened."

"Such as?" Mama said.

"Adela had a fainting spell. For a while, I thought I might have to call an ambulance."

"What's the Lalaurie Mansion?" Taj asked.

"A house in the Quarter where the people who owned it abused and tortured the slaves there," Mama said. "Though it's closed to the public, it's still quite a tourist attraction. What caused Adela's fainting spell?"

"Proximity to the mansion, though I didn't realize it at the time," I said. "Adela recovered once I got her away from the house. We went to see Madeline Romanov, and it was Madeline who suggested the Lalaurie Mansion may have been the cause of Adela's distress."

"And Madeline Romanov is . . . ?" Taj said.

"A former Catholic nun who lives in the Quarter," Mama said. "She owns Madeline's Magic Potions where she sells mystical-related souvenirs to the tourists. She is also, by all accounts, a witch and the best fortune teller in town."

"She wouldn't tell my fortune," Adela said.

"Because some fortunes are best left untold," I said. "Madeline has a raven named Calpurnia who lives in her courtyard. The intelligent bird can talk.

She flew into the courtyard while we were there and became excited and agitated when she saw Adela. She called her Aisling."

Taj stared across the table to where Adela was tinkling the ice in her glass of vodka.

"Is that true?" he asked.

"Yes," Adela said.

"How do you explain that?" Taj asked.

"No idea," Adela said. "I'd never seen that bird before in my life. From what Wyatt says, Madeline is used to dealing with gullible tourists. Maybe it was a hoax."

Taj and Mama turned their stares to me. "Madeline's not a charlatan. She had no idea we were going to knock on her door and no way to cause her raven to react to Adela the way she did. It's too much of a coincidence that Calpurnia linked Adela to someone named Aisling. There must be something to it."

"That is strange. What did Madeline think about it?" Mama asked.

"That Adela and Calpurnia are connected to the abuse and torture at the Lalaurie Mansion."

"Surely Calpurnia isn't that old," Mama said.

"If humans can have past lives, then why can't animals?" I said.

"I don't know," Mama said.

"I don't either," I said. "I trust Madeline's intuition. When we left there, I decided to find out more about the place."

"Go on," Mama said.

"Allemands wasn't far away. We went there hoping to find Armand and Madam Toulouse," I said.

"Experts on everything dealing with New Orleans," Mama said when Taj gave her a quizzical look. "What did you expect to learn from them?"

"I thought they might know some things about the Lalaurie case that isn't common Internet knowledge."

"Did they?" Mama asked.

"Lots more. Madam Lalaurie was of Irish descent, and Madam Toulouse told us it was common for the rich locals to have indentured servants from Europe as well as slaves from Africa and the Caribbean. That would explain why someone of Irish descent was living in a Creole household in the French Quarter."

"Is there more?" Mama asked.

"Yes," I said. "Madam Toulouse knew all about the murder at the Hotel Montalba."

"So there really was a murder?" Mama said.

"A chambermaid discovered the headless body of the woman in the bathtub. They buried the headless body in the Charity Hospital Cemetery. You won't believe who had the room the night of the murder," I said.

"Tell us," Mama said.

"Madam Lalaurie's third husband, Dr. Leonard Louis Nicolas Lalaurie."

"No way!" Mama said.

"And the murder occurred the same night the Lalaurie Mansion burned and the tortured slaves were discovered."

"The mansion burned?" Taj said. "Didn't you say you and Adela walked past it when she had the fainting spell?"

"It's not the same mansion where the Lalaurie's lived. The present house was built several years after the original one burned almost to the ground," I said. "A fact French Quarter tourist guides never tell their customers."

"Probably because they don't know," Mama said.

"So a mansion that's not there anymore caught fire and burned to the ground? How did the slaves escape the fire?" Taj asked.

"Rescuers saw the flames and hurried to help,"

Mama said. "They managed to get the servants out of the house. They also found a torture room. The people in that room were there for only one reason—to be tortured and even killed by their sadistic owners."

"Were the Lalauries taken into custody and charged with murder?" Taj asked.

"They escaped a mob bent on punishing them for the heinous acts they committed," I said. "Madam Lalaurie reportedly died in France. I have no clue what happened to her husband. According to Armand, Madam Lalaurie and her husband were both politically connected. It's possible they were spirited away before the angry mob could deal with them."

"A typical situation present to this day in New Orleans. Still despicable," Mama said.

"One last thing," I said. "Armand identified the symbol on Adela's chest as a Baron Samedi veve, though he said it was done by someone other than a mambo or houngan."

"That's what Mama thinks," Taj said. "We were talking about it less than an hour ago. You never told me why these veves are drawn in the first place."

"To summon a loa or deity for assistance," Mama said.

"Are they always tattoos?" Taj asked.

"They are usually pictures drawn on the ground using a powder such as flour, salt, gunpowder, or whatever. Once drawn, money, whiskey, or something considered valuable is placed on top of the veve in hopes of securing the loa's assistance."

"What does any of this have to do with Adela and me?" Taj asked.

"Madam Toulouse told us the Lalauries had an African overseer who helped them control the slaves," I said. "His name was Taj, and he was tall enough he could have played in the NBA."

"You gotta be shitting me!" Taj said. "Other players respect me, and I've never backed down from a fight. Doesn't matter because I'm not cruel and I've never abused or tortured anyone."

"Wyatt isn't suggesting you have, Baby," Mama said.

"Then what is he suggesting?"

"Wyatt?" Mama said.

"Maybe in a past life, you and Adela both lived in the original Lalaurie Mansion. The one that burned the night the woman was murdered at the Hotel Montalba."

"Wyatt believes it was me who was murdered," Adela said. "I think he's full of shit."

"I have my reasons. The demon was dragging a woman's head by its long red hair. I could swear it was Adela's head. If that's true, then she was murdered by Dr. Leonard Louis Nicolas Lalaurie."

"If I was dead, then how am I alive now?" Adela asked.

"Because it was you during a past life," I said. "What connects you and Taj are your twin veves. Someone or something put them on your chests to try and curry favor with Baron Samedi. Maybe it worked, and spiritual powers have brought you two back here to New Orleans."

"For what purpose?" Taj asked.

Outside, heavy rain was pelting Mama's old roof. I felt the storm's intensity as Adela, Taj and Mama's stares bored inquisitive holes in my soul.

"Redemption," I said.

Chapter 29

Everyone at the table had grown quiet as I finished my rambling narrative. The cats had returned to their snug beds as the storm outside continued to rage. Mama topped up Adela and Taj's glasses and then started a new pot of coffee for me.

"What now?" she asked when she returned.

"I feel certain we've found a tangible link with the events that occurred at the Lalaurie Mansion. I've checked all my live sources. I think it's time to chase the dead ones."

"Maybe you'd better explain," Mama said.

"Use your magic music box. See if you can summon a spirit from the Lalaurie Mansion," I said.

"You know I don't like using the music box. Even if I did, I'm not sure who to summon," Mama said.

"Yes, you do. If Adela and Taj lived past lives in the Lalaurie house before the fire, then you can use them to summon their spirits. If they didn't, then it'll be no harm, no foul."

"I don't know," Mama said. "You know how powerful and dangerous the music box is. I'd hate to unleash its powers without knowing for sure we'd achieve positive results."

"The only way to be sure is to try it," I said.

Taj grew agitated with the talk of spirits. "Maybe you better explain a few things to Adela and me," he said. "What is this magic music box?"

"I'll show you," Mama said.

She disappeared into another room, returning with an ornate box constructed of polished wood, an antique jar, and a red velvet pouch. She placed the three objects on the table.

"Is that your music box?" Taj asked.

"Much more than just a music box. It's a priceless relic."

"It's so beautiful," Adela said. Is it really magic?"

"Monks, shrouded in mystery, constructed this medieval music box during the Early Middle Ages."

"For magical purposes?" Adela asked.

"Christianity was in its infancy in Europe. During the Early Middle Ages, Christianity was little more than a mixture of folk religion and paganism. Monks and other holy men still practiced magic. This music box was created, among other things, to summon spirits of the dead."

Taj was frowning. "Does it work?"

"Of course it works," Mama said. "Stow your cynicism and trust me when I tell you this music box has magical powers."

"I'm trying my best to believe," Taj said. "It just seems so foreign to me."

"When monks created this music box, the practice of magic was rampant. They had knowledge of secrets that are long since lost," Mama said. "Powerful secrets."

"Such as?" Taj said.

"The magic of this music box has the power to summon the dead."

"No one practices magic anymore. If they could

do so much with it, why did they stop using it?"

Adela winced when I said, "Because the ones who used it were damned as witches or wizards and burned at the stake, or tortured on the rack."

"How did you come by such a powerful instrument?" Taj asked, ignoring my comment.

"I can't tell you," Mama said. "All I can confirm is its powers are so great, I've only used it once and it's quite frightening."

"It is impressive looking, I'll give you that," Taj said. "I just can't wrap my head around what makes it magic."

"I understand your doubt," Mama said. "I can only give you a simple explanation because I don't fully understand it myself."

"Please do," he said.

"Everything in the world can be described using mathematics. The universe is the most complex mathematical formula, and music is rooted in mathematics. Some say the arrangement of musical notes in Gregorian chants results in particular responses. One all-powerful chant is the musical equivalent of the universe's mathematical formula. When performed in a specific manner, certain chants can unlock the powers of the universe."

"Then why don't today's scientists know about this?" Taj asked.

"There was little written history during the Dark Ages. Practically everything people knew then has since been lost. The ancients knew lots of things that aren't common knowledge in our modern world."

"But we are so much more advanced now than we were then," Taj said. "Surely, we know everything they did."

"Maybe not. Wyatt wasn't far off with his burning at the stake comment. People were afraid of magic and fearful of the people who practiced it.

Those who practiced magic had to hide their abilities or chance being killed."

"Surely we have enough knowledge to replicate what uneducated monks knew," Taj said.

"Do we?" Mama said. "Knowledge begins with a single seed. If that seed is lost, is it ever possible to recreate again?"

"Most people have hard times believing anything they haven't seen with their own eyes," I said. "Even, then they try to explain anomalies away."

Adela looked the other way when I glanced at her.

"If your music box is so powerful, then why not share it with the powers-that-be?" Taj said.

"Magic is power," Mama said. "The monks guarded their magic with their lives because not only can it unlock the secrets of the universe, it could also destroy it."

"Okay," Taj said.

Mama chuckled as she finished her vodka in a single swallow and then filled her glass to the brim.

"No more questions and no more explanations. This music box will never leave me. Now, either we're all in on using it, or else I'll return it to its proper place of keeping."

"You sound so dire," Adela said.

"For good reason," Mama said.

"This is starting to sound like there's risk involved," Taj said.

"There is," Mama said. "When Wyatt and I used it to summon a spirit of the dead, I wasn't sure if either of us would survive. Employing its immense power should never be taken lightly, and only done as a last resort."

"Is that what this is?" Taj asked.

"Though we're close, I'm not sure we've reached that point yet," Mama said.

"I haven't been this excited about trying

something new in a long time," Adela said. "Count me in."

Casting a grave stare at Taj, Mama said, "In or out?"

"Will it hurt my basketball chops?" he asked.

"No, but if you don't hurry and make up your mind, I'm going to break both of your legs."

Taj grinned. "Why not? It can't kill me."

"Don't be so sure of that," Mama said.

"I trust you," he said. "You know what you're doing."

"Don't be so sure of that, either," she said. "Hold out your hands."

Outside, the wind had picked up, rain pounding the windows and wooden shutters. Mama lit a single candle on the table, turned off the CD player, and extinguished all the other lights. From the velvet pouch, she removed two necklaces with polished black stone pendants.

"Put these around your necks," she said.

"What is it?" Adela asked.

"The stone is psilomelane, also known as the Crown of Silver. It's a metallic mineral with magical properties. It'll help induce the trance I'm going to put you into."

"You're putting us into a trance?" Taj said.

"That's exactly what I'm going to do," Mama said. "I thought you said you trust me."

"I do trust you. I just don't like anesthetics."

"This isn't the same," she said. "When you awaken from the trance you'll have no anesthetic hangover."

From the antique jar, Mama shook something into Adela and Taj's awaiting hands.

"What is this?" Taj asked.

"Mushroom. Chew it up and wash it down with your wine.

"If it's psychedelic I'll get in trouble with the league."

"One last time, are you in or out?" Mama said.

"I'm all in," he said. "But taking illegal drugs could end my career."

"We're not doing this for recreation," Mama said. "Chew the mushroom. I'll give you an antidote and something to cleanse the remnants of the drug from your system later."

"What about me?" I asked.

"No magic mushroom for you. I need you to be cognizant and help me make sense of the spirits if we are successful in summoning them. Put these in your ears. In case you don't remember, the music is deafening."

Mama handed me a pair of soft rubber earplugs. "What about you?"

She showed me her own pair. "I was all but deaf for days after the last time we used this box. That's when I bought these earplugs. Adela and Taj won't need them."

Adela was grinning. "I've never tried magic mushrooms."

"You'll be in a trance, so don't expect much. You may not know anything until the spirits are gone."

"That sucks," Adela said.

"I can't do this without you and Taj. Tell me when the drug begins to take effect. Until then, I won't start the music box."

Taj and Adela didn't need to tell Mama the psychedelic drug had begun working. Their heads were soon drooping, their eyes closed, their arms off the table and hanging by their sides.

"I'm going to put my cats in their beds outside on the back porch," Mama said. "They won't be happy but the porch is covered, and they'll be safe from the storm and the cacophony of the music box."

When Mama returned, she signaled for me to insert the earplugs. After winding the music box, she opened the carved top of the ancient instrument. The inner workings began to turn and the metallic, though dulcet notes of an unknown melody began to play. The sound of the storm raging outside the house soon became little more than background noise. Though the earplugs blocked most of the melody, I could clearly hear the plucked tones resonating inside the medieval wooden cabinet.

The single candle burning on the table provided dim light to the room. The wax dripping down its side had turned blood red as the music grew ever louder. Even with the earplugs firmly inserted, I could tell the difference. A hazy cloud began to form in a dark corner of the room.

Because of the hallucinogenic mushroom I'd consumed the first time Mama had employed the music box, I remembered little of the former experience. Now, lucid and coherent, I began to see pentagrams and pentacles floating around the room.

A poisonous viper, causing me to recoil before it slithered to the floor, fell from the ether onto the tabletop in front of me. I was starting to wish I wasn't quite so coherent when two shadowy figures began to appear.

Once fully formed, I saw a huge man, his skin as black as coal, his face, neck, arms, and bare chest covered with tattoos and tribal markings. The other person was a girl, probably no older than fifteen or sixteen. She had long, red hair and a milky complexion. Though there was some resemblance, I could see neither spirit was either Taj or Adela.

"Who summoned us here?" the spirit of the large black man asked.

"Voodoo mambo Mama Mulate. What is your name?"

"I am Taj, and this is Aisling. You have not

answered my question. Why have you summoned us?"

"For answers. Did you live in the Lalaurie Mansion?"

"We were both victims of that vile place," Taj said.

"Then I need to hear your story," Mama said. "Will you tell it to me?"

"For what purpose," the spirit said.

Mama didn't answer his question. "Do you know what a veve is?"

"Yes," he said.

Our Taj was in a stupor beside Mama when she opened his robe and revealed the symbol on his chest.

"Have you ever seen this or one like it before?"

"Yes," he said.

"The young woman with the long red hair has a similar veve on her chest. The Lalauries also victimized these two people. Now, they need your assistance. Will you help them?

"I'll help," the female spirit said. "That woman looks like my mama."

"Where shall we begin?" the giant black man asked.

Chapter 30

The single candle on Mama's table flickered and died. It mattered little because a ghostly glow filled the room. Candlelight wasn't all that was missing. Silence had replaced the dulcet tones of the magic music box and the storm raging outside the house.

Taj and Adela, their eyes closed, had slumped forward in their chairs. Also closed were the eyes of the two spirits whom Mama had summoned. Mama was wide-awake and so was I. As we watched, a billowing cloud engulfed the room. The cloud parted to reveal a French Quarter courtyard, circa 1834.

Aisling's long red hair bounced as she crossed the slate floor of the French Quarter Courtyard. Even during winters in New Orleans, palms, ferns, and baskets of hanging flowers combined to form a lovely, enclosed garden. The two-storied building surrounding the courtyard kept it hidden from the people passing outside on the sidewalk. Aisling hated the long dress and petticoats her mother made her wear.

"You must take care not to wear anything provocative," her mother had told her.

At least the dress was yellow, Aisling's favorite

color.

Aisling loved the courtyard and the garden and spent as much time there as she could. Today, she was looking for Calpurnia, the majestic raven who called the courtyard home.

Except for Aisling's mother and the Lalauries, everyone else living in the large house was black. Moreover, they were all much older than she was. Shasa, the old cook was her best friend. Shasa fancied herself a voodoo woman. She wasn't, but having come from Haiti she did know lots about the subject. Aisling had magical powers. She'd known of her powers since she was a child. Aisling sensed she could do far more than she'd ever tried.

Except for her mother and Shasa, Aisling's only other friend was the raven, Calpurnia. Calpurnia could talk. Aisling had discovered she could also communicate. When Calpurnia wasn't flying around the French Quarter, she usually occupied a perch suspended from the building's second-story balcony. Today, she was missing from her perch and Aisling was concerned.

"Calpurnia, where are you," Aisling said.

Thinking she'd heard the bird's cackle around one of the courtyard's many nooks, Aisling walked around the corner to investigate. She found the raven on the shoulder of a man working the flowerbeds with a hoe. Aisling stopped in her tracks.

For a long moment, she stared at the bare upper body of the young man. His skin was light brown, his muscles rippling as he worked the beds. He turned when Aisling spoke.

"That's my bird. What are you doing with her?"

When Aisling saw the young man's face, she realized he was not much older than she was. After catching a glimpse of her, he lowered his gaze. Aisling continued staring at his chiseled chest and regal facial features.

"Didn't you hear me?" she said.

"I'm sorry," he said, not glancing up to look at her. "Your bird was helping me weed the flowerbeds. We just kind of hit it off and I didn't know she belonged to anybody."

"Calpurnia belongs to no one," Aisling said. "I've never known her to take up with anyone but me."

"Animals like me," the young man said. "Like I said, I'm sorry."

"I'm not mad because Calpurnia likes you. I just want to know why you won't look me in the eye."

"I can't," he said.

"And why can't you?" she asked.

"Because you are white. We aren't supposed to look white people in the eye."

"We?"

"We darkies," he said.

"That's absolutely crazy," she said. "You aren't much darker than I am."

"Don't matter none. You're white, and I'm a nigger."

"My mama told me never to use that horrible word. She would kill me if she ever caught me saying it," Aisling said.

"Your mama must be a special person," the young man said.

"Yes, she is. Calpurnia, come to me."

The raven ignored Aisling, staying on the young man's shoulder. Taking Calpurnia on his wrist, he propelled the bird into the air.

"Go to her," he said. "You'll get me in big trouble."

Calpurnia's feathers ruffled before flying to Aisling's awaiting wrist. The young man continued to keep his eyes averted.

"You're rude, you know it," Aisling said. "And now you've turned my raven against me."

"I'm sorry, I didn't mean to."

"You can at least look at me," she said.

"I can't. I told you why."

"There's no one in the courtyard except for us. I promise I won't get you in trouble. Please look at me."

"But you're white," he said.

"My mama's a servant here, just like you."

"Is your mama a slave?"

"No, but she's indentured," Aisling said.

"What does that mean?"

"Mama is Madam Lalaurie's cousin. Madam Lalaurie brought us from Ireland when my daddy died. Mama has to work for the mistress until she's paid the price of our passage here."

"How long will that be?" he asked.

"Don't know. I'm fifteen, and we've been here for three years now. My name is Aisling. What is yours?"

"Darius," he said.

"How long have you been here, Darius?"

"The mistress bought me yesterday at the slave market on St. Charles."

"Shasa says the slave market is a horrible place. That's all she would tell me. Is it true?"

"It's true," he said.

"Please tell me about it," Aisling said.

"You are way too young," he said.

"I'm as old as you are."

Darius hesitated as if trying to recall something he'd successfully forgotten, or at least put out of his memory for a while.

"They have a pen behind the market where they keep the slaves until time to sell them. The men, women, and children are stuffed into the pen where there's barely room to stand. There's no place to go to the bathroom, and I can't even tell you how bad it smelled.

"They fed us nothing but bacon ends to fatten

us up. The water was hot and the bacon half-cooked and spoiling in the sun. Almost everyone was sick and throwing up.

"People died in the pen waiting to be sold. When they did, the guards would drag their bodies out and throw them into a cart. They took the bodies to the middle of the river and dumped them."

"That is so awful," Aisling said. "I'm sorry you had to go through such horror."

"It wasn't as bad for me as it was for the men and women separated from each other and their kids. One woman clawed her face so bad when they took her son the guards killed her to make an example of her."

"I'm so sorry," Aisling said.

"It's okay," Darius said. "I'm young and strong and got no family to lose."

Determined to change the conversation back to a less painful topic, Aisling wiped away her tears with the sleeve of her yellow dress.

"Where did you come from?"

"I lived my whole life at a sugar plantation down River Road."

"You look so healthy. Shasa told me there's no harder work than cutting cane under the hot Louisiana sun."

"Shasa is right about that," Darius said. "I was lucky and worked as a gardener. The mistress was looking for a gardener. That was part of the reason she bought me."

"What's the other reason?" Aisling asked.

"To sleep with her," Darius said.

"Are you kidding?"

"Wish I was. That ugly woman makes my stomach turn worse than thinking about the slave pens on St. Charles."

"Are you going to do it anyway?" she asked.

"I got no choice," he said.

"You still haven't looked at me," Aisling said. Darius raised his head. "That didn't kill you."

"I'm not afraid of dying," he said.

"Then what are you afraid of?"

"Getting beaten so bad you can't walk. Hurting so bad you wished you was dead," he said.

"You've never been beaten like that, have you?" Aisling asked.

"No, but I seen others who have. Grown men crying like babies."

"Mama says it's okay to cry."

"No, it ain't. No matter how bad you're hurting, you can't ever let them know," he said. "My friend Kalifa taught me that."

"Who is Kalifa?" Aisling asked.

"An old man I knew. Kalifa came straight from Africa. The overseers called him Zeke, but he was always Kalifa to me. He was the only father I ever knew. Kalifa said no matter how bad things get, you should keep your dignity."

"What happened to Kalifa?" Aisling asked.

"The overseers made an example of him and cut off his hand with an ax. Didn't matter none because he never changed expression. The overseers killed him for it."

"I'm so sorry," Aisling said.

"It's not your fault. If I get tortured and killed, I want to leave this world with Kalifa's dignity."

"I would never hurt you for any reason," Aisling said.

"I know you wouldn't," he said. "I've never seen hair or eyes like yours."

"Red hair and blue eyes. Everyone says I look like my mama."

Darius turned his gaze back toward the ground. "Guess I better get back to work," he said.

"How old are you, Darius?"

"Don't know," he said.

"It's just mama and me," Aisling said. "We got

nobody else."

"You told me your mama is Mistress Lalaurie's cousin."

"That woman is evil," Aisling said. "She treats us like dirt under her feet. Only reason she hasn't got rid of us is it would make her look bad to her other Irish relatives."

"I'm sorry," Darius said.

"How many people are in your family?"

"Ain't got no family," Darius said.

"Where's your mother?"

"We was separated when my brother and me was just kids."

"You have a brother?" Aisling asked.

"Twin brother," he said.

"Where is he?"

"Don't know. The master sold him to another plantation."

"When was the last time you saw your mother and brother?" Aisling said.

"When I was about knee-high," he said.

"That's so horrible," Aisling said. "I don't have a sister. If I did, I couldn't imagine not ever being able to see her again. My mama is young and almost like my sister. If I were to lose her, I would die."

"No, you wouldn't," Darius said. "You have to guard your feelings. Don't ever get too close to anyone, cause you or they might get sold. You can't make friends either because tomorrow you may never see them again."

"You can't think that way," Aisling said. "I would kill myself if I lost my mama."

"Life is cruel, but you can't let it ever get the best of you. Right now, I better get back to work. Don't want to wind up with scars all over my back."

"I like you, Darius. You're the only person my age I can talk to."

"Don't matter. You mustn't talk to me. You'll

get us both in trouble."

"I'm not going to worry about that. Will you be here tomorrow?" Aisling asked.

"The mistress said I'm the gardener now. I got the job long as I keep the place green and pretty."

"I love this courtyard and come here every day. If I need to talk to you and someone is around such that I can't, I'll send you a message by Calpurnia."

"How can you do that?" Darius asked.

"I told you she is smart. No one knows how smart except me. She understands what I say, and she can talk."

"You sure?" Darius said.

"Want to see?"

"Yes."

"Later on from now, tell her to find me. I'll give her a message and send her back to you. You'll see," Aisling said. "Our friendship will be a secret between only you, me, and Calpurnia."

Darius nodded, and then returned to hoeing the flowerbeds.

Chapter 31

Dr. Leonard Louis Nicolas Lalaurie stood at the window of his upstairs bedroom. Seeing him staring out at the courtyard below, his wife Madam Delphine Lalaurie walked over to see what he was looking at. As she reached the window, she saw the redheaded girl in a yellow dress disappear around the corner.

"You'd like nothing better than to bed that pretty young white girl, wouldn't you?"

"You're one to talk," he said. "I saw the mulatto boy you bought yesterday at the market. I'm sure you have similar plans for him."

"Don't worry about what I do," she said. "Except for her, I don't give a tinker's dam about whoever, or whatever you bed. That particular girl is a relative of mine, and it wouldn't be proper. If word got out, I would lose face in the community."

Dr. LaLaurie was two inches shorter and fifteen years younger than his wife, Delphine. Slight of frame, he looked as if he'd never done a hard day's work in his life. Pomade slicked down his brown hair, short except for the pigtail tied with a black bow. His only impressive features were his extra-long fingers and delicate hands. They were all he needed to wield either whip or scalpel, and he was quite proficient at both.

Delphine Lalaurie's black wig sat precariously over her graying hair. When she became angry or flustered, a common occurrence for a woman who rarely smiled, the wig would often become cocked on her head. Along with the excess rouge and lipstick she used, it imparted her with a cartoonish look. Known for hosting lavish fetes, none of her guests ever mentioned Madam Lalaurie's comic book appearance to her. Still, it didn't keep the topic from being common knowledge around town.

"After our dinner with the governor tonight, I'm going to practice my surgical technique on one of the slaves," Dr. Lalaurie said. "Will you join me?"

"You know I will," she said. "There's no one better in bed than you after you've performed with the scalpel. It gets you so hot."

"You like cutting as much as I do," he said. "Hot sex and skillful surgery are the two things we both have in common. Maybe that's why I love you so much."

"Just don't ever cross me, or there will be part of your anatomy I will surgically remove," she said.

Dr. Lalaurie grinned. "I also made a purchase at the market yesterday. The woman is in the cage in the garden, awaiting her appointment with us later tonight in the Dark Room."

Madam Lalaurie left rouge and lipstick on Dr. Lalaurie's face when she kissed him.

"I can't wait, my darling," she said. "Now, I must attend to the kitchen and make sure that black bitch Shasa is preparing the feast tonight for our important guests."

Madam Lalaurie never went anywhere in the mansion without her whip. She had ten slaves to help her with the chores which needed doing around the large house. She kept more slaves than she needed because it was always a good thing to make an occasional example. A bullwhipping in the courtyard went a long way to strike fear in the hearts of her slaves. They were all expendable. All of them except for Shasa.

Shasa was the best cook in New Orleans. Her culinary creations were legend. No dinner party ever passed without at least one of the guests offering lots of money for the talented old woman. Delphine loved the accolades her lavish dinner parties always garnered but hated that Shasa was the star of the show, and not she.

One of the richest persons in all New Orleans, Delphine didn't need any more money. Though she wallowed in the acclaim her cook had brought her, she hated the old woman for having power over her. Because of her hatred, she tortured Shasa every chance she could.

Delphine entered the kitchen to find Shasa sitting on the floor, her arms gathered around her knees as she sobbed. Leather cracked as Delphine lit into her with the whip.

"What the hell do you think you're doing?" Delphine said. "You have a feast to prepare, so get the hell off the floor!"

Shasa was short, her bony frame swallowed up by the plain brown dress she wore. Her bushy hairdo liberally sprinkled with gray made her seem even smaller than she was. The old woman scooted away from the whip, trying without much success to protect her face from the flying leather.

Remembering her guests, Delphine had to restrain herself from beating the slight old woman to death. Taking a deep breath, she somehow managed to regain her composure when she caught up to the little woman.

When Shasa was in the kitchen, Madam Delphine kept her chained by the ankle. The long chain allowed her access to all parts of the kitchen but would let her go no further. When Shasa had to relieve herself, she had to do it in a can in the corner. Once, in an angry snit, Madam Lalaurie had dunked her face into the can.

Delphine wanted to punish Shasa. She also needed the cook available to prepare dinner for her guests arriving later that evening. Seeing a pot of water boiling over an open flame, she knew what she had to do. Grabbing the old woman's hand, she wrestled her to the boiling pot and plunged her left hand into it.

"Don't you cry out, don't you dare!" Delphine said.

The boiling water on Shasa's hand produced pain like she'd never before felt. It didn't matter because she knew if she cried out the mistress would hold her hand in the water even longer. When Delphine finally released her grip and let Shasa wrench her hand from the boiling pot, blood was pouring down her face from where she had bitten through her lower lip.

"You're not hurt you horrible black bitch," Delphine said. "Get your lazy ass off the floor and get dinner started. My guests are arriving in four hours. If you don't have the feast of all feasts prepared by then, I swear by God, I'll personally skin you alive."

Madam Delphine Lalaurie went stomping out of the kitchen just as Aisling entered. Seeing Shasa slumped on the floor and bleeding, Aisling ran to her, putting her arms around her shoulders and hugging her.

"Oh my God! What did that evil woman do to you?"

Blood was dripping down Shasa's neck, and she was holding her left hand. The hand was already swollen and puffy, and as red as boiled crawfish. Aisling ran to the cabinets, returning with a crock of honey. Without asking, she plunged Shasa's hand into the gooey substance.

Tearing cloth from her petticoats, she used the strips to bandage Shasa's hand.

"The honey will lessen the pain and help the burn begin to heal," Aisling said.

Aisling used more cloth from her petticoat to staunch the blood on Shasa's face.

"Your lip needs stitches," she said. "Hold the bandage tight. I'll go get Mama."

Aisling and her mother Adela soon returned to find Shasa still sitting on the floor.

Aisling was as tall as her mother. Both had long red hair. They could almost have passed as sisters. From behind, they were all but impossible to tell apart. Adela had a brandy bottle and held it to the old woman's lips until she had drunk enough to quickly intoxicate her.

"This will hurt though the brandy will provide some relief while I put stitches in your lip," Adela said.

"I got to get to cooking," Shasa said. "The mistress has people coming for dinner. She said she'd skin me alive if I don't have a feast prepared for them."

"I told Taj what happened," Aisling said. "He's coming with Danke and Estelle. Mama and I will help, too. You may have to show us how, but we'll get everything ready for you."

Adela knew the brandy was working because Shasa's words were slurred when she said, "You girls are angels sent straight from heaven."

"Open your mouth and don't talk," Adela said, her Irish brogue prevalent. "I'm going to sew up this cut as fast as I can. Will you be okay?"

"Damn, Baby," Shasa said. "I can't hurt no more than I already do."

Taj arrived with Danke and Estelle as Adela tied off the thread, applied a soothing poultice on the wound and then bandaged it with gauze and tape. Estelle and Danke grabbed Shasa's arms and helped her into a chair. Shasa continued to sob.

"Something else is wrong, isn't it?" Aisling said. "Please tell me what it is."

"James, my son," she said. "He been killed in the fields down River Road."

"How do you know?" Aisling said.

"I feel it all the way to my very soul. James dead and I ain't ever going to see him no more."

"I'm so sorry," Aisling said, gently hugging the old woman.

"Can I have some more brandy?" Shasa asked.

Adela handed her the bottle. "Drink it all. Taj can raid the liquor cabinet and get us more."

Taj was the largest man Aisling had ever seen. His skin was black as coal and covered with tattoos and tribal markings. Though he looked mean as hell, he was one of the kindest and gentlest persons Aisling had ever known. He kept his compassion hidden from the Lalauries who considered him their enforcer.

Danke and Estelle, dressed similarly to Shasa though not nearly so slight of frame, were two middle-aged black women who had somehow managed to survive in the Lalaurie household. Scars on their faces and many more on their bodies testified to the abuse both of them had endured. Danke began to cry as she held Shasa's head in her hands.

"I'm okay, Baby," Shasa said. "You're gonna have to help me cook tonight."

"We ain't going no place," Estelle said. "You just keep sitting right there and tell us what to do. We'll get it done for you."

The wonderful aroma of Creole cooking soon filled the kitchen. Taj had brought more brandy, and Shasa was quite drunk, though still coherent enough to direct the preparation of the food. The menu included oyster artichoke soup, sauteed redfish with crab and oyster dressing, and bread pudding with cognac sauce as dessert. Shasa was pleased.

"You girls cooked a regal meal fit for a king, or the madam's cousin, the governor of all the colonies. I hope she don't find out I didn't cook it, or she'll be dragging me to the Dark House to skin me alive."

"We ain't telling nobody," Estelle said. "Far as the mistress will ever know, you cooked everything with your one good hand."

Shasa chuckled as she lifted herself with some difficulty from the chair.

"You girls get the hell out of here. The mistress will return soon, along with the waitstaff. You don't need to be here," Shasa said. "I'm drunk as hell, and right now I don't give a damn."

Danke and Estelle kissed Shasa and hurried out the door leaving only Aisling to tend to the old woman.

"I used plants from the garden to prepare this salve," Aisling said, rubbing some on Shasa's lip. "It'll help you heal. I'll redress your burn tomorrow and bring more salve."

Shasa smiled for the first time that night as she caressed Aisling's cheek with her one good hand.

"Ain't nothing ever gonna heal in this house. Way too much evil afoot," she said. "You were my angel tonight, Baby. I promise you now, one day I'm going to be your angel."

When Aisling reached the little room where she and her mother lived, the curtain was pulled between her bed and her mother's. Knowing Taj was in bed with her mother, she listened to their noisy lovemaking.

Tonight, she had other things on her mind: the young man she'd met in the courtyard, the most handsome person she'd ever seen in her life.

Tomorrow, she would return to the garden and pay another visit to the boy named Darius.

Chapter 32

Shasa was feeling better the following morning when Aisling went to change her bandages. She'd even cooked Aisling's favorite omelet. Aisling was taking the last bite when Calpurnia came flying through the open window and landed on her shoulder. Shasa waited a moment before commenting about Aisling's expression.

"Baby, you got a funny look on your face. What did the bird just tell you."

"There's a new boy named Darius working as a gardener in the courtyard. He's the dreamiest boy I've ever met. He sent Calpurnia to find me. I'll be back later to check on your wounds."

Calpurnia flew ahead as Aisling ran down the stairs to the courtyard. She found Darius tending the ferns hanging from a second-story balcony. They both smiled when they saw each other.

"Good morning," Darius said. "You were right about Calpurnia. She understands every word I say."

"She told me," Aisling said. Darius' smile disappeared when she asked, "Do you like it here now?"

"I gotta show you something," he said.
"What is it?"

"You'll see," he said as she followed him into one of the garden's many hidden nooks. "I couldn't sleep last night after meeting you. I walked outside for a breath of fresh air and heard something. I found this cage."

"It's so big," Aisling said. "What do they keep in it?"

"People," Darius said. "I hid in the bushes when I saw the master and mistress take a woman from the cage and lead her into that building."

Darius pointed at a door secured by two padlocks. Hidden in the farthest nook of the courtyard, Aisling had never noticed it.

"What's in there?" Aisling asked.

"Don't know for sure. They shut the door behind them, and I listened with my ear to it."

"What did you hear?" Aisling asked.

"Screams, horrible screams," he said. "I waited in the bushes until they came out. The master and mistress were carrying the body of the woman. There's a dry well over there. That's where they threw the body."

Aisling's hand went to her mouth. "My God! They killed her?"

"Worse than that," Darius said.

"How do you know?"

"This morning, I lowered a rope and went down into the well to have a look," he said.

"And?" Aisling said.

Darius shook his head. "She was dead. What else they did to her you don't even want to know."

"That's awful," Aisling said

"Her body wasn't all I found down there. It was a boneyard. I counted a dozen skulls."

"What'll we do?" Aisling asked.

"What can we do?" Darius said.

⬥

Dr. Lalaurie waited in his study as Taj entered the door along with Adela.

"Here she is, Mastah," Taj said.

"Leave us," Lalaurie said. "I'll handle things from here."

Taj returned to the hallway, shut the door, and then made a pretense of walking away. He didn't, putting his ear to the door instead to try and hear why Dr. Laulaurie had ordered him to bring Adela to his study. The door was thick, and he could hear nothing.

Adela stood in the doorway, wondering like Taj why Dr. Lalaurie had summoned her to his study.

"Sit," he said, pointing to a chair in front of his desk. "Madam Lalaurie left this morning for an extended visit to Paris. While she is gone, I have some specific things I intend to do. The number one thing on my list is to make love to your daughter."

"That's out of the question," Adela said. "Aisling is only fifteen. She's a virgin."

"That's about to change," Dr. Lalaurie said. "Madam Lalaurie's boat sails today. Tomorrow, I have reservations for the bridal suite at the Hotel Montalba."

"Madam Lalaurie won't allow it," Adela said. "We are related to her."

"The madam will never know. When she returns, you and your waif will be onboard a ship bound for Ireland."

"You can't do that. We have no family left in Ireland and no place to go," Adela said.

"That appears to be your problem and not mine. Have your daughter ready tomorrow evening to spend the night with me at the Hotel Montalba."

"And if I don't?"

"Madam Lalaurie and I have a room where we punish slaves who disobey us. Aisling will spend the night with me tomorrow, and you'll be on your way back to Ireland, or I will make love to Aisling tomorrow night with or without your assent. If you try to defy me, you will see the inside of the punishment room, and Aisling will join you there after I have had my way with her. Your choice."

Adela's flash of anger changed quickly to fear and then a feeling of utter hopelessness.

"Take me instead," she said. "Aisling's just a child.

"And that's precisely why I want her and not you. Have Aisling ready tomorrow. You may go now."

Adela was crying when she ran out of the study. Dr. Lalaurie followed her out the door and then went upstairs to his bedroom. When he opened the curtains and looked out the window to the courtyard, the first thing he saw was Aisling in the embrace of the mulatto boy his wife had just purchased at the market.

Dinner was finished, Shasa cleaning the kitchen when Adela and Taj joined her. Adela was crying. From her puffy red face, she'd been doing so for some time. Shasa put her arms around Adela, hugging her to her bony chest.

"Baby, what's the matter?"

"Madam Lalaurie's on her way to France and that monster husband of hers is bent on taking Aisling's virginity."

"The mistress won't allow him to get away with that. She and Aisling are related."

"He intends to either send us back to Ireland or else to torture and kill us in that torture chamber of his."

"Where does he plan to take Aisling's virginity?" Shasa asked.

"He has a room tomorrow night at a hotel in the Quarter. You have to help us stop him, Shasa."

Shasa walked to the window and stared out. For the first time that month, it was raining. Shasa stuck her injured hand out the open window letting the cold rain soak the bandage. When she returned to the kitchen table, she had a look of resolve on her face.

"Well?" Taj said.

"You have to take Aisling's place."

"How can I do that?" Adela asked. "He knows what I look like."

"It's almost Mardi Gras. You and Aisling are about the same size, and you both have long red hair. Wear a Mardi Gras mask. If you're clever, he'll never know the difference."

"But what will it matter? When he discovers my ruse, he'll simply go through with his threat of dealing with us in the torture room."

"That's why you're going to have to kill him," Shasa said.

"But how will I do that?"

Shasa went to the cabinet and returned with a butcher knife. "With this."

"How will I conceal the knife from him? Adela asked.

"Baby, do you know what a veve is?"

Adela shook her head. "No, I don't."

"It's a symbol used to beg the assistance of a particular voodoo loa. It's usually drawn on the ground with flour or some other powder. Offerings to the deities are placed on top of the veve. If the loa accepts the offering, he will grant your request."

"What does that have to do with anything?"

"I need to tattoo a veve on your chest. The only veve I know how to draw is Baron Samedi's. If the Baron accepts your offering, he will ensure that evil man's death."

"If I'm the offering, shouldn't the veve be on my back?" Adela asked.

"If Dr. Lalaurie were a normal person with normal desires," Shasa said. "He isn't. He will turn you on your stomach and take you from behind.

When he does, you'll be the offering between the veve and him."

"How do you know this?" Taj asked.

"He's had almost everyone in this house at one time or other," Shasa said. "His perversions are well known."

"It all sounds too dangerous to me," Taj said. "Why don't I just kill him?"

"Because it would result in your death and both Adela and Aisling's when Madam Lalaurie returns. This way, she'll never know who killed Dr. Lalaurie."

"How will this work?" Adela asked.

"Strip your clothes off in front of him and keep your mask on. Show him your titties but cover the veve with your hand. Talk in a child's voice. He'll think of it as foreplay, and it will only serve to further excite him. Hide the knife under the pillow, in the bed."

"Can't I just stab him in the back?" Adela said.

"Baron Samedi will only accept your offering once he is on top of you. We need his help to make this work."

"How will Adela get rid of the body?" Taj asked.

"She won't," Shasa said. "She'll leave it there and steal out of the hotel."

"But the desk clerk will see me when we check in to the hotel," Adela said.

"Wear a long coat with a hood. The master won't protest because he doesn't want anyone knowing he's checking in to the hotel to have sex with a fifteen-year-old relative of his. When the mistress returns, she'll have no reason to believe anyone here had anything to do with the killing."

"What if it doesn't work?" Taj said.

"It has to work," Adela said. "I can't allow that monster to touch my baby girl."

"Then bare your chest, and I will tattoo the veve on you," Shasa said. "This will take a while because it has to be a mirror-image of the true veve."

"Why is that?" Adela asked.

"Because if it isn't, the veve will be upside down when Lalaurie flips you over. Though it might work anyway, we can't take that chance."

"When you finish with her's, put one on my chest," Taj said.

"What purpose will that serve?" Shasa asked.

"Maybe nothing. If all else fails, the veves might help us find each other in another life," the big man said.

Shasa spent the next hour tattooing the intricate reverse veve on Adela and a normal Baron Samedi veve on Taj. When the old woman finished her task, she bade the couple good luck and farewell. When they reached Adela's room, they found Aisling in tears on her bed.

"Baby, what is the matter? Why are you crying?"

"That monster Dr. Lalaurie has Darius locked in the cage in the garden. He's going to cut him up in his butcher shop."

"No, he won't," Taj said. "We have a plan."

Aisling wiped away her tears. "What plan?"

"Tomorrow night I'm going to a hotel in the Quarter with Dr. Lalaurie. He'll think I am you."

"Me?"

"The perverted maniac wants to defile you. I'm going to take your place."

"Oh no, Mama, I won't allow it. He'll kill you."

Adela showed Aisling the knife. "He will not because I will kill him first."

"He'll just take the knife away from you and use it to carve you up," Aisling said.

Adela opened her blouse and showed Aisling the veve. "No, he won't because I have divine power on my side. Taj has a similar veve on his chest."

"I won't let you do this," Aisling said. "I

couldn't bear it if you were killed. Let me do it."

"I can't," Adela said. "When the monster arrives tomorrow evening for you, we must use illusion on him. Trick him into thinking I am you."

"How will we do that?" Aisling asked.

Adela took Aisling's face in her hands. "I have a plan. I think we can make it work. You must be an actress, a great actress or the plan will fail, and we all will die. Will you help me with this?"

"Only if you let Shasa tattoo a veve on my chest," Aisling said.

Chapter 33

Adela and Aisling waited for Dr. Lalaurie's inevitable knock on their door. They'd sat on the side of Aisling's bed in each other's arm for what seemed like hours.

"Mama, I'm so scared," Aisling said.

"Don't be, Baby. Everything will turn out all right."

"I know. I just can't stop shaking. I don't want to lose you."

"No one's losing anybody," Adela said. "We've planned this down to the finest detail. We even have Shasa's voodoo on our sides."

"She told me, and she also told me not to worry. I wish I could do that. I can't."

"Time to stop worrying about it," Adela said. "I hear someone coming down the hall, and it's probably Dr. Lalaurie." Adela kissed Aisling's forehead. "Will you be okay?"

"I'll try," Aisling said.

"I love you, Baby."

"I love you, Mama."

Darkness had begun to fall, shadows creeping over the courtyard outside the window. When the knock came, Adela opened the door. It was Dr. Lalaurie.

"You know what I'm here for," he said.

"You won't have to wait. Aisling is ready," Adela said.

"Then bring her to me," Dr. Lalaurie said.

Aisling stepped from behind the door dressed in a long black coat, a hood covering her head and a Mardi Gras mask over her face.

"Why is she in a mask?" Lalaurie asked.

"It seemed like the right thing to do," Adela said. "Someone at the hotel might recognize her. You don't want anyone to know you're taking a fifteen-year-old relative up to your hotel room."

Lalaurie hesitated before answering. "Probably a wise idea. Remove your mask and coat. I need to see your face."

Aisling lifted the mask and removed the coat to reveal a red dress slit all the way up her long legs. Dr. Lalaurie took a deep breath as someone in the hallway tapped his shoulder. It was Taj.

"Mastah, I have questions that need some answers and will require no more than a few minutes of your time. Can we talk about it?"

"Not now. Whatever it is you have to say will have to wait until tomorrow," Lalaurie said.

"It will only take a moment," Taj said.

"I said, it will have to wait."

Taj persisted. "Just one question, that's all I ask."

"I have other things on my mind."

"But . . ."

"Stop it. I will not tolerate disobedience. Enough, I said. Be gone with you, now."

Dr. Lalaurie had turned away from the door for less than thirty seconds. It was all the time Aisling needed. Slipping the red dress over her head, she gave it, along with her coat and mask to her mother.

With deft hands, she helped her put them on. Dr. Lalaurie didn't notice the costume change as he grabbed Adela's hand and pulled her out the door. Once they were gone, Aisling put her arms around Taj and began crying again. Too busy leading whom he thought was a fifteen-year-old girl down the hallway, Dr. Lalaurie didn't notice.

"You have my blood boiling my young pretty, so let us make haste. Tonight may not be long enough for me to quench my desire for you. I don't want to waste a moment."

A carriage waited outside the Lalaurie Mansion on Royal Street, and the driver dropped them off in front of the Hotel Montalba, the tallest building in New Orleans. Dr. Lalaurie identified himself to the man at the front desk, and then he and Adela proceeded upstairs. Adela had yet to speak a single word.

A serving cart with a bottle of champagne and two glasses waited for them in the center of the large suite of rooms. Dr. Lalaurie ogled Adela's fiery red dress and hair after helping her remove her coat. Aisling's breasts weren't exactly flat but were still much smaller than her mother's. Adela was praying Dr. Lalaurie hadn't caught on to her ruse. As the little madman had other things on his mind, he didn't seem to have.

"As Act One of our night together we shall first enjoy a bottle of the finest champagne," Dr. Lalaurie said.

Lalaurie seated her in a chair, uncorked the bottle of champagne, and then made a production of pouring each of them a glass.

Adela said, "I've never tasted champagne."

"Good," Lalaurie said. "This is the bridal suite, and tonight you are my bride. Before the evening ends, you will experience the heights of rapture and the depths of despair."

Lalaurie's comment sent a shiver up Adela's spine as she sipped her champagne across the table from the man whose smile had begun turning satanic. It seemed he had much more in mind than just the deflowering of a fifteen-year-old girl. She knew she'd have to act soon.

"And now, I want you to remove your mask," he said.

Adela answered in her best child's voice. "Mama said the mask would make the sex act much more exciting and you should remove it only at the moment of climax."

"An excellent idea," he said. "What else did your mama tell you?"

"She said I'm lucky to experience my first time in bed with such a fine gentleman."

"Did she now?" Lalaurie said. "Anything else?"

"That you're one of the smartest and most handsome men in all of New Orleans."

"I don't believe a word you say," Lalaurie said. "It doesn't matter, because I like hearing it."

"This is the most beautiful room I've ever seen," Adela said. "It must have cost a fortune to rent it for the night."

"Very perceptive," Lalaurie said. "This suite of rooms is a special place. I've planned this night for many months."

"Do you mind if I have a look around?" Adela asked.

"I welcome your enthusiasm," Lalaurie said.

Adela finished her champagne before leaving the table and looking in the bathroom. A regal porcelain tub dominated the floor finished in black and white tile. Following a quick glance, she went to the four-poster bed."

"I've only ever dreamed of sleeping in something so fabulous," she said.

"Don't get your heart set," Lalaurie said. "If I have any say in the matter, you won't get much sleep in it tonight."

"You are funny," Adela said.

Knowing she had the knife secured in a pocket in her dress, she inched around Lalaurie and crept over to the bed. Making a pretense of mussing the sheets, she used the ruse to slip the knife under the pillow.

"I've never had sex before," she said. "Please don't hurt me," she said.

Lalaurie's comment again left an uneasy feeling in Adela's stomach.

"That is a request I cannot promise to grant," he said.

Deciding to take the initiative, Adela climbed on the bed, sprawled against the pillow, and spread her arms.

"I'm ready to make love to you," she said.

"Oh no, my dear girl. The time isn't right. I have other plans for you before we consummate the final act."

Dr. Lalaurie had brought his black leather medical bag with them from the mansion. Retrieving it, he removed his instruments, arranging them on the serving cart. From a medical vial, he filled two shot glasses and took them to the bedside.

"Drink it, my dear," he said.

"What is it?" Adela asked.

"Nectar from the magical garden of the god Morpheus," he said.

"What does it do?" she asked.

"It creates the most golden euphoria you will ever experience," Lalaurie said. "Our time together will last longer and be all the more exciting. Now drain your glass."

"I don't understand," she said.

Lalaurie downed his shot. "Drink the potion and stop with your inane comments," he said.

When Adela put the shot glass to her lips, Lalaurie watched closely, making sure she drained all of the liquid. Lalaurie touched a drop that had rolled off her lips and put it into his mouth.

"Now what?" she asked.

"If you are the person I think you are, tonight will be the best of your life."

"And if I'm not?" she said.

"Then you are in line for a bit of suffering," he said. "I'm going into the bathroom to prepare your bath. The water must be extra warm, so you enjoy it while I luxuriate in the sight of your young body."

The morphine Dr. Lalaurie had given Adela began to work as he disappeared around the corner, the euphoria he had mentioned already beginning to flush her cheeks red. In all of her life, she'd never experienced anything like the warmth spreading through her body.

Adela took a deep breath, trying to regain control of her senses. As she did, she thought of Aisling, Taj, and Shasa. She suddenly had doubts, serious doubts, if she would have the wherewithal to kill the little lunatic when the opportunity presented itself.

Placing her hand under the pillow, Adela felt for the hilt of the knife, her heart beating faster when she didn't immediately find it. When her fingers locked around the bony hilt her hand was trembling, her thoughts filled with doubt.

Should she creep into the bathroom and attempt to plunge the sharp knife between Lalaurie's shoulder blades? The progressive euphoria was locking up her resolve, preventing her from doing anything other than to close her eyes. The first sight she saw when she opened them was Lalaurie's smile that had grown more sinister than before.

"Come with me," he said. "Your bathwater is drawn. I have waited too long to see your body."

Adela's fears had vanished, and so had her logic. It didn't bother her that Lalaurie had transferred his surgical instruments to a table in the bathroom, or there was a drain in the black and white tile floor. She was tripping, and even the imminent possibility of her own death failed to disturb her.

Only the flickering light of seven black candles illuminated the bathroom. Had Adela been more cognizant, she would have appreciated the dimness. It didn't seem to matter as she unbuttoned the long red dress and let it drop to the floor.

Dr. Lalaurie watched as Adela entered the tub. Steam wafted toward the ceiling as she sank into the water up to her neck. Somewhere, deep in her soul, she knew she would never make it to the bed. At that moment, she was beyond caring.

The kitchen at the Lalaurie Mansion was dark. No one had come to release Shasa from her chain. She was sitting on the floor, her head in her hands, crying. As she waited in the darkness, she heard a scream and instinctively knew where it had come from. After rising off the floor with some difficulty, she made her way to a storage cabinet.

Coal oil lamps lighted the kitchen at night. The sooty fuel always caused Shasa to cough. Tonight, she didn't care. Finding a coal oil can in the closet, she took it to the oven still hot with glowing coals. Taking a handful of ashes from the hearth, she began drawing a Baron Samedi veve on the floor. When she finished, she sat in the middle of the intricate symbol. Taking the can of coal oil, she poured it over her head.

Shasa was distraught, of that there was no doubt. She waited until the coal oil had soaked into her dress, then reached into the hearth with her hand and extracted a glowing coal. She didn't wince as she held the coal to her heart, waiting until it ignited the oil, and then her dress. She'd drawn her veve on the floor and was giving herself as the offering.

Shasa closed her eyes and crossed her arms as

the ensuing blaze ignited her dress. Fire, quickly spreading to the walls and dry wood engulfed Shasa's old body. As it did, she prayed Baron Samedi would accept her offering and change her fate, and that of Taj, Aisling, Adela, and all the other wretched humans, trapped in the Lalaurie's house of evil.

Chapter 34

As Shasa's dress caught fire and began to burn, a dark cloud engulfed the ensuing scene. The music grew so loud I could hear it even through my earplugs. As the spirits of Taj and Aisling faded into nothingness, there remained only total silence and complete darkness. I popped the plugs out of my ears and shook Mama Mulate's arm to make sure she was still cognizant.

"Shasa," Mama said. "Let's revive these two and then we have work to do.

Waking Taj and Adela took some effort. Mama slapped cold water on their faces and shook them gently until they'd regained consciousness. When they did, they both looked as if they'd survived a beating.

"What the hell did you do to us? I've never had a headache like this," Taj said. "Feels like a mule inside my skull trying to kick his way out."

Mama gave them each two tablets.

"What is it?" Taj asked.

"Aspirin," she said. "You'll feel better in a bit."

"What happened?" Adela asked.

"I channeled two spirits. Wyatt and I witnessed scenes from the night you were murdered, and the Lalaurie Mansion burned."

"You know I love you, Mama," Taj said. "I hope you're not pulling our legs on this one."

"Wyatt and I know what happened, where your veves came from, and why you are here. Let's get dressed."

"Aren't you going to tell us, first?" Taj asked.

"You'll know everything we know in due time," Mama said.

It was still raining outside, my clothes damp when I exited the bathroom. Taj and Adela were experiencing the same problem

"Try not to fret," Mama said. "We are going to get even wetter when we go back out."

"Surely this can wait until tomorrow," Taj said.

"I'm so tired I'm about to drop," Mama said. "There's nothing I'd rather do than wait until tomorrow. We can't because tomorrow may be too late."

"Can I at least finish my glass of wine before we go?" Taj asked.

"Then slug it down and bring the bottle with you. We may need it," Mama said. "When you finish, call a cab. Have them pick us up."

"At this hour?" Taj said.

"You have the card of the man who took us to the cemetery. Call him. He didn't seem particular about what hours he worked."

"Where are we going?" Adela asked.

"To the cemetery. I have a feeling someone is waiting there for us."

Mama had a closet filled with clothes from past relationships. Even Taj found a raincoat that fit him. The cab arrived shortly, and I grabbed the front seat. Mama, Taj, and Adela piled in back.

For as late as it was, our cabbie looked wide awake. He fingered the pencil stub resting on his ear.

"Wait, don't tell me," he said. "St. Louis Cemetery No. 1."

"You're a mind reader," Mama said. "Wish you could stop the rain."

"I ain't figured how to do that just yet. If I could, I wouldn't be driving this hack at all hours of the night."

"I hear that," Mama said. "We won't be gone long. Will you wait for us?"

"I still remember the tip that big boy here laid on me the last time. I'll wait."

Wink, the cab driver parked near the entrance to the cemetery. As if someone was expecting us, we found the front gate open. Old iron hinges creaked as we pushed through the door and walked toward an ephemeral light piercing the darkness. It was coming from a storage shed.

"That's the same building where I first saw Sam," Taj said.

"Good," Mama said.

"How would he have known we were coming?" Taj asked. "We didn't know ourselves until a half-hour ago."

"He's here," Mama said. "I sense his presence."

Lightning, illuminating the eerie old crypts surrounding us, flashed through the rain falling in torrents. After booming thunder died away, we heard a voice calling to us from inside the shack.

"It's me, Sam. Come in here."

The door closed behind us, shadows dancing on old brick masonry as coals from a pot-bellied stove flickered and popped. Sam was dressed in jeans and an old work shirt. The lighted stub of a cigar protruded from his lips. Even in the dim room, he was wearing dark glasses. Bedclothes draped an old cot, a pillow hanging off the edge. The only other furniture on the dirt floor was a couple of derelict chairs. Heavy rain continued blowing through the door Sam had left ajar.

"We brought you something," Mama said, handing him the bottle of wine.

Sam removed the cork, took a swig, and then plopped down on the cot.

"Not bad," he said. "I was wondering how long it would take you to return to the graveyard."

"Pardon my skepticism," Taj said. "I was born, but I wasn't born yesterday. This is starting to feel like a setup."

"No setup," Mama said. "You and Adela were lovers in a past life. Aisling was Adela's daughter. They all lived in the Lalaurie Mansion. Madam Lalaurie and her husband were sadistic murderers. They had a killing room where they routinely tortured people to death."

"Adela's not black," Taj said.

"Madam Lalaurie brought Adela and Aisling to New Orleans after Adela's husband had died. Though Adela and Madam Lalaurie were related, Adela served as an indentured servant and was little more than a slave."

"This is crazy," Taj said. "I'm not the least bit attracted to Adela. How could we have been lovers in a past life?"

"Because she isn't Adela," I said.

Taj was growing angry, his fists clenched. "Then who the hell is she?"

"She's Aisling," I said. "That's why Madeline's raven recognized her."

"Bullshit!" Adela said. "I know who I am."

"Do you?" I said. "Your veve is identical to Taj's. Your mother's veve was a mirror image of his."

"How in hell would you even know that?" Adela asked.

"We'll tell you later how we know," Mama said. "You're here tonight because an old woman named Shasa sacrificed herself to give you a chance to save your mother from a horrible fate."

Adela grew silent. Taj was still raging. "I'm like Adela and calling bullshit on this whole affair.

Where did you come up with Sam? Is he just some old wino you gave a bottle of Mad Dog to play a part?"

Sam's cigar had gone out. A flame shot from his finger to relight the stogie.

"The first time we met you had a bloody voodoo doll with you," Sam said. "Remember what the owner of the voodoo museum told you about the doll?"

"He said it was my doll and somebody had put a hex on me," Taj said.

"You remember how you got the doll?"

"I'm starting to believe this whole thing is a hoax," Taj said.

"You don't believe your own eyes? You saw me materialize when Mama summoned me that night in the cemetery," Sam said.

"Maybe it was just illusion," Taj said.

Sam grabbed him by the neck, lifting him into the air.

"Is this illusion?" he asked. Taj's eyes had grown large when Sam lowered him to the floor. "Adela, here, knows magic. Make him levitate."

Adela shook her head. "I have no clue what you're talking about," she said.

Taj began rising off the floor, not stopping until he bumped into the ceiling.

"Is this an illusion?" Sam said.

"Put me down," Taj said.

When Sam flicked his wrist, Taj dropped to the floor. "That's the problem with you young people," he said. "You don't believe in nothing except the here and now. If it weren't for Shasa, I'd wash my hands of you."

"Who paid to have me hexed?" Taj asked.

"The incarnation of Dr. Leonard Louis Nicolas Lalaurie," Mama said. "Another reason why we need Sam's help."

"I just don't know," Taj said.

"Then take Adela and go back to the hotel," Mama said. "Wyatt and I will return your retainer tomorrow."

"Adela?" Taj said.

"What happened to my mother?" Adela asked.

"She was murdered by Dr. Lalaurie because her veve never had a chance to work," Mama said.

"You have your veves because Taj thought it would help you find each other in a future life," I said. "Instead, you found Aisling. Adela, your lover, was murdered."

"How do you know she isn't Adela?" Taj asked.

"Like you said, you and Adela, here, don't have even the slightest sexual attraction. Aisling's veve, unlike her mother Adela's, is a normal image. Aisling knew magic and could use it. Adela knew nothing about magic. You are Aisling and not Adela."

"She is Aisling. She's known it all along," I said. "Her mother, Adela was murdered trying to protect her."

"Okay," Taj said. "Now that I know about the past lives Adela and I led, guess we can go about our business."

"Not that simple," Mama said. "You need to unravel the curse."

"What I want to know is how this curse is going to affect me," Taj said.

"It already has," Sam said. "You wouldn't be in New Orleans if it wasn't for the curse. Next time, the demon may kill you."

"Adela is also a victim of the curse," I said. "The same madman who cursed you also cursed her. If he hadn't, she wouldn't be here now."

"I can handle my own problems," Adela said.

"Can you save Darius and your mama from horrible deaths?"

"Who is Darius?" Taj asked.

"Someone who had a strong emotional connection with Aisling. A boy who Dr. Lalaurie had caged in anticipation of torturing and killing."

"All those things happened almost two centuries ago," Taj said. "What good does it do to worry about it now? Isn't that how you feel, Adela?"

Sam answered for Adela. "Aisling is a special being. She's an Irish witch and knows lots more than you think she does. Her magic is powerful, though not powerful enough to travel back in time."

Adela's eyes began turning red. "If there were a way to change time and save my mother and Darius from horrible deaths, I would do it."

"There is a way," Sam said.

"You can help me travel back in time?" Adela asked.

"Wyatt can. He's a Traveler," Sam said. "I'll accompany Wyatt to the portal. The rest is up to him."

Adela grabbed my arm. "You must take me with you."

Chapter 35

The rainstorm ended the moment we stepped out of Sam's shack. The eyes of the cabbie named Wink grew larger when Sam climbed into the front seat. Unlike the persona he had exhibited in the shack, he'd donned an old tuxedo jacket and a top hat and looked just like the voodoo Loa Baron Samedi. It took Wink only a moment to notice.

"Hey, this ain't Halloween, and it's too early for Mardi Gras," he said.

"What's your name, boy?" Sam asked.

Something in Sam's voice alerted Wink to the possibility his costume might be something more than an act.

"Don't mind me," he said. "I always talk too much. Where to?"

"Charity Hospital Cemetery," Sam said.

"You mean the Katrina Memorial?"

"Same location, different cemeteries," Sam said. "I told you where we want to go."

"Except for an empty patch of dirt and a single headstone, there ain't a damn thing to see at Charity Hospital Cemetery," Wink said.

"You got a mouth on you," Sam said. "Why don't you shut the hell up?"

"Yes sir," Wink said.

The entrance to the cemetery, near the intersection of Canal and City Park Avenue, wasn't far from where we'd come. Still, it was starkly different from St. Louis Cemetery No. 1.

"Where are all the crypts?" Taj asked.

"This was New Orleans' original Potter's Field. If you were a derelict and no one claimed your body, you were buried here. If you died of cholera, influenza, or yellow fever, you were likely buried here," Mama said.

"After Charity Hospital bought the property," I said, "they began interring their medical cadavers in this cemetery. Before Katrina, there was a simple iron cross and a single stone monument for the bodies donated to science. Now, there's a Katrina Memorial, some walkways and two large crypts."

"Not very big," Taj said. "How many bodies are buried here?"

"More than you might imagine," Mama said. "Maybe as many as one-hundred-fifty thousand bodies are interred beneath that little patch of land."

"You gotta be kidding," Taj said.

Sam glanced into the back seat at Adela. "It's where your mama is buried," he said.

"That's so sad," Adela said. "There's no dignity in a mass grave."

"You're wrong about that," Sam said. "This piece of ground is hallowed. There's no less disrespect than if they'd been buried in the most regal crypt in New Orleans."

"How do you know?" Adela said.

"Because I know where every body in New Orleans is buried. Your mama's remains are the portal that'll launch you back in time."

We left Taj and Mama in the cab with Wink and stood outside the massive iron gate that said Charity Hospital Cemetery. As we stood in the darkness, the gate creaked open. We followed Sam inside.

As we plodded across the damp earth, the clouds parted, revealing a full moon sitting low in the starless sky. It was a blood moon, its creepy color illuminating many piles of dirt, each one marked by a flag, where someone had recently dug.

"Do they still bury people here?" Adela asked.

"Haven't for years," Sam said. "Archeologists dig and use ground-penetrating instruments to study the bodies." He chuckled. "They should have just asked me."

Spirits of the dead were rising up through the damp earth, surrounding us as we trodded to a far corner of the cemetery. Each one of them seemed to want to touch Baron Samedi. The Baron stopped when he reached a spot near the fence surrounding the little patch of ground.

"Your mama is buried about ten feet from here. Wyatt is an old hand at time travel. Since you've never done it before, there are things you need to know."

"Like what?" Adela said.

"The flesh can travel through time, though not your clothes. When you enter the portal, you'll be transported to the last place you were before your mama died. You'll reach the past naked, the way you came into this world, and you won't be the same person you are now."

"Who will I be?" Adela asked.

"The person you were then. You gonna be all right?"

"You're not talking me out of this if that's what you mean," Adela said.

"That's not all," Sam said. "Once you get there, and finish what you're going there to do, you'll have to return to the exact spot where you entered. There's one last little detail."

"What?" I asked.

"You need to return to that spot before dawn. If you don't, you'll be trapped in the past for eternity. Are you ready?"

"I'm ready," Adela said.

"Then take Wyatt's hand and start walking toward the fence. When you reach your mama's grave, you'll be transported to another time and another place."

Foggy spirits caressed us as Adela clutched my hand and pulled me toward the fence. Before we'd gone ten steps, my senses went totally dark, almost as if I'd died. When my eyes cleared and I could see again, I was in a tiny bedroom with two beds separated by a sliding sheet. I was quite naked, and so was the person holding my hand.

Aisling screamed when she opened her eyes and saw me. Grabbing the sheet from one of the beds, she quickly covered herself. I yanked a sheet from the other bed. When she spoke, Aisling's voice was probably an octave higher than normal.

"Who are you?"

"I'm Wyatt."

"What are you doing in my room?" she asked.

"I'm here to help you."

"Then why were we naked?" she said.

"We were just transported through time from the future. We lost our clothes in the process."

"You are crazy," she said, backing away from me until she touched the wall.

"We don't have much time, and you have to trust me on this. Your mother is in grave danger; you, Taj, Shasa, and everyone in this house are in danger. We have to act quickly. Can you find me something to wear?"

Aisling must have heard something in my voice because she disappeared for a moment behind a screen. She was dressed when she stepped out again and began rummaging through a wicker chest. I changed behind the screen into a shirt and pants that were woefully large. Neither of us had time to worry about it.

"Is my mama okay?" Aisling asked.

"I hope so," I said. "Right now, we have things to do here. Point me toward the kitchen, and you go find Taj."

Aisling showed me the way to the kitchen and then ran in the other direction. I burst through the kitchen door in time to see Shasa, in tears and chained by the ankle. She was sitting on the floor, pouring coal oil over her body. I called out to her.

"Shasa, no!"

My warning wasn't in time as she'd already lit the oil. Coal oil apparently has a high flash point because it didn't immediately burst into flames. Still, it would only be a moment before her dress caught fire and she would die a painful death. I grabbed the chain and pulled.

Smoke billowed up from the fire as I pulled on the chain, trying to yank it loose from the wall. Just as I thought it was too late, Aisling and Taj came rushing through the door.

"Taj, I need something to cut the chain."

Taj had already thought about it and was carrying an ax. He smashed through the chain as Aisling and I tried to put out the fire. Taj knew what to do. Finding a bucket of sand, he began pouring it on the flames. Once the fire was out, the four of us stood in the smoky kitchen, Aisling, Taj, and Shasa embracing.

"No time," I said. "Before Lalaurie kills Adela, I have to go to the Hotel Montalba."

"I'm going with you," Taj said.

"Me too," Aisling said.

"First, we have to rescue Darius from the cage in the garden, along with everyone else. Though I can't explain how I know, this house will be burned to the ground before morning comes."

"I got the keys," Taj said.

The house was huge, the wood floors echoing, as we raced downstairs and out into the courtyard. The light of the full moon was shining down on the tiny cage. Darius was holding his head when Taj inserted the key and rattled open the door.

"You're free, boy. Now, we need your help." Taj tossed him the hefty keychain. "Open all the doors and help get the people out of the Dark Room."

Taj rousted the shay driver from the stable and helped him rig the wagon.

"Take us down Royal to Hotel Montalba," Taj said.

There was no traffic on the street as our driver trotted the horse down Rue Royal. The night clerk was asleep behind the counter as we hurried up the stairs to the thirteenth floor where Taj kicked open the door to Room 1313.

The next thing I knew, Aisling, Taj, and I were standing on the black and white tile floor of the bathroom. Adela was in the steaming tub, her long red hair damp. Dr. Leonard Louis Nicolas Lalaurie was standing behind her with a surgical scalpel in his hand. When Taj made a move toward Lalaurie, the mad little doctor put the scalpel to Adela's neck.

"What the hell are you doing here?" Lalaurie said.

"Leave her alone," Taj said. "If you want to kill somebody, then kill me instead."

"Come here, and I'll do just that," Lalaurie said.

"Taj, no!" Aisling said.

Grabbing Aisling's shoulders, I shook her. "Stop him, Aisling," I said. "Use your magic."

Aisling glanced first at me and then at her mother. Raising her arms, she pointed her fingers at Lalaurie, bowed her head and closed her eyes. Lalaurie glanced up as if he'd just seen a ghost and released his grip on Adela. Taj was already there. Water drenched the tile floor as he grabbed Adela's wrists and yanked her out of the tub.

Lalaurie could do nothing about it. His right arm had stiffened, his eyes growing ever larger as he struggled to keep the scalpel away from his neck. He was screaming bloody murder as he decapitated himself with his own scalpel.

Lalaurie's body tumbled into the tub, the steaming water turning red. Adela, Taj, and Aisling were in an embrace as Lalaurie's head rolled across the tile, coming to a halt at our feet. Aisling kicked it across the floor.

"What do we do with his head?" Aisling asked.

"Throw it out the fucking window," I said.

Grasping the hair of the disembodied head, Aisling hurried into the next room, raised a window and threw it out.

"Baby," Adela said. "Who is this man?"

"No time to explain," Aisling said.

Aisling found Adela's long red dress and helped her pull it over her wet hair. The night clerk awoke long enough to see us rushing out of the front door. Our shay was waiting on the street in front of the hotel. Up Royal Street, we could see flames licking the horizon. Taj took control of the reins and had the horse in a fast trot. Flames were pouring out of the roof of the Lalaurie Mansion as Taj reined the horse to a stop.

A group of neighbors and all of the household slaves stood on the sidewalk watching. I found Shasa and pulled her aside.

"How did the house catch fire?" I asked.

"I went back to the kitchen to get something. Madam Lalaurie was there. She'd missed her boat and had returned home. When she realized what was happening, she attacked me with her whip. Her dress burst into flames. She was screaming at me when she fell over the banister."

"Baron Samedi answered your prayer," I said. "Does anybody know Madam Lalaurie was in the house?" I asked. When she shook her head, Shasa's gray hair flickered in the light of the fire. "Then don't ever tell anyone. Not even Taj or Adela."

Shasa gave me a knowing nod as Aisling, Taj, and Adela reached us. The mansion was in flames, the sun beginning to dawn, as I stepped toward the burning house.

"I have to go now," I said.

Adela and Aisling clutched my hands. "You can't go in there. You'll be burned to death," Adela said.

"No choice," I said. "I'm glad you're all safe. It's now or never for me. Aisling, are you coming with me?"

"I don't know who I was in another life. I know who I am here. This is where I'll stay."

I kissed Aisling's forehead, pulled loose from her grasp and sprinted toward the house. Before I had entered the burning building, she called to me.

"Go with God," she said.

Flames licked the walls, smoke filling the house, as I ripped off the shirt and held it over my mouth and nose. As I hurried up the stairs, I knew God was my only hope. I could see the door to Aisling's room at the end of a long and fiery hallway. The last thing I remembered was pulling open the door and diving inside.

Chapter 36

I opened my eyes in the Charity Hospital Cemetery. A new day had dawned, and wispy spirits caressed me before disappearing into the damp earth. My clothes lay in the mud, and I quickly got dressed. The front gate was still open as I hurried toward it. Mama was waiting for me on the sidewalk.

"Oh, Wyatt, I've been so worried. Where's Adela."

"Adela was really Aisling, and she chose to stay."

Wink wasn't smiling when we reached the cab. "Your fare is getting more expensive by the minute."

"And I have no money," Mama said.

Mama, Wink, and I were the only ones in the cab. "Where's Taj?" I said.

"Gone," Mama said.

"Where did the big basketball player go?" I asked.

"Ain't nobody here but the three of us," Wink said.

I fished through my wallet, looking for some of Taj's retainer I had stashed there. Taj's money was gone. The twenty-two dollars I found wasn't enough to pay our fare.

"Take us to Bertram's Bar on Chartres," I said. "I have money upstairs in my room."

Bertram was up, waiting on a customer when we entered the bar.

"Where you two been?" he asked.

"Detective work," I said as we hurried upstairs.

My cat Kisses met us at the door, and I quickly opened a can of cat food for her.

"I put my share of Taj's retainer in the upper drawer," I said, pointing.

As I finished feeding Kisses and was giving her a few full body strokes, Mama rummaged through my underwear drawer.

"There's nothing in here," she said.

"You sure?"

"Nope, nothing. What now?"

"Back downstairs."

Bertram had coffee waiting for us when we reached the bar.

"You been mud wrestling?" he asked.

"Something like that," I said. "Can I borrow some money for a few days?"

"What for?"

"No questions, please. There's a cab waiting outside and his meter's running."

Bertram handed me a wad of cash from beneath the bar.

"When you gonna pay me back?" he asked.

"Soon as I can," I said.

"Yeah," he said. "I believe you, but I believe you're lying." Mama followed me to the door. "You two coming back? Eddie's in town. He found a cache of the rum that's so good. We're celebrating later on."

"We'll have to see," I said as we walked out the door.

Wink was waiting, the motor of his cab running. The sun was rising, tourists beginning to prowl the early morning streets.

"Well?" Wink said.

"Drop us off at the Upper Pontalba Building."

Wink looked visibly perturbed but drove the short distance to one of the buildings flanking Jackson Square. He was considerably happier when I paid his tab and added a nice tip.

"Who do you know who lives here?" Mama asked.

"Armand and Madam Toulouse. Maybe they'll have some answers for us.

Artists, mimes, tourists, and pigeons were already occupying Jackson Square as we reached the front door of the Pontalba and rang a bell. A squawky voice sounded through the speaker.

"Who the hell is it?"

"It's me, Armand. Wyatt Thomas."

When the buzzer sounded, we entered the hallway and walked up a short flight of stairs to Armand and Madam Toulouse's apartment. Armand was waiting for us at the door.

"Mama Mulate," Armand said. "What a pleasure. Come in here. You're just in time for breakfast."

Armand was dressed in house slippers and a plush burgundy bathrobe. It marked the first time I'd seen him in anything other than black. We followed him into one of the most sought after places to live in all of the Big Easy. Known as the oldest apartment complex in the United States, Armand, and Madam Toulouse's domicile was anything but old and rundown.

Madam Toulouse was cooking at a restaurant-style six-burner stove that must have cost them a small fortune. She was also dressed in a plush burgundy bathrobe, and her usual bouffant hairdo was relaxed and draped over her shoulders.

"Wyatt," she said. "And Mama Mulate."

Madam Toulouse scooted the pan away from

the flame and rushed to give Mama a big hug.

"Better cook enough for two more, Baby," Armand said.

"You know it," she said. "No one goes away from my house hungry."

We didn't. We were soon sitting at a beautiful wooden dining table drinking coffee and eating Eggs Benedict. When we'd finished, Armand refilled our cups from the pot on the stove.

"Now, tell us what's so important you felt you had to talk with Madam Toulouse and me before nine in the morning."

"Taj Davis," I said.

"What about him," Armand said.

"The Pels are in town tonight. Is Taj playing?"

Armand stared at me as if I'd just asked him something crazy.

"What the hell are you talking about? The Celtics aren't in town tonight."

"We traded Zee Ped to Cleveland for Taj Davis," I said.

"What planet are you living on? Taj Davis never played for the Cavs. He's a Celtic," Madam Toulouse said.

"You sure you're on the wagon?" Armand said.

"I was just pulling your leg. I do have a couple of other questions for you," I said.

"Hit us," Madam Toulouse said.

"Do you know anything about a murder at the Hotel Montalba which occurred almost two centuries ago?"

"Madam Toulouse knows all about it," Armand said. "She researched the case when she worked at the Notarial Archives."

Madam Toulouse made a face when I asked, "Who was murdered?"

"Don't know," she said. "They found the body of a naked man in the bathtub. His head was missing. It was never found."

"Could it have been the body of Dr. Lalaurie?"

Madam Toulouse gave me one of her patented looks. "Funny you should ask. The dead man had registered using an assumed name. Though no one believed him, the clerk who'd checked him in swore it was Dr. Lalaurie."

"The murder happened the same night the Lalaurie Mansion burned," Armand said. "Dr. Lalaurie disappeared and was never seen again, probably to avoid abuse and torture charges for the way he and Madam Lalaurie had treated their slaves."

"Did Madam Lalaurie flee to France?" I asked.

"That's the word on the street," Armand said.

"And you don't believe it?" I said.

"Not long ago, someone found a plaque in St. Louis Cemetery No. 1 which seemed to indicate she was buried there," Madam Toulouse said.

"What happened to the Lalaurie's slaves?" I asked.

"They were all manumitted and became part of the city's free people of color population," Madam Toulouse said.

"Do you know anything about an Irish woman and her daughter who had lived with the Lalauries?" I asked.

"They were related to Delphine Lalaurie and her cousin who at the time was the governor of Louisiana and Florida. The governor took them with him to Florida," Armand said.

"Do you know what happened to them after they moved away from New Orleans?" I asked.

"They must have prospered because there's a dormitory named after one of their ancestors at the University of Florida," Armand said. "I know because I lived there while I was attending college."

Armand nodded when I asked, "You from Florida? I didn't know."

"Lots of things you don't know, Cowboy,"

Armand said.

The sky was blue, not a single cloud in the sky as we left Armand and Madam Toulouse's Upper Pontalba apartment.

"Guess that answers all my questions," I said. "It's almost as if Taj and Adela were never here."

"They weren't, except for you and me. We may as well keep it to ourselves. No one will ever believe us anyway," Mama said.

"Sure seems that way," I said.

"So sad," Mama said. "That handsome man, Taj Davis, is out of my life forever, not to mention our lost twenty-thousand dollar retainer."

"When I told the story about seeing the demon, Adela kept telling everyone I was only dreaming. Right about now, I'm not so sure she was wrong."

"Oh, Wyatt," Mama said. "Sometimes there's not an ounce of difference between reality and a bloody nightmare."

"At least the rain has stopped," I said. "And Eddie's back in town. I'll bet he has a story to tell."

Mama put her arm through mine and turned us toward Bertram's. "Then let's go get drunk."

End

About the Author

Born on a sleepy bayou, Louisiana Mystery Writer Eric Wilder grew up listening to tales of ghosts, magic, and voodoo. He's the author of twelve novels, four cookbooks, many short stories, and Murder Etouffee, a book that defies classification. His two series feature P.I.s adept in the investigation of the paranormal. He lives in Oklahoma, near historic Route 66 with wife Marilyn, three wonderful dogs, and one great cat. If you liked *Garden of Forbidden Spirits*, please check out the rest of the French Quarter Mystery Series, the Paranormal Cowboy Series, and all of Eric's other books.